"Josh, good ~~to see you,~~ Rebecca said, forcing a smile

He gave her that crooked grin of his, the one that showed his dimples, and immediately called her on the lie. "Are you sure?"

Hell, no. "I'm trying to be positive," she said, clasping her hands in front of her because she suddenly didn't know where to put them. Katie and Mona—and everyone else—were watching avidly.

He settled his black felt cowboy hat farther back on his head. "So this truce thing is for real."

"I guess," she said with a shrug.

"Because I gotta tell ya, that fiasco at your sister's wedding was…" He shook his head and let his breath go all at once.

"I can't believe you'd even bring that up," Rebecca responded, bridling. "You made me take out the punch fountain."

He cocked his head. "You're the one who tripped me in the first place."

"I didn't even touch you!"

"Wait a second," Katie broke in. "That wedding was the most exciting thing this town has seen in the past three years. If you two call a truce, life's going to be pretty boring around here. Who will Rebecca have to fight with?"

Dear Reader,

Welcome back to Dundee, Idaho, where in *A Baby of Her Own* (September 2002) Delaney and Conner finally worked out their differences. Now that the scandal involving "good girl" Delaney has died down, it's time to mix things up again. And Delaney's best friend, Rebecca, is the perfect woman to do that. She's high-strung and unpredictable; in fact, you could say Rebecca's middle name is "Trouble." It's going to take a strong hero to tame her. But I think she's met her match in Josh. I hope so, at least. I fell in love with him myself!

I always enjoy hearing from readers. Please feel free to contact me at P.O. Box 3781, Citrus Heights, CA 95611. Or simply log on to my Web site at www.novak.com to leave me an e-mail, check out future book signings, learn about my upcoming releases and win some fabulous prizes.

Brenda Novak

Books by Brenda Novak

HARLEQUIN SUPERROMANCE

899—EXPECTATIONS
939—SNOW BABY
955—BABY BUSINESS
987—DEAR MAGGIE
1021—WE SAW MOMMY KISSING SANTA CLAUS
1058—SHOOTING THE MOON
1083—A BABY OF HER OWN

HARLEQUIN SINGLE TITLE
TAKING THE HEAT

brenda novak

A HUSBAND OF HER OWN

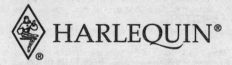

HARLEQUIN®

TORONTO • NEW YORK • LONDON
AMSTERDAM • PARIS • SYDNEY • HAMBURG
STOCKHOLM • ATHENS • TOKYO • MILAN • MADRID
PRAGUE • WARSAW • BUDAPEST • AUCKLAND

ISBN 0-373-71130-1

A HUSBAND OF HER OWN

Visit us at www.eHarlequin.com

Printed in U.S.A.

DEDICATION

To my first son, Trey, who, at eight years old,
already exhibits the dignity of a confident man. He is my
anchor in the storm of life, holding fast, always at peace—
an echo of my father. If you forget everything else I've ever
taught you, Trey, remember this: my love is everlasting.

ACKNOWLEDGMENT

Thanks to Michael Star,
www.AstrologyZine.com/attract-women-Scorpio.shtml
for his astrology information and horoscopes.

CHAPTER ONE

"YOU WANT TO *WHAT?*" Rebecca Wells pulled away from where she'd been leaning on her kitchen counter and clutched the telephone tightly, hoping she'd heard wrong the first time. She was supposed to be at work by nine, in twenty minutes, but this call took precedence over everything else.

"I think we should wait until the end of January," her fiancé, Buddy, responded. He sounded tentative, as though he feared she might not accept this news well. Probably because she'd lost her temper last time. He'd postponed the wedding twice already.

"The end of January is almost four months away, Buddy," she said, and was immediately proud of how calmly she'd spoken. Too bad Delaney had gotten married and wasn't living with her anymore. Rebecca felt certain her best friend would have applauded her efforts.

"That's not so long, babe. What're another few months? It won't change anything in the long run, right?"

Change anything! It would change *everything*. Rebecca had been counting the days until she could leave her small hometown behind. She wanted to move to Nebraska with Buddy so Mrs. Whipple couldn't pass her on the street, shake her head and mumble, "Poor Mayor Wells. Who would've thought he'd get stuck with such a daughter?" So Mrs. Reese couldn't frown disapprovingly as she sat in the beauty shop across from where Rebecca was working, recounting the occasion when Rebecca had purposely dyed her hair blue. So Delaney's Aunt Millie couldn't constantly remind her of the day she ran away with Johnny Red, the leader of a biker gang that had once passed through town.

On second thought, being reminded of Johnny probably wouldn't have bothered Rebecca. He'd been dangerous and reckless and incredibly sexy. Except he'd sent her packing in only three days—that was the humiliating part. Everyone in town had assumed even a man like Johnny Red couldn't tame Rebecca Wells. They didn't realize that next to Johnny, she looked like a saint.

Stretching her neck to relieve some of the tension, she took a deep breath. She needed to loosen up or she was going to blow this conversation. The last time she'd let Buddy feel the full force of her disappointment, he hadn't called for almost a week.

"Now I'm going to have to explain to the whole town that I'm not getting married for my birthday, and I'm going to have to say it's because your great-aunt can't make it until after Christmas?" she said.

A sense of accomplishment swept through Rebecca despite her dismay. She'd just managed another reasonable statement. She was doing amazingly well, considering her track record, but the strain was taking its toll. Just last week, she'd promised Delaney that she'd given up smoking for good. But a cigarette seemed almost imperative to her success here. If only she hadn't destroyed every pack in the house in the fervor of her good intentions.

"Are you saying that my great-aunt isn't enough of a reason to hold off?" he asked. "She's very important to me, Rebecca."

Rebecca had a few things to say about the relative importance of a great-aunt, but she bit them back. Opening the kitchen drawer that housed the Ziploc Baggies, aluminum foil and plastic wrap, she retrieved her nicotine patches and smoothed one on her arm. "They'll think you're getting cold feet," she pointed out.

"I'm not getting cold feet. We met only nine months ago. And we've seen each other in person…what? A handful of times? I think most people understand that a long-distance relationship sometimes develops a little more slowly."

Except their relationship hadn't developed slowly. From almost the first moment they'd met on the Internet last January, they'd been talking about getting married. They'd grown close very quickly.

Unfortunately, Rebecca was afraid their relationship might be fading just as fast. And she couldn't figure out why. She knew she was a little temperamental, but it wasn't as though Buddy was likely to do any better. Only five feet six, he was at least fifty pounds overweight. He had blond hair and kind blue eyes—Rebecca loved both his hair and his eyes—but his face showed traces of years-old acne, and he had a big nose. He certainly wasn't someone who would normally have turned her head. Especially because she was five feet ten, one hundred thirty pounds, and nearly five years older.

It was the differences in their basic natures that she thought of as the truly positive factor in their relationship. Nothing riled Buddy. On a scale of one to ten, the intensity of his emotions fell somewhere below a one. He immediately and completely withdrew from any and all confrontation. Rebecca, on the other hand, had never backed away from a fight in her life. Until today. "Stay calm," was quickly becoming her silent mantra.

"I don't understand why you keep doing this," she said, still admirably rational. "Are you having second thoughts about us?"

"No...not really."

Not really? She considered asking Buddy if she could call him back after she made a cigarette run. Only she was already too engrossed in the conversation to walk away from it now.

"I just...I don't see any need to rush into anything," he was saying.

"We wouldn't be rushing," she responded. "We'd simply be going ahead with our plans. Why can't we show your aunt the video when she comes to town? I mean, weddings aren't all they're cracked up to be. It'll be more fun to get to know her in a relaxed atmosphere."

"It's not just my aunt."

"You said you weren't having second thoughts about us. At least, I think that's what you said. You said 'not really.' I don't know what I'm supposed to make of that. I guess it means you *could* be having second thoughts, or you could be having *some* second thoughts or—"

"You're putting words in my mouth," he said. "I'm thinking about the advantages, that's all. We'd have more money if we waited, and I'll have saved up a few more days' vacation time."

"What about me?" Rebecca slapped a nicotine patch on her other arm. "I've already given my notice at Hair And Now, and Erma has a new girl I'm supposed to train starting in a few weeks. There won't be enough business for her if I keep my current clients. Besides, the lease is up on my house and—"

"Has anyone else come forward to rent it? Maybe you could talk your landlord into letting you stay another few months."

Wasn't he listening? She didn't *want* to stay any longer. She didn't want to see the doubt in her father's eyes when she told him the wedding had been postponed a third time.

And she sure as heck didn't want to share such news with her three perfect sisters, all of whom had husbands and families of their own. They'd paved the road before her with such high expectations she'd never measure up. And everyone down at the Honky Tonk, the redneck bar that served as the center of Dundee's weekend entertainment, was already placing bets on whether there'd really be a wedding. She couldn't have the whole town laughing at her. Not again.

"The invitations are at the printers," she said. She could feel the reassuring adhesive of both nicotine patches clinging to her skin but somehow it wasn't the same as a smoke.

"You could probably catch them if you called right away," he replied.

"Maybe, maybe not. Maybe we should just forget about the wedding and elope."

"Elope?"

His voice had definitely gone a bit high, but Rebecca barreled on. "Yeah. Let's fly to Vegas and do it. Forget the cake and the flowers and the food. Forget the guests!"

"My mother would kill me."

"Why? My parents are the ones who've already spent a lot of money." Her parents had been so excited that she was finally getting married, they'd promised to give her the same kind of wedding they'd provided for her sisters, even though she was thirty-one. The vein in her father's forehead had momentarily appeared when she mentioned the cost of her dress, but her mother had quickly quelled whatever he was about to say with one of her magical warning glances. He'd nodded vacantly and walked away, and they hadn't discussed the expense of the wedding since.

"See?" Buddy said. "We can't elope. Your parents would be furious."

"Some things, like the food and hall and the photographer, we can still cancel. The rest I'll pay for myself, a little at a time.''

"And the memory of having your father give you away and all that?''

"I don't think my folks care whether or not I have a wedding. They just want me to be happy.''

"That might be true. But I'm an only child and my father died when I was eight. It's perfectly understandable that my mother would want me to do things the traditional way.''

Rebecca was beginning to feel a little desperate. He had an answer for everything, but they weren't answers she could understand. Two people who were madly in love wanted to be together as soon as possible. They didn't put off their wedding for a great-aunt. It was the one time in life a couple was allowed to be selfish.

Or maybe she was getting carried away by the emotion of the moment. Maybe she wasn't thinking like other people. It had happened before.

"Okay,'' she said, shifting to damage control. "What if I move out there and we live together until the wedding? That should make everyone happy.''

"Um…I don't think so. My family wouldn't like it.''

"Your *family* wouldn't like it? What about you, Buddy?''

He immediately picked up on the edge in her voice. "There's no need to get upset, Beck. Would you please calm down?''

Calm down? How could she respond any more calmly and still have a pulse? "What do you want me to say?'' she asked. "I can't help that I'm not happy about this.'' As a matter of fact, the bubble of her anger was rising inexorably toward the surface, and she feared she'd no longer be able to hold it back. Worse, she could barely remember why it was important to do so. If Buddy didn't love her, all the soft-spoken words in the world wouldn't change a thing. And he couldn't love her if he was putting everyone else's feelings before hers.

"Just try to understand," he said.

She pinched the bridge of her nose. "I want to know what's really going on."

"There's nothing going on. I want my aunt to come to the wedding. Reading anything more into this would be blowing it out of proportion."

"What about *my* family? They've been making hundreds of scrolls with that silly romantic poem we chose."

"Which we'll use…eventually."

"Eventually." Rebecca felt as if her hold on the rope that was supposed to rescue her from Dundee had just grown a little more tenuous.

"I've got to go," Buddy said.

"Wait! I want to talk about this. I admit I'm upset, but I think I have good reason to be."

Silence.

"Buddy? Answer me, dammit. Not every conversation we have has to be pleasant. That isn't even realistic."

Nothing.

"What if one of my aunts can't make it in January? Do we put if off again? We can't possibly accommodate everyone."

"Let's talk about it later, okay?"

"Why?"

"Because maybe by then you'll have cooled off."

"And maybe not. Can't you work with me here? I'm disappointed and frustrated and—"

"And I'd talk to you now if I thought it would help, but arguing won't solve anything," he said. "Come on, Beck. I'm just asking for a few more months. What's the rush?"

He didn't get it, and Rebecca knew she couldn't explain it to him without dredging up her past. Which she definitely didn't want to do. She was moving to Nebraska to start over. "I thought we were in love," she said.

"We are in love. And we're going to be just as in love in January, right?"

How could she answer that without conceding it would be okay to wait? "I guess."

"At least, I'm still going to be in love with you," he added, and Rebecca felt herself soften. She didn't want to wait any longer to be married, but if it would make Buddy happy, how could she refuse? "Okay," she said at last.

"Great." She could hear the smile in his voice. "I knew you'd understand. You're the best, babe, you know that? Listen, I've got someone at the door, so I'll have to call you later."

Rebecca slouched into a chair at the kitchen table and started peeling off the nicotine patches she'd plastered on herself. "Fine."

The phone clicked and a dial tone filled her ear. Hanging up, she sat in a stupor for several seconds, waiting for her emotions to reach some kind of equilibrium. She'd behaved admirably. She'd succeeded in remaining calm and should be proud of herself for that. But it was hard to celebrate when Buddy was still postponing their wedding. She'd have to tell her family and friends. She'd have to make new arrangements at work and with her landlord. She'd have to withstand all the snide remarks she was bound to receive at the Honky Tonk.

Propping her chin on her palm, she gazed dejectedly out the window at the front drive. *Everything will be okay,* she told herself. This wouldn't be the first time the whole town had snickered behind her back. Folks still told and retold the crazy things she'd done over the years, even though some stories went all the way back to her childhood. But she always managed to smile through the telling. And she'd keep on smiling. The trick, of course, was never to let anyone know how much it hurt.

CHAPTER TWO

"MARTHA CALLED EARLIER, said you wanted me to come over for dinner so you could talk to me about something," Rebecca said. Dropping her car keys on the counter, she plopped onto a stool in the middle of her parents' large white kitchen.

Her mother, wearing a cherry-print apron over her June Cleaver dress, was busy chopping onions at the center island. A puzzled expression knotted her brows as she glanced up. "Who's Martha?" She grimaced as understanding dawned. "Oh, you mean Greta."

"There's a little Martha Stewart in all of us. Some of my sisters just have more than their share."

"There's nothing wrong with being a good homemaker," her mother replied.

"I would've agreed with you—" Rebecca toyed with the fresh fruit that graced the bowl at her elbow "—but Greta lost me when she tried to make roses out of the ends of her toilet paper. Presentation *isn't* everything. Some things are meant to be functional. Next thing we know, she'll be trying to camouflage the commode." She took a bite out of an apple and was mildly surprised when her mother didn't insist she wait until after dinner. "So what did you want to say to me?"

Her mother scooped the onions she'd been chopping onto a plate. "I just wanted to tell you that I found some pretty candles I think will work well for the wedding. They're vanilla-scented.''

The way her mother's eyes settled on her, then shifted quickly to her task again, suggested she had more to say. But mention of the wedding was enough to make Rebecca uncomfortable. She'd called the printer in Boise this morning and managed to talk them into holding her order, but she hadn't mentioned the latest wrinkle in her love life to anyone closer to home. When her sister called earlier to set up dinner, she'd thought tonight might be a good time to talk to her parents. But her mother was preparing a lot of onions. Probably she wasn't the only one coming to dinner.

''Can I help?'' she asked.

''Sure. Grab a bowl and start cutting up vegetables for a salad. Everything's in the bottom drawer of the refrigerator.''

''I may be less like Martha Stewart than your other daughters, but even I know where to find the veggies,'' Rebecca grumbled, crossing to the fridge and pulling out the romaine lettuce. ''Who's coming tonight?''

''Greta and the kids.''

''She told me she had a headache.''

''She called just before you came. She's feeling better.''

''And Randy?''

''He has to work.'' With a population barely reaching 1,500, Dundee had only two full-time firemen. Randy, husband of the sister closest to Rebecca in age, was one of them.

''I'll miss him,'' Rebecca said, making little effort to mask her sarcasm.

Her mother arched a reprimanding eyebrow at her. ''That's not a very nice tone to use regarding Randy. He's your brother-in-law.''

He'd also been sidekick to Josh Hill all through high

school. But then, her parents didn't understand her feelings toward Josh, either. They'd worshipped him ever since his family moved in across the street twenty-four years ago. Especially her father. From the beginning, if Josh got into a brawl at school or skipped class to catch frogs in the nearby creek, her father would say, "He's all boy, isn't he?" And there was no mistaking the pride in his voice. In high school, if Josh was caught with his hand up Lula Jane's blouse or sticking his tongue down Betty Carlisle's throat behind the bleachers, her father wouldn't go on about the evils of promiscuity. He and Josh's father would dismiss it with a wink and a nudge, then slap Josh on the butt and tell him he played one helluva football game.

Maybe the double standard wouldn't have bothered Rebecca so much if her father hadn't wanted a son so desperately. But she knew, as the youngest, she'd been Doyle Wells's last hope for a boy, and he wasn't happy she'd failed him. The suspicion that he'd rather have the boy across the street than his youngest daughter had soon made Josh the bane of Rebecca's existence. She'd immediately set out to conquer and defeat—or at least to prove that anything he could do, she could do better. If Josh climbed a tree, she climbed higher. Once she fell and broke her arm and he had to run for help, but that didn't put an end to the rivalry that raged between them. Her humiliation only escalated it. If Josh hopped a fence, or waded through the creek on his way to school, ruining his clothes, she proved she wasn't afraid to do the same.

Though her father generally reacted with something far less than pride, she did have a few moments of glory. On Josh's ninth birthday, when he received his first two-wheeled bicycle, she challenged him to a race around the block and somehow managed to beat him. Her father was absolutely beaming when she crossed the finish line; his father was not.

So much for glory days, Rebecca thought as she immersed the lettuce in cold water and started ripping it into pieces. Sheer determination couldn't make up for Josh's advantage in size and strength forever, so Rebecca had been forced to find other areas in which to assert herself. If Josh ran for student body president, she ran against him—and lost. If Josh took debate, she challenged him on the other side of the argument—and thanks to her sharp tongue, usually won. If Josh made honor roll, she tried for Principal's List—and most semesters fell laughably short.

Fortunately life with Josh as part of the community eventually achieved a sort of precarious equilibrium. Once they graduated from high school, he went off to college in Utah and she went to massage school in Iowa before changing her mind and going to beauty school, instead. When they both returned to Dundee, they pretty much left each other alone. Until that hot August night a year ago last summer. What happened then, Rebecca couldn't explain. She didn't even want to think about it. She could only concede that Josh had come a long way since the age of eight. He was now six-four and two hundred pounds of lean hard muscle—which she knew because she'd had the pleasure of exploring nearly every inch of him.

"Are you going to answer me?" her mother prodded.

Rebecca's throat had gone dry at the memory of Josh's bare chest. "What was the question?" she asked, shoving his image from her mind.

"I want to know why you don't like your brother-in-law."

She shrugged. "I don't have to like him. I'm not the one who married him." Shaking water off the leaves, she tossed them into the bowl she'd removed from one of the glass-fronted cupboards. Like everything else—the sink, the counters, the appliances and the tile floor—the cupboards were so white the reflection of the setting sun, streaming unchecked through large square windows running along the entire back of the house, nearly blinded her. The windows and the shiny new kitchen were the results of a recent renovation. The old kitchen had been avocado-green and brown—a color scheme Rebecca hoped would never gain popularity again.

Her mother scraped the onions into a frying pan and added a pat of butter. "But he's a great guy. What's not to like?"

"Nothing. Forget it," Rebecca said.

"Now that you've brought up it up, I'd finally like to know."

"The memories we have of each other from high school aren't the most pleasant, that's all."

"What memories?"

Most of them had far more to do with Josh Hill than Randy, but Randy had been constantly at Josh's elbow, which meant he was included. "We had a few run-ins," she said vaguely.

"Because he was a friend of Josh Hill's?"

Unfortunately the conversation was drifting toward Josh and she wasn't sure she could stop it. "Maybe."

"So we're not really talking about Randy. We're talking about Joshua."

"No, I'm not talking about Josh. I never talk about Josh," Rebecca responded.

Her mother found a spatula in the drawer and began stirring the sizzling onions. "Well, perhaps it's time you did," she said. "I've always wanted to get to the bottom of this feud between you two. We love Josh and his older brother. His parents are good friends of ours."

Rebecca sighed. "I know. But it's too late to improve relations between Josh and me, so don't get it in your head to try. The bad blood between us is old, old news."

"That might be the case, but I want you to bury whatever grudge you're holding against him."

"Are you kidding?" Rebecca paused in her knife attack on the radishes. The sudden absence of her rapid *thump, thump, thump* made the silence seem loud. "What's the point? We run into each other a lot, but it's only in passing. We could go on like this indefinitely. There's no reason to change anything."

"Now there is. You'll soon be seeing each other more than in passing."

"That sounds pretty specific. When?" And Rebecca had thought Buddy's news was the worst she could receive.

"Your sisters are planning an anniversary celebration for your father and me. It's in two weeks."

The scent of her mother's grilled onions became almost overpowering. "Somehow I knew you didn't invite me over to talk about candles."

"I did find some good candles," her mother said.

Rebecca retrieved two stalks of celery from the fridge, washed them and started chopping them on the cutting board. She realized she could probably avoid the subject of Josh by using the candles to segue into Buddy's postponement of the wedding. But the words stuck in her throat when she envisioned what her experience at the anniversary party would be like if she mentioned her latest setback too soon. "Heard you and Buddy are waiting a few weeks longer… You think that boy really knows what he wants?… Musta figured out what he was getting himself into, huh?" (said with a hearty chuckle).

Deciding that it would be much better to wait until after her parents' anniversary, she plunged back into the subject of Josh Hill. "What does this party have to do with me and Josh? We can attend the same function without causing a scene."

Her mother looked less than optimistic. "Like you did at Delia's wedding?"

Rebecca threw the core of the lettuce in the trash compactor. "Is that what this is all about? You blame me for what happened at Delia's wedding? I've told you, it wasn't my fault."

"Then whose fault was it?" her mother wanted to know. "You can't blame Josh, not when you were the one who tripped him."

"He only *thought* I was going to trip him. He overreacted." She'd said so before, but no one seemed to care.

"Regardless, he fell into the cake and took the whole food table down with him." Her mother winced at the painful memory.

"I told you, it was his mistake."

"Maybe. But you're the one who darted away from him at the last second and ran smack into the punch fountain, dousing your poor sister. She was so sticky, she had to miss the end of her own reception to change and shower. By the time she and Brad left on their honeymoon, her eyes were swollen, her nose was red from crying, and her hair and dress were ruined."

"Okay, the punch part might've been my fault," Rebecca conceded. "Josh grabbed at me when he fell and I was trying to get away so he couldn't pull me down with him."

"Better you fall in an undignified heap than the bride gets sprayed with punch. It wasn't a pleasant thing for Delia to—"

The door banged open as her father strode in from the garage, briefcase in hand, and whatever her mother was about to say was immediately lost in the human power surge. Loud, authoritative and supremely confident, her father commanded respect simply by being. The fact that he'd been the mayor of Dundee since Rebecca was in high school, was well over six feet and resembled Billy Graham certainly didn't hurt. "Did you tell her?" he demanded the moment he spotted Rebecca.

Her mother gave him one of her famous warning looks and cleared her throat. "Actually, Doyle, we were just getting around to—"

"Tell me what?" Rebecca interrupted, meeting her father's direct gaze. He might not approve of her, but she wasn't going to flinch in his presence like everyone else. And she sure as heck wasn't going to use her mother as a go-between.

"That you're not invited to the anniversary celebration unless you can behave yourself," he said point-blank. "I've had it with this thing between you and Josh Hill. I won't have you embarrassing me again." With that, he stalked from the kitchen, presumably to change out of his suit.

Rebecca put down the knife she'd been rinsing and let her wet hands dangle in the sink. "Not everyone sees Josh Hill through the same rose-colored glasses you do, Dad," she called after him.

"That would only be you," he hollered back. "Everyone else in this town knows Josh for what he is—an ambitious young man with a shrewd business mind. That boy's going to make something of himself someday. You wait and see."

"And I'm not? Is that what you're implying?"

He didn't answer. He didn't have to. Though Rebecca loved her profession, she knew that in her parents' opinion, a hairstylist—even an accomplished hairstylist—could never compare to a successful horse breeder like Josh. Josh

Hill had somehow been able to win the love and approval she'd always craved, especially from her father. But what bothered her most was that he'd done it so effortlessly and so long ago. How could she compete with someone so well entrenched in her father's affections?

She hadn't been able to compete with Josh at seven. She couldn't compete with him now. She wasn't even sure why she kept trying.

After finishing the salad, she set it on the table and retrieved her keys.

"Where are you going?" her mother asked, alarmed. "Aren't you staying for dinner?"

Rebecca pictured the moment her sister and the kids arrived; she pictured sitting across the table from her father. "No, Dad already took care of what you both wanted to say. Consider me warned," she said and headed for the entry.

"Rebecca?"

She paused.

"He doesn't mean to sound so harsh, honey," her mother said softly.

"Oh, he meant it all right," she said. Rebecca wasn't sure about a lot of things—why Buddy kept putting off their wedding, why she'd gone home with Josh a year ago last summer (and how she'd even started dancing with him in the first place), why she didn't really fit into her own family. But she knew her father had meant every word.

REBECCA SAT on her back step as darkness fell, and lit up a cigarette. She'd managed to get through yesterday without smoking, despite Buddy's call, but one visit to her parents' house and—POOF—there went her resolve. What difference did it make, anyway? She couldn't change her stripes. Even if she decided to become a nun, the good folks of

Dundee would find something to criticize, her father chief among them.

At least she'd come by her reputation honestly. She'd raised eyebrows in Dundee more times than she could count and had certainly given Josh a run for his money in their younger days. She still remembered filling his locker with pincher bugs, spray-painting "Josh Sucks" on the sidewalk in front of his house and telling everyone that his penis was a mere three inches long (without adding that she was going by information gleaned ten years earlier in a classic "I'll show you mine if you show me yours").

Contrary to popular belief, however, he was hardly blameless. He'd retaliated by jamming her locker so she couldn't open it, which made her fail an English test because she couldn't turn in the essay she'd written the night before. He and Randy stole a pair of panties from her gym locker and ran them up the flagpole. And Josh had offered to give her a more current measurement of his penis. She'd refused, of course. But plenty of other girls had come forward to vouch for something far more impressive than three inches. Taken with his football prowess, even her accusation of a small penis wasn't enough to dent Josh's overwhelming popularity.

Rebecca was the only one, it seemed, who didn't worship Josh Hill. And that hadn't changed over the years. No matter what happened, her father remained one of his staunchest supporters.

A staunch supporter of the *enemy*. She grimaced and took another drag on her cigarette. About Josh, her father always said, "He's made his parents proud, hasn't he?" About Rebecca her father always said, "God tries us all."

Oh well, nothing in Dundee was going to matter when she moved to Nebraska, she told herself. But that line of reasoning didn't pack the same power it used to because she was no longer sure she'd be moving to Nebraska. Buddy had left several messages on her answering machine today, but she didn't feel like returning them. She felt like sitting on the steps, smoking one cigarette after another, watching the moths hover about her porch light. Autumn was here. The leaves were turning, the days growing shorter. Rebecca had always loved the crisp mountain air, and she wondered if Nebraska was very different. She'd only visited there once, the past spring....

If she did move, she'd miss autumn in Idaho. And she'd miss Delaney.

Picking up the cordless phone she'd carried outside with her, she dialed her best friend at the ranch where Delaney now lived with her husband, Conner Armstrong.

"You're smoking again," Delaney said, almost as soon as she answered.

Rebecca exhaled. "That's the first thing you've got to say to me?"

"You promised me you were going to quit for real this time."

Rebecca removed her cigarette and watched the smoke curl up into the sky. "Yeah, well, that was before I went over to my parents' tonight. Be grateful I'm only smoking."

"Something happen at your folks?"

After another long drag, Rebecca stubbed out her cigarette, then stretched her legs. "Nothing new. How's the pregnancy?"

"The doctor says everything looks fine."

"Good. Hard to believe you're almost ready to pop. The past few months have gone fast." In fact, considering that Rebecca and Buddy had been engaged before Delaney even met Conner, time had streaked by. Delaney was starting a family; Rebecca was trying to work up the nerve to tell everyone her wedding had just been postponed *again*.

"I'm big enough that it's getting a little uncomfortable," Delaney complained. "I've lost my toes."

Rebecca thought she wouldn't mind gaining twenty-five pounds and losing sight of her toes if it meant a baby. "Guess that goes with the territory, huh? Did you ever find the dressers you were looking for?"

"Conner told me to buy new ones. But I'm having fun hunting for bargains. It keeps me occupied while he oversees the building of the resort. Maybe I'll drive to Boise next week and visit a few garage sales, see what I can find. You're off Monday. Want to go with me?"

Rebecca's call-waiting beeped before she could answer. "Hang on a sec," she said and hit the flash button. "Hello?"

"Rebecca?"

It was her father. She sat up and shook another cigarette out of the package, knowing instinctively she'd need one. "Yeah?"

"I just talked to Josh Hill."

She froze mid-motion. "Why do I get the feeling that comment is somehow related to me?"

"Because it is. I asked him to call a truce between the two of you."

Rebecca stuck the unlit cigarette in her mouth and found her lighter. "You didn't," she said, speaking around it.

"I did." A brief, unhappy hesitation. "Are you smoking again? I thought you'd quit."

Dropping her lighter in her lap, she quickly pulled the cigarette from her mouth. "I have."

"I hope so. That's such a nasty habit."

"Why did you call Josh, Dad? There's no reason to ask for a truce."

"After what happened at Delia's wedding?"

"That was an accident. We haven't done anything to each other on purpose for years." Barring the night they'd gone to Josh's place from the Honky Tonk, of course. They'd done a few things to each other then—and would probably have done a lot more if they hadn't been interrupted. But that night didn't count. Feverish groping didn't fall in the same category as their earlier dealings.

"I'm tired of being afraid to have you two in the same room," her father replied.

"Is that what you told him?"

"That's what I told him."

"And he said…" Rebecca toyed nervously with her lighter, flipping the lid open, closed, open, closed. *Click, click…click, click.*

"He agreed to let the past go."

"He did?"

"That's what I just said, isn't it? Now, what do you say?"

Click, click…click, click.

Words were cheap, Rebecca decided. Why not let her father feel as though his intervention had solved everything? "Okay."

"Okay, what?"

"Okay, we're calling a truce."

"Good." Her father sounded inordinately pleased. "I told him I could convince you."

"You've done a bang-up job, Dad. Is that all?"

"Not quite."

Rebecca hesitated, fearing she hadn't heard the worst of it yet. "What do you mean by that?"

"As a gesture of good faith, he's stopping by the salon tomorrow for a haircut."

Rebecca coughed as though she'd just swallowed a bug.

When she could speak, she said, "But he always gets his hair cut at the barbershop."

"Not tomorrow. Tomorrow he's coming to you. He'll be there at ten. Good night."

"Wait," she cried. "I can't cut his hair."

"Why not?" her father asked, his voice now gruff. "You agreed to the truce, remember?"

Collecting her cigarettes and lighter, Rebecca stood and began to pace across the small porch. "Of course I *remember,* but…but tomorrow's Saturday. I'm booked solid."

"Not at ten in the morning you're not."

"How do you know?"

"Because I was your first appointment, and I just gave him my slot."

Her heart sank. "You sure you want to do that, Dad?"

"Positive."

"But this is crazy. How does my cutting Josh's hair cement this…little truce of yours?"

"Consider it a trial run for the anniversary party. If you two can get through tomorrow without killing each other, we'll all breathe a little easier."

Rebecca propped the phone on one shoulder and shoved a hand through her new Ashley Judd hairstyle, frantically trying to think of some way out. But her father didn't give her a chance to argue further. He surprised her by saying, "You're doing the right thing, Beck. And stay away from those damn cigarettes." Then he hung up.

Shocked, she blinked into the dark yard for several seconds, not knowing what to think.

"Was that Buddy?" Delaney asked as soon as she switched back over.

"It was my father."

"Everything okay?"

"No. Absolutely not."

"Why?" Delaney asked. "What's wrong?"

"I'm supposed to cut Josh Hill's hair tomorrow."

Silence met this statement, followed by, "You're kidding, right? Josh is going to put himself at your mercy when you've got a pair of scissors in your hands?"

Rebecca bit her lip and sighed as she headed back inside the house. "I guess we'll see, huh?"

CHAPTER THREE

REBECCA GLANCED NERVOUSLY through Hair And Now's large front window as the clock ticked inexorably toward ten. The weather was cool and clear with a slight breeze—another perfect autumn day. Not many people were out and about yet, but Saturdays typically started slow at this end of town. Three blocks away at the bakery, there'd be a crowd wanting coffee, donuts and muffins. Starbucks might be taking over the planet, but the citizens of Dundee still patronized Don and Tami's Bakery.

Maybe Josh wouldn't show, Rebecca thought hopefully, noting the dearth of traffic. If he stood her up, she could shrug when she next saw her father and say, "I was perfectly willing to make peace, Dad, but he never arrived." And then she'd look innocent for a change.

Perfect. She smiled as she began readying her station with rods and tissues for the permanent wave she'd be giving at eleven, imagining the look of disappointment on her father's face if for once Josh failed him. This whole truce thing could end up working in her favor. She could feign disappointment in his stubborn refusal to put the past behind them and—

The bell rang over the door, causing Rebecca's daydream to dissipate. She knew without turning that Josh had arrived. The murmur that ran from Katie, the other stylist, to Mona, the manicurist, to Nancy Shepherd, who was having her nails done, would have told Rebecca even if her sixth sense did not.

But her sixth sense was working just fine. Somehow she could always tell when Josh was around. He made her feel clumsy, nervous, unattractive.

No wonder she didn't like him. Anyway, despite her wishful thinking, she'd known all along that he'd appear. He'd never been one to back down from a challenge.

Rebecca cleaned her combs and scissors before looking up. She needed a moment to gather her nerve. Josh was so much easier to hate when he wasn't within ten feet of her. Ever since she'd made the mistake of going home with him that one night, something had changed. She wasn't sure exactly what it was, but it made their relationship—or *absence* of a relationship—very complex. She supposed kissing a man the way she'd kissed him, as though she longed to climb inside his skin and live there for the rest of her life, tended to confuse the issues.

"Hi, Josh, what brings you in today?" Mona asked. At least fifteen years his senior, Mona had a handful of children at home as well as a husband, but the pitch of her voice suggested she could still appreciate a handsome man when she saw one. And Josh was definitely handsome. He had thick blond hair that fell carelessly across his forehead, skin that tanned so easily he was golden-brown before anyone else even thought of bringing out their summer clothes, and intelligent green eyes that sparkled with more than enough mischief to keep a woman guessing.

Fortunately Rebecca had long ago perfected her immunity to his rugged virility. She couldn't really explain her brief lapse that fateful August 16th, but she was still Rebecca Wells. Josh Hill was never going to get the best of her.

"I have an appointment this morning," he told Mona.

"You're Katie's first client?"

"He's not *my* ten o'clock," Katie said. "Unless there's been some mix-up, I'm doing a perm for Mrs. Vanderwall. And Erma's not coming in today. She's off visiting her sister in Boise."

From the corner of her eye, Rebecca saw Josh shove his hands in the pockets of his Wranglers. "Actually, I'm here to see Rebecca."

"You're joking, right?" Mona was chuckling as she spoke, as though he *had* to be joking. Everyone in town knew that putting her and Josh together was like putting a match to gasoline.

Rebecca cleared her throat and faced them fully. If she waited any longer to acknowledge Josh's presence, he might realize she wasn't quite up to her usual self.

"Josh, good to see you," she said, forcing a smile.

He gave her that crooked grin of his, the one that showed his dimples, and immediately called her on the lie. "Are you sure?"

Hell, no. "I'm trying to be positive," she said, clasping her hands in front of her because she suddenly didn't know where to put them.

He settled his black felt cowboy hat further back on his head. "So this truce thing is for real."

"I guess," she said with a shrug.

"Because I gotta tell ya, that fiasco at your sister's wedding was…" He shook his head and let his breath go all at once.

"I can't believe you'd even bring that up," Rebecca responded, bridling. "You made me take out the punch fountain."

He cocked an eyebrow at her. "You're the one who tripped me in the first place."

"I didn't even touch you!"

"Wait a second," Katie said. "That wedding was the most exciting thing this town has seen in the past three years. If you two call a truce, life's going to get pretty boring around here. Who will Rebecca have to fight with?"

"She doesn't need me," Josh said. "She's always been her own worst enemy."

Katie started to chuckle, but Rebecca gave her a look that said "shut up or pay later." Katie covered her mouth with one hand in an effort to hide her amusement. But Rebecca wasn't fooled. She would've said something to the effect that she wouldn't be around to entertain everyone much longer. Except she felt a little unsure of that right now. And Mrs. Vanderwall entered the salon just then, offering the perfect distraction.

"Your ten o'clock is here," Rebecca said pointedly to Katie and narrowed her eyes at Mona long enough to remind her that she had a client, too. As Mona finally bent over Nancy Shepherd's hands, Nancy said, "Don't look at me, I didn't say anything," and Rebecca turned back to Josh. "I should've known you'd make this difficult."

His devil-may-care grin reappeared. "I thought that's how you like things."

"I don't like things difficult."

"Yes, you do. The harder the better."

Rebecca was fairly certain he didn't mean what he'd said as a sexual innuendo, but his words still brought visions of August 16th. He'd been as aroused as she had—which was the only saving grace about the whole experience. She might have embarrassed herself by nearly sleeping with the enemy but, if memory served, the attraction had been very mutual. "I'm not the one who rained on your parade," she said.

"Excuse me?"

"*You* moved in across the street from *me*."

"That's what you hold against me?" he cried. "That I moved in across the street from you? How the hell was I supposed to help that? I was eight years old, for crying out loud."

She hadn't really meant what she'd said, of course. He hadn't ruined her life by moving in across the street. He'd ruined her life by being everything her father had ever wanted. But trying to explain that would sound equally ridiculous. She was thirty-one. Her father's preference for Josh shouldn't bother her anymore.

"Never mind," she said. "Are you planning on staying or what? Because you don't have to, you know. I'll just tell my father that you chickened out at the last minute. I'm sure he'll understand."

"Chickened out?" he repeated.

She smiled sweetly. "Isn't that what you'd call it?"

"I'd call it an issue of trust. The thought of you standing over me with a sharp instrument strikes fear into my heart."

"Oh, come on. You'd have to have a heart for that," she said, and thought she heard Mona snicker.

Josh rubbed his chin as though she'd just delivered a nice left hook. "You certainly haven't changed much," he said sulkily.

"You have good reason to worry," Mona muttered from where she was sitting at her station up front, filing Nancy's nails.

"I bet five bucks he won't stay," Nancy piped up.

"I'll put ten on that," Katie said.

"What's the bet?" Mrs. Vanderwall had been too busy trying to straighten her girdle so she could sit down to pay much attention to what was going on around her. At eighty, her hearing wasn't what it used to be. Katie started to explain, but she only got partway before Mrs. Vanderwall waved her to silence. "Never mind the rest. It doesn't matter. No one's a match for Rebecca. I'll put twenty on *her* getting the best of *him*.''

Rebecca wasn't flattered by this show of support. She wasn't *that* much of an ogre, was she? Sure, she'd lost her temper a few times in the past. Once she'd blackened Gilbert Tripp's eye when he backed into Delaney's car, but he'd deserved it. He'd tried to drive away before she and Delaney could get out of the Quick Mart, and when Rebecca finally chased him down, he'd blamed the accident on Delaney's parking. Their argument had quickly escalated and the next thing Rebecca knew...well, she'd let one fly. But she didn't doubt Josh would have done the same!

"Forget it," she told him. "I'm not out to get the best of you or anyone else. Just go down to the barbershop and buy yourself a haircut." Her voice had gone flat. She cleared her throat and tried to put more inflection in it. "I'll tell my father you stopped by and everything went fine, okay?"

He stared at her for a long moment without speaking. She lifted her chin and threw back her shoulders, praying he wouldn't realize that her friends' banter had stung. She was tired of being the bad guy, tired of being a laughingstock. But as long as she remained in Dundee, there was no escaping her reputation.

"Okay?" she repeated when he didn't respond.

He started to move. She thought he was going to swing around and head right back out, onto the street. But he didn't. He strode across the salon, doffed his hat and planted himself decisively in her chair.

"You've probably got a big day," he said. "We'd better get busy."

Rebecca blinked at him. She could've sworn he'd decided to stay for her sake, to silence the others. But that couldn't be. That would take intuition and an unusual degree of sensitivity, and this was Josh Hill. The Testosterone King. The boy who wrote, "For a good time call anyone *but* Rebecca Wells," on the bathroom wall at the A&W, starting a whole section of graffiti about her, none of which was very flattering. His staying probably had more to do with proving to everyone else in Hair And Now that they'd been foolish to bet against him—why would anyone do that? He was the great Josh Hill.

The others grumbled about being wrong but finally returned to minding their own business. Rebecca nodded in acknowledgement. "Fine. It shouldn't take long."

Spine so rigid she was surprised it didn't creak when she moved, she draped her cape over his broad shoulders, covering his polo shirt and most of his blue jeans. As she fastened the collar, her fingers brushed his neck and he swiveled to look up at her.

She raised her hands to show him she held nothing sharp. "Just fastening the cape," she said.

"I didn't think you were going to stab me," he grumbled.

"You jumped." What else would make him react that way? She'd barely touched him. In any case, she wasn't going to argue the point. She was too determined to get through this as quickly as possible.

"What would you like me to do for you?" she asked.

"*Do* for me?" he repeated as though the question somehow surprised him.

"To your hair." Stepping on the lever, she lowered the chair as far as possible. She was tall, but he was several inches taller. She needed to accommodate his height. "What would you like me to do to your hair?"

"Just give it a trim."

"Okay. You don't want me to shampoo it, though, right?" She reached for her spray bottle. "We'll be done much faster if we just wet the hair down and go from there.''

He leaned away from her. "Isn't shampooing included in the price of a cut?''

Rebecca hesitated, spray bottle in hand. "Um, yes, it is, but...I'll give you a discount. A good discount.''

"No, thanks,'' he said. "I'll have the full treatment.''

"O-k-a-y. Sure.'' She glanced from Katie to Mona to see if they'd done something to challenge him, thereby causing him to prolong the agony, but they seemed engaged with their own clients.

Setting the spray bottle on top of the rolling cart that held most of her supplies, she took a deep breath. She'd shampooed hundreds of people without a second thought. But she didn't want to shampoo Josh. "Then...uh...you need to come back here with me.''

He stood and followed her past the short row of old-fashioned hairdryers, shelves of products and racks of hair magazines to the sinks at the very back of the salon. Waving him into a cushioned seat on her left, she levered the adjustable black vinyl chair so he could lie with his neck resting comfortably in the crook of the porcelain bowl.

Mostly decorated in pink, with a wide stripe to the wallpaper and a black canvas awning over the door, the salon was about as feminine a place as Rebecca could imagine. It smelled of bleach and acrylic and perm solution—a virtual self-improvement paradise into which few men ever ventured. Until recently, anyway. With the growing popularity of spiked, bleached hair among young boys, Rebecca's male clientele had grown sharply.

But Josh looked out of place all the same. His body was too big for the chair, which had been designed twenty years earlier for women, and his well-scuffed boots and the slightly frayed hem of his jeans provided a notable contrast to the muumuus and cotton print dresses Rebecca generally saw sticking out from below her plastic cape. He smelled different, too. More…evocative. A blend of warm skin, leather and soap reminded her of that night a year ago last summer when she and Josh were dancing at the Honky Tonk. While they were swaying to the music, he'd put his hands possessively on the small of her back, drawing her closer, and then he'd kissed her neck just below the ear-lobe.…

A shiver ran down Rebecca's spine, and she quickly forced her mind back to the present. She didn't want to think about that. That night was an exception, the only exception, to the way she normally felt about Josh. And it made her nervous again.

"Remember when you taped up that *Playboy* centerfold inside my locker our senior year?" he asked, out of no-where.

His comment took Rebecca off guard. She didn't know how to respond. If she said no, they'd both know she was lying. If she said yes, they'd be back on adversarial ground. "It was just a joke," she said, mumbling slightly in hopes he wouldn't pursue the conversation.

"Someone reported me to the principal before I even knew it was there and I got suspended for three days."

She adjusted the water temperature. "Three days? That's not so long."

"It was during finals," he added dryly.

She stretched her neck, hoping he wasn't going to re-count their other shared experiences. "Those were crazy days."

He made a face. "That's all you have to say?"

"What do you want? An apology? It was years ago."

"Thanks for the sincere remorse."

Remorse. Rebecca was too apprehensive for remorse.

The prospect of touching her childhood nemesis was causing an odd reaction in her body. She was trying to convince herself it was revulsion, but sweaty palms and a racing heart weren't the most indicative symptoms.

Wetting his head, she poured shampoo into her palm and began to work it through his hair. She told herself to stick to the same routine she gave all her clients—a thorough ten-minute head massage, followed by a gentle raking of the scalp with her nails. She was a professional, after all, with a background in massage therapy, and he was paying for her services.

But somehow she couldn't maintain any emotional distance. Having Josh right there, so accessible and pliable beneath her hands, changed the whole experience.

Feeling a stab of guilt for having such a strong reaction to him—in spite of her engagement—she cut the massage short and quickly rinsed his hair. Then she slapped on some conditioner, nearly spraying him in the face when she went into rinse mode again.

"What'd I do now?" he asked as she sat him up so fast she nearly gave him whiplash.

"Nothing," she said, tossing a towel into his lap. "Why?"

He swiped at the water that was running down from his temples and dripping onto the cloak. "That was some shampoo. I've never seen anyone snap into fast-forward like that."

She smiled to cover the craziness inside her. "Well, you know me."

He raised his brows. "Somehow you always manage to surprise me."

"YOU KNOW, IF WE TOOK a little more off the top, we'd make the most of the cowlick you've got right here," Rebecca said.

Josh shifted his gaze from the look of expectation on her face to his own reflection. One of Rebecca's hands held up a section of his hair, the other clutched a pair of scissors. "Are you setting me up?" he asked.

That cowlick had been a nightmare for him when he was a kid. His mother had waged her own personal war against it, usually armed with a jar of Dippity-do. Up until the time he was six or seven, she'd plastered his hair to his head, making him look more like a young executive than a first-grader. Fortunately it hadn't taken him long to learn how to compensate for her efforts by visiting the bathroom before class and using the sink to rinse his hair. His bangs always stuck up once they dried, but he hadn't minded that. What he'd minded was the perennial "wet look" and the way his mother had constantly licked her fingers and combed his hair down, even in public.

Rebecca rolled her eyes. "It's only hair. If I botch it too badly, you can always shave your head."

"That's supposed to make me feel better?"

"Come on, don't be a wimp. Bald is in. And I'm not going to mess up. I have my reputation to consider."

"Your reputation is what frightens me."

She sent him a pointed look, and he couldn't help smiling. After the shampooing incident she'd calmed down a bit and seemed to be hitting her rhythm. But when it came to Rebecca, nothing was ever the way he thought it would be, so he had no idea how long the peace might last.

"Do what you think is best," he told her, even though it went against his better judgment to give her so much freedom. Especially when he remembered the time she put gum in his hair while he and Randy were having a sleepout in the yard.

He chuckled as the clippings from his hair fell all around him.

"What's so funny?" she asked.

"I was just thinking about that time you snuck over and—"

"Never mind."

"Wait," he said. "I was just going to see if you remembered putting gum—"

"No."

Obviously she didn't want to discuss the past, but that incident and several others, while horrific enough at the time, seemed pretty funny now. Couldn't she see how immature and stupid they'd been? "Don't want to take a walk down memory lane, huh?"

"Not with you."

"Why not? You have to admit some of that stuff is funny."

"Hilarious," she grumbled. "Only no one seems to remember what *you* did."

"What'd *I* do?" he asked.

"You know what you did. Quit playing the innocent."

"At least I feel bad about my terrible behavior," he replied.

"I'll bet."

She was right, of course. He didn't feel any worse than she did. She'd pulled pranks on him; he'd pulled pranks on her. After so many years, there was no way to sort out blame—and the thought of even trying to do it bored him. He didn't care anymore. So why didn't they just forgive and forget? They were both adults, with separate lives to lead. Yet every time he passed Rebecca on the street or saw her somewhere like Jerry's Diner, he got the feeling they had unfinished business between them.

Probably because of that night over a year ago—even

though nothing had ultimately happened. He'd gotten Rebecca to go home with him. He'd even managed to remove her clothes, along with most of his own. Then his brother had come home and at the slamming of the front door, she'd suddenly scrambled to her feet, dressed, grabbed her purse and hurried off. He'd been two seconds away from the best sex of his life, so crazy for her he almost begged her to stay. Except he'd known it wouldn't do him any good. It was as if she'd suddenly come out of a trance and realized who she was with. After that, she didn't want him anywhere near her.

But his preoccupation with Rebecca was just an ego thing, he assured himself. Something to do with conquering her at last. She was the girl in school who thumbed her nose when he passed in the halls or booed when he threw a touchdown. He'd wanted to make her a believer. That was all. He'd only come today hoping to put all that behind them so they could finally achieve neutrality.

Unfortunately, it wasn't that easy with Rebecca. She held too much against him, even though he'd never set out to make a real enemy of her. For a few years when he was a kid, he'd thought it fun to torture girls by putting spiders in their hair or chasing them home from school with a craggy old stick he claimed to be one of his dead grandmother's bones. But his grandmother hadn't even died at that point. And Rebecca had never been intimidated by that kind of stuff, anyway. The one time he'd put a spider in her hair, all the other girls had screamed, but not her. She'd calmly scooped it up and set it gently on the ground. Later she'd dredged up a garter snake and slipped it down the back of his shirt when he wasn't looking. He'd liked snakes, so that part was actually kind of cool. What wasn't so cool was that a girl had beat him at his own game.

Still, he'd always liked Rebecca's toughness. She was

different from the other girls. More stubborn. More prideful. He'd never seen determination on a person's face like he'd so often seen on hers—usually when they were competing in some way. He knew how badly she hated to lose, but she'd never let him see her cry. If he beat her at something, she'd jut out her chin and tell him he'd had a stroke of luck. Or she'd challenge him again. Sometimes he let her win just because he was tired of being goaded to give her another chance.

So, all in all, he supposed what had happened when they were young probably wasn't so different from what happened to a lot of kids. In elementary school, boys occasionally pinched girls, pulled their hair, whatever. It was the "cooties" stage, and girls turned up their noses at boys, too. Rebecca just never forgave him as they grew older. There were times when he'd tried to seek her out, tried to win her over, but it made no difference at all.

He remembered one time in particular, right before his first game as starting quarterback for the varsity football team. He was only a junior and had yet to prove to the town that his dad, who was head coach, hadn't put him in because of the family connection. The senior who'd been planning to start that year was furious about losing his position. So were his folks. They'd stirred up all kinds of trouble around town, which threatened his father's job, and Josh knew the only way to silence the critics was to play the best game he'd ever played in his life. He was feeling the pressure of it all when he spotted Rebecca standing near the bleachers. He caught her eye, thinking if he could only get her to smile at him, just once, everything would be okay. But she'd cast him that "who gave you the right to breathe" look and turned away.

Fortunately, he'd thrown for over two hundred yards,

including three touchdown passes, and they'd won the game. No thanks to Rebecca.

The other girls in town came around, though. In the second grade, he'd pulled Beth Paris's ponytails countless times, yet she'd ended up asking him to take her to the Homecoming Dance when they were seniors. And she'd wanted to do a lot more than dance. Certainly no hard feelings there.

Forget about Rebecca, he told himself, growing cranky. It'd been twenty-four years since he'd met her, and he was just as confused by her now as he'd ever been. Men who thought women were complicated creatures didn't know the half of it—unless they knew Rebecca Wells.

"You don't like it?" she said, sounding for the first time in all those twenty-four years as though she wasn't quite sure of herself.

"What are you talking about?"

"The expression on your face. You look like you're ready to choke someone."

He wondered what she'd say if he told her she was the one he was thinking about choking. She probably wouldn't be surprised. If she wasn't so engrossed in cutting his hair, she'd most likely be thinking about choking him, too. That was the way it was between them.

"Looks good," he said, even though he couldn't tell a whole lot while it was still wet. It just seemed shorter.

She set her scissors down on the vanity and retrieved her blow-dryer from a holster-like holder. "You're lucky to have that cowlick," she said. "It gives your hair some lift here, off the forehead, and adds a lot of body."

"Yeah, well, you might mention that to my mother the next time you see her standing in line at the drugstore to buy Dippity-do," he said. "Maybe I won't get a jar for Christmas this year."

"If I came within ten yards of your mother, she'd probably shoot me."

"Now that you mention it, she is a little bitter," he admitted. "I guess I'm stuck with the Dippity-Do."

"If it depends on me, you are," she said and switched on the blow-dryer. The resulting whir left Josh to his own thoughts again, but only for a few minutes. Soon Katie interrupted them by tapping Rebecca's shoulder. "Your father's here," she hollered over the noise.

CHAPTER FOUR

"THERE YOU ARE, my boy," Mayor Wells boomed, cutting across the salon.

Rebecca turned off the blow-dryer. Josh brushed the hair off his drape and stood to shake hands. "Good to see you, sir. You're looking fit, as always."

Dundee's mayor tapped his rounding middle. "Ah, the weight catches up with you eventually. Be forewarned. But you don't have to worry about that until you find someone to cook for you. When are you and that cute little Mary planning to tie the knot?"

He and Mary Thornton had been dating since Mary's divorce was final six months ago. Glen, her ex, had taken off for the big city almost a year before that, and Mary and their nine-year-old son, Ricky, had moved back in with her parents. Word had it that Glen was too busy chasing skirts to be a very conscientious father. Whether Glen was chasing skirts or not, Josh knew Ricky never heard from him. So Mary was understandably a little anxious to provide her son with a new and improved role model.

Josh had no doubt *he* was the role model she had in mind, but he wasn't entirely convinced he was going to let her lead him to the altar. He loved Ricky. Most of the time he liked him better than Mary. But he doubted the enjoyment he received from knowing her son was enough of a basis for marriage.

He opened his mouth to say that he and Mary had no

plans, but Doyle's attention had already shifted to Rebecca. "So you came through, huh?"

A certain strain around the mouth and eyes told Josh Rebecca wasn't happy to see her father. "I told you I would," she replied.

Doyle considered Josh's hair. "Well, it's not blue. That's a good sign."

Josh couldn't help glancing in the mirror, even though he'd been watching the entire process. Rebecca had actually given him a good cut. Though she hadn't quite finished, his hair was dry enough now that he could see what it was going to look like, and he was impressed. He'd been settling for the cut Ed down at the barbershop gave almost everyone who walked in, but she'd added a touch of style that was a welcome change.

"It's definitely not blue," he said, refusing to allow her too much credit.

"Did you stop by for a reason?" Rebecca asked her father.

The mayor smiled. "Just wanted to see how things were going down here."

"Well, we haven't killed each other yet, if that's what you were worried about."

Doyle turned just enough to exclude Rebecca from the conversation. "I hear you and your brother have yourselves another million-dollar stallion out at the ranch. That's five now, isn't it? Good for you. You're making quite a name for yourself in the Quarterhorse business."

"Things are going well, thanks," Josh said.

"How's the resort coming along?"

A *chung* indicated Rebecca had just shoved the blow-dryer back into its holder. In his peripheral vision, Josh saw her fold her arms, cock one leg and glower at her father. "I'm only an investor," he said, "so I'm not involved in the day-to-day management. But it seems to be doing well under Conner's hand.''

"Who would've thought that Armstrong fella could turn his life around and manage to pull off a project of this size? It's sure gonna do the community some good. Yes, sir." He shook his head. "Gives a father hope, doesn't it?"

At this Rebecca rolled her eyes and although Josh caught the insult in what Doyle said, he pretended not to notice. Whatever was going on between father and daughter had nothing to do with him. He'd agreed to the truce. He'd done his part. After he paid for his haircut, he was off the hook until the anniversary party.

"By the way, Rebecca's gettin' married and moving to Nebraska in a few weeks," Doyle went on. "Did she tell you?"

A coughing fit seized Rebecca. She quickly excused herself by mumbling something about needing a drink.

"I've heard a rumor to that effect," Josh said as they both watched her march to the back of the salon and duck into a small room.

"I thought I'd never see the day," Doyle confided.

"She's an attractive woman," Josh said, oddly defensive, although he couldn't say why. He used to feel a little smug when people made derogatory comments about Rebecca. And considering the fact that she'd be out of his life soon, out of town completely, he really didn't have a stake in whether or not her father appreciated her physical attributes or anything else.

"Oh, the problem isn't her looks," Doyle said. "Least not anymore."

Though she'd been far too thin and lanky in high school, Rebecca had filled out since then. Josh didn't think she'd ever be curvy, exactly—her breasts were high and small, her hips a little too narrow to be ideal. But he happened to like the way she was built.

He imagined her as he'd seen her last summer, lying on his bed with most of her clothes on the floor. Sure her breasts were small, but they were well-shaped and firm. And all the angles that had made her features appear exaggerated when she was young had evolved into...an arresting face, he decided, the perfect setting for her expressive eyes. Perhaps her top lip was a little too thin, but Josh couldn't see how any man could hold that against her. Not when she kissed with such abandon. When her defenses were down, and she was looking up at him as she had that night, without the usual distrust and resentment, she was actually quite beautiful.

"It's that temper of hers," Doyle was saying. "Why would anyone want to put up with her?"

Josh could have added an "amen" to that. Poor sap probably didn't know what he was getting into. But he wasn't going to involve himself by stating an opinion. "What's her fiancé like?" he asked, hoping to spin the conversation in a new direction so he wouldn't have to comment on Rebecca's suitability as a wife.

Doyle shoved his hands into the pockets of his khaki slacks—his nod to casual dress for the weekend—and jingled his change. "He's not from around here. She met him on the damn Internet, not that I'm complaining. At least she's got herself a man. Lord knows no one around here was willing to take her on. But I worry." He jingled his change some more as he seemed to mull over his concerns. "He's too mild-mannered for her, if you ask me."

"But you like him?"

"I've only met him once. I don't really know him. And I'm afraid she doesn't, either. He certainly isn't the type I would've expected her to choose." Doyle leaned a little closer and spoke out of the side of his mouth. "He's not much of a man, if you get my drift. He's soft. A bookworm. Doesn't look like he's done a hard day's work in his life. Once a few months go by, I have no doubt she'll be leading him around by the nose." He straightened. "And on top of everything else, he's younger than she is."

"He is? By how much?"

"Too much."

Too much? What was that supposed to mean? Curiosity prompted Josh to ask, but he overrode the impulse. Now that he'd done the right thing in coming here, he just needed to bide his time until she got married and moved. Resolution at last.

"But we're happy she's finally found someone and is settling down," Doyle went on. "Maybe she'll get turned around yet, like that Armstrong fella."

"You told me on the phone last night that she'd mellowed," Josh pointed out.

The other man grinned. "Had to tell you something to get you down here. We've got that anniversary party coming up. Her poor mother couldn't survive another embarrassing ordeal like the last one."

Josh cleared his throat. What had happened at Delia's wedding was more his fault than Rebecca's. Rebecca hadn't even touched him. "I think she has mellowed…a little," he said, because honesty demanded it.

"She's mellow only when it suits her. Yesterday she stormed out of the house again. I should be used to it by now."

"What does her fiancé do for a living?"

"Something with computers. Likes his job and doesn't want to leave. Least that's why they told me they'll be living in Nebraska."

Rebecca was on her way back. Doyle bowed his head

closer and lowered his voice, "Could be worse, I guess. Booker Robinson's in town. She could've hooked up with him."

Booker had visited Dundee for the summer once while he was in his teens. He'd come to stay with his Grandmother Hatfield, or Hatty as everyone called her, because his parents couldn't handle him. And he'd left quite an impression—on everyone. As a typical red-blooded American boy, Josh had figured he knew how to cause trouble. But his version of raising hell was good clean fun compared to Booker's.

"Did you say Booker's back?" Rebecca asked.

Doyle grimaced. "Now I've done it."

"When'd he get back?"

"I don't know the exact day he rolled into town. Louise over at Finley's Grocery saw him when he came in last Tuesday."

"And he's staying? For longer than a couple of weeks?"

"He told Louise he's here to take care of Hatty now that her health is failing." Doyle nudged Josh. "More likely he's hoping for an inheritance."

"He hasn't called me," Rebecca said, as though she wasn't really listening.

"I'm sure he will," her father said. "If I know him, he'll be looking for a partner in crime. But if you talk to him, you might want to tell him that I'm having Chief Tom keep an eye on him. He won't get away with anything this time."

"Would you give him a break, Dad?" Rebecca said, her patience obviously slipping. "He's been gone for…what? Twelve years? He was just a kid back then. I'm sure he's changed by now."

Josh couldn't help noticing that her father's verbal jab had included Rebecca, what with the "partner in crime" reference, but she said nothing in her own defense. Had she become so used to belittling remarks that she didn't even bother to respond?

He didn't want to think so. That threatened to pull him out of the "neutral zone," and, when it came to Rebecca, he wasn't about to abandon his central objective: to achieve peace, a sense of finality and very limited future involvement. The truce between them was already tenuous; he definitely shouldn't overstep his bounds. She wouldn't thank him for becoming her defender.

"If I know Booker, he hasn't changed enough," Doyle replied. "But I'll let you two finish up. Good to see you, Josh. You ever get a chance, stop by City Hall and I'll take you to lunch. And don't forget the anniversary party."

"Thank you," Josh said. "I won't."

He and Rebecca watched her father go without saying anything. Josh had nothing to say. He didn't like Booker, didn't want Rebecca to connect with him any more than her father did. He didn't like the fact that she was marrying someone who sounded so ill-suited to her—and so young. More than anything, he didn't like the condescending way her father had just treated her. But there wasn't a damn thing he could say or do about any of it because what happened in Rebecca's life was none of his business.

Tossing a twenty on her vanity, he jammed his hat on his head.

"You don't want me to finish?" she asked in surprise.

"It's fine the way it is," he said and walked out.

TALL, WIRY AND SLIGHTLY BOWLEGGED, with a head of thick dark hair that fell low on his brow, often shading his eyes, Booker T. Robinson hadn't changed much. He'd grown, of course, several inches from the look of him, and he'd filled out. But judging by the tattoos on his arms, the calluses and scars on his hands, and the long jagged scar on the right side of his face, the years hadn't been kind to him. Even the clothes he wore, a plain black T-shirt with a front pocket and tattered blue jeans, added to his tough-guy image.

He was a rebel, all right. But Rebecca liked him. Probably because he was one of the more honest people she'd met. At least he was generally honest with himself. He wasn't a pillar of the community. He probably never would be. But he didn't care what other people thought and he didn't pretend to be something he wasn't. He cussed and smoked and sometimes drank to excess. He said what he wanted to say and he offered no apologies or excuses.

Rebecca had never been happier to see anyone in her life. She sank into the white wicker chair on his grand-mother's porch, put her feet up on the railing and felt at home in her own skin for the first time in months.

"I couldn't believe it when my father said you were in town. Why haven't you called me?" she said.

He handed her the cold beer he'd offered her when she first came to the door and carried his own to the porch swing a few feet away. Popping the cap, he took a long drink and sat down before answering. "I wasn't so sure you'd be excited to see me. Your father was always one of those law and order types."

"Yeah, well, he still is. If he gets the chance, he might try to run you out of town. But don't take it personally. And don't let anything he does reflect on me."

He chuckled. "I see you two are still close."

Rebecca remembered the way her father had treated her in the salon that morning compared to the way he'd treated Josh—*stop by City Hall and I'll take you to lunch*—and felt her temper rise. But she didn't want to talk about it. She'd been trying to forget Josh ever since shampooing his hair had felt like a sexual encounter.

She took a sip of her beer. "You ever marry?"

"No."

"Kids?"

"No. You?"

"None so far. I am getting married, though. I just don't know when."

"That sounds promising. Who's the lucky guy?"

"Name's Buddy. Lives in Nebraska."

He nodded.

"What do you do for a living?" she asked.

"Nothing right now."

This time the silence felt awkward, and Rebecca knew she'd treaded too close to something he wasn't willing to discuss. So she backed off. "Haven't you been going stark-raving mad out here with only your grandmother for company?"

"Not yet. I only got in last weekend, and Granny's kept me busy fixing up the place." He gazed out over the meadowlike yard. "It's prettier here than I remembered."

The Hatfield property *was* pretty. Set away from Dundee, back in the mountains, it consisted of several wooded acres. The house, a simple white A-frame as old and charming as the one on *Little House on the Prairie,* had a wraparound porch with a hint of fancy woodwork at the windows and doors. A detached garage sat off to one side, at the end of a long drive, and a stone path led through the backyard, past a root cellar and a neatly tended vegetable garden, to the back porch.

"My dad said you've come to look after Hatty," Rebecca said. "Does that mean you're staying for a while?"

He pulled a pack of cigarettes from his shirt pocket and lit one, then offered one to her.

She almost grabbed it. She wanted to. But Josh didn't chew or smoke. In the bad habits department, as in all others, she didn't compare favorably to him, and she hated that.

"Figured it was the least I could do for all the years she's spent trying to reclaim my soul from the devil," Booker said. He set the cigarettes on the arm of the swing—within easy reach—when she refused them. "Fortunately, she's a lot better off than she let me believe. I think it was all a ruse to get me out here. But now that I'm here—" he shrugged "—I think I'll stick around. For a while, anyway."

"So did she ever manage to reform you? Are you a better man?" Rebecca shifted farther away so the smell of his smoking wouldn't tempt her beyond her endurance.

"I don't think I've changed a whole hell of a lot. But then, I'm getting the impression that neither have you."

"Even you?" she cried. "What does a girl have to do?"

He laughed outright. "What are you talking about?"

"I've been trying to change. I've been trying for years, but no one's even noticed, except maybe Delaney. If anything goes wrong, I still get the blame. When Josh Hill knocked over the food table at my sister's wedding, did anyone say, 'That Josh Hill, you just can't invite him anywhere.' N-o-o-o. You know what they said? They said they should've expected something like that with *me* around. All I want is to live my life without the extra baggage, you know? I mean, I'm thirty-one years old. How long is it going to take for people to forget my past sins? Will I ever live them down?"

"Why would you want to?" he asked.

He wasn't getting it. Of course he wouldn't. He was Booker Robinson, and to him a bad reputation was a mighty fine thing to have. He'd worked hard to establish his own.

"Forget it," she grumbled. "You don't understand."

"Yes, I do."

"What?" She leaned forward. "What do you understand?"

"That they're getting the best of you."

"Who?"

"The critics."

"They're not critics. They're my friends, my family."

He tipped his bottle at her. "That doesn't mean they're not critics, babe. Why don't you tell them to go to hell?"

"Oh, great solution," she said. "Thanks."

He finished his cigarette, dropped it on the porch floor and ground it out. "You are what you are. You can't apologize for that."

They fell silent while they drank their beer and watched the sun set.

"What ever happened to Delaney?" he asked when it was almost dark, his body a mere shadow in the swing. "She still around?"

"She's pregnant."

"Married?"

Rebecca folded her arms and leaned back. "Yeah. She married Clive's grandson, Conner Armstrong."

"Who's Clive?"

"He's the old guy who owned the Running Y Ranch. Conner owns it now. He's in the process of building a big resort and golf course."

"No shit. Delaney's rich, then?" he asked.

"Not yet, but if everything goes the way it should, she will be. So will Josh and Mike Hill. From what Delaney has told me, they've invested quite a bundle in the project."

"Josh again, huh? This name seems to come up quite often with you."

"Not really. You just caught me on a bad day."

"From what I remember, he was a pretty decent football player. He ever go pro?"

"No. He played for the University of Utah for a few years. But once he got his degree he returned home. His brother was already out of school and wanted to partner up, buy some land and start a breeding business."

"And that's what they did?"

"That's what they did."

"What kind of degree did Josh get?"

"I think they both majored in animal husbandry."

Booker hooked an arm over the swing and scowled. "What the hell is that?"

"It's the degree most everyone around here gets," Rebecca said. "Not that I know a whole lot about it. I went to massage school, realized I couldn't make a living doing massage, at least in these parts, then went to beauty school. I've never seen the inside of a university."

"That makes two of us."

"Did you know Josh very well?" she asked.

"No." Rebecca couldn't see for sure, but she thought Booker was frowning. His voice, when he spoke, confirmed it. "I've never much liked him, though," he said.

Rebecca laughed. "Neither have I. So what are you doing later? Want to head over to the Honky Tonk?"

CHAPTER FIVE

"WHY WOULD I WANT to see Booker Robinson?" Delaney asked.

Rebecca propped the telephone against her shoulder and turned sideways to contemplate her reflection in the mirror behind her bedroom door. She wanted to look good tonight; she *needed* to look good. After the past few days, it was time for an emotional comeback.

"Because he's an old friend."

"He's not an old friend of mine."

Rebecca rotated to the back, checking her behind. Did her butt look big in these jeans? Maybe she should go for the tight black slacks, the ones that rode low on her hips and showed the tattoo she'd gotten to mark her thirtieth birthday. Though she had no romantic designs on Booker, he was just the type of man to appreciate a purple butterfly near her navel. "He's been gone twelve years. He might have changed," she said.

"You saw him today. Has he?"

She peeled off the jeans and wiggled into the black slacks. "No. Not a bit."

"So why are you hanging out with him?" Delaney asked with a chuckle.

Because Buddy had just postponed the wedding again, her own parents didn't want her to come to their anniversary party, and Josh... Well, Josh was partly to blame as well. She just couldn't figure out why. "Beats the hell out of sitting home, doesn't it?"

"Not when you're seven months pregnant."

"Come on, Laney. You haven't been anywhere with me in ages. Bring Conner to the Honky Tonk and have a soda. You can still be in bed by midnight."

"I'll think about it," she said, but her words slurred at the end as if she was yawning. "How'd it go with Josh this morning?"

"Fine."

"That's a pretty mellow reaction. Are you on some type of sedative?"

"You know I don't do drugs."

"Then he must not have shown."

"He came, I cut his hair, my father stopped by to make me feel like crap, and that was it."

"And?"

Rebecca sucked in her stomach and reconsidered her reflection. Better. "What more do you want to hear?"

"I want to hear about this supposed truce. Is it real?"

"Who knows? If you ask me, the only thing that's changed is Josh's haircut."

Covering the phone, Delaney spoke to someone in the background, probably her husband. When she came back on, she said, "Well, you won't even remember Josh Hill in a few weeks. You and Buddy will be getting married and moving on to bigger and better things."

"Um, not exactly... Just a sec." Rebecca held the phone away from her ear long enough to pull a tight-fitting sweater over her head. It was black, too, with three-quarter-length sleeves, and hit her midriff in just the right place to make the most of her low-riding pants. Not bad, she thought. "Actually I *won't* be getting married in a few weeks," she said, returning to the conversation.

"What?"

"Buddy wants his great-aunt to attend."

"Did you say *great-aunt?*"

"I did. And she can't come until January." She turned her attention to her hair. She liked the blond highlights she'd put in it much better than her natural dishwater color or the fluorescent auburn it had been a few months ago. But she'd had Katie give her a pretty short cut, which didn't leave her a lot of styling options. Grabbing a bottle of mousse from her dresser, she settled for putting some life into it.

"But you were going to celebrate your birthday in Cancun while you were on your honeymoon."

"Guess I'll be doing something else for my birthday."

"Are you okay with waiting?" Delaney asked.

"I'm excited to think that now I might be here when you have your baby, but other than that, I'm not happy about it." Rebecca wandered into the bathroom, leaned close to the mirror above the vanity and started applying mascara to her lashes. "But I can't *make* him marry me on my birthday, you know?"

"You could give him an ultimatum," Delaney pointed out.

"Believe me, I've thought about that."

"And?"

"He might tell me to take a hike. Then I'd have to spend the rest of my life living right here in Dundee."

"That's not necessarily true. You could meet someone else. Or strike out on your own in a big city somewhere. If Buddy's not as committed as he should be, maybe it'd be better to find out now."

"No, thanks. I think I'd rather go out with Booker."

"Why? That's only avoiding the issue."

"So I'm avoiding it. I need to get out of the house. I've

been spending all my weekends sitting on the couch, talking to Buddy on the phone. Or at the computer, communicating through e-mail and instant messaging. I can't face another four months of this.''

There was a slight hesitation. ''You'd never allow yourself to get *involved* with Booker, though, would you?''

''No way. I'm still engaged. Besides, it wouldn't be right to sleep with someone just because your father would hate it.'' Rebecca dug through her cosmetics case and came up with some jewelry. Holding a pearl earring to one ear and a large silver hoop to the other, she tried to decide which one looked best. ''Anyway, Booker and I are just friends. It was you he always liked, remember?''

''He tried to corrupt me. That doesn't necessarily mean he liked me.''

The hoops. Much sexier. ''Come on,'' Rebecca said. ''He wouldn't corrupt just anybody.'' She abandoned the bathroom in favor of digging through the shoes in her closet. ''You think I should wear flats or something with a heel?''

''How tall is Booker?''

''About my height.''

''Perfect. Wear the dominatrix boots with the six-inch heels. That'll let him know who's in control.''

Rebecca came up with a pair of flats. ''I don't think he'd be intimidated by the dominatrix look. I think he'd probably like it. But I'd rather not feel like the Jolly Green Giant tonight.''

''Your height's never bothered you before.''

''It doesn't bother me now. I'm creating a different look.''

''If you're not getting married until January, what are you going to do about the house?'' Delaney asked. ''Isn't your lease up soon?''

"Yeah. I'll have to call Mr. Williams and see if he'll give me an extension."

"I don't think he will, Beck. His son and daughter-in-law and their two little monsters have been living with him for the past couple of weeks. I think he's promised them the house when you move."

"You're kidding."

"I'm not. I heard him say something to Lisa down at the bank about how happy he was going to be to have his space back once Peter and Carla move out."

"That means I'll have to find another place," Rebecca said, sinking down on the bed.

"I'm sure Aunt Millie would let you move in with her and Uncle Ralph for a few months," Delaney said.

Aunt Millie and Uncle Ralph had adopted and raised Delaney. They were good folk, the best, but Rebecca had no illusions that she could live peaceably in the same house with them. She already had to visit Aunt Millie once a week to do her hair, which nearly caused her to have a claustrophobia attack inside the first ten minutes—usually when Aunt Millie told her she was too thin *for the hundredth time.* "Are you trying to cheer me up, or what? You know Aunt Millie would snoop through my things and try to hold me to a curfew."

"I just want you to know you've always got somewhere to stay. You could even come out here to the ranch."

"Wouldn't Conner love that." Rebecca retrieved the perfume from her dresser, squirted some into the air, then stepped into the shower of spray. She didn't want to smell like a perfume factory; tonight she was aiming for *subtle.*

"He wouldn't mind," Delaney said.

"No, thanks. I'm not pathetic enough to move in with my newly married friend."

"It's just temporary—"

"Don't worry, I'll figure something out." Tomorrow. She'd figure something out tomorrow. Tonight she was going to forget all her troubles and go dancing for the first time in months. "Are you meeting me at the Honky Tonk or what?"

"You're really going?"

"Of course."

"Then I can't let you go alone."

"I'm not going alone. I'm going with Booker."

"Exactly. I'll be there in an hour or so."

As soon as Rebecca hung up, the telephone rang. She eyed it with distrust. Ignoring a ringing phone went against her basic nature. She had sort of a "no run, no hide" policy; anything less smacked of cowardice. But she didn't want to talk to Buddy or her father or one of her perfect sisters. Not right now. Tonight she was feeling good and going out.

She managed to keep herself from picking up but hurried into the kitchen to adjust the volume on the answering machine. She breathed a sigh of relief that she'd used some restraint when she heard Buddy's voice.

"Beck? Where are you? Are you mad at me? What's wrong? I haven't heard from you. I thought we worked everything out, so what's with the silent treatment? If you're that upset about the wedding, maybe we could move it up a couple of weeks. I'll talk to my aunt. Give me a call, okay?" *Beep, click.*

"A couple of *weeks?* Jeez, that's nice of you, Buddy," she grumbled and went for her coat.

When she had her purse as well, she called Booker. "I'm on my way."

"I'll meet you there," he said and hung up.

"OH, MY GOD! Would you look at her?" Mary said, straining to see through the crowd. "She's got a tattoo on her belly."

"You're kidding. A tattoo? Of what?" Across the table from Josh, Candace made her date, Leonard Green, move so she could see the dance floor.

"Seems to be a butterfly. She's over there with Booker Robinson," Mary answered. "You know he's back in town, right? He drove past me on that motorcycle of his a few days ago."

"You already told me," Candace replied.

Mary watched for a few seconds in silence. "You think they're sleeping together?"

Josh had been trying to ignore the conversation—just like he'd been trying to ignore Rebecca—ever since he'd arrived at the Honky Tonk. But he couldn't hold his tongue any longer. "No," he said flatly. "She's not."

"How do you know?" Mary asked, her tone eager.

Candace pursed her lips in obvious skepticism. "They look like they're sleeping together to me."

"I thought she was engaged," Leonard said. Until that moment, Josh hadn't realized Candace's date was even listening. He'd been too busy craning his neck to see over the half wall that separated their table from those playing darts.

"She's engaged, all right," Mary said. "But I wouldn't put anything past Rebecca. She likes guys on motorcycles, remember? Besides, her fiancé isn't from around here, so how would he know?"

Josh felt his jaw clench as he put his beer on the table. "She *isn't* sleeping with Booker. She didn't even know he was in town until this morning, okay? Can we cut her a little slack?"

Mary frowned at the impatience in his voice. "What's wrong with you, Josh? I thought you didn't like her."

"I have better things to do than spend the whole evening gossiping about Rebecca's every move," he said.

A pouty expression claimed Mary's face. "Boy, are you touchy tonight."

"I'm just tired of talking about Rebecca as though she's the devil incarnate. She's not *all* bad, you know."

Candace arched her brows. "She's not?"

"No. For one, she has more grit than anyone I've ever met."

Mary and Candace exchanged a look. "Whatever you say, Josh," Mary told him.

"I'm serious. Do you remember when we were in the seventh grade and Buck Miller was teasing Howie Wilcox?"

"Candace and I weren't in junior high then."

"I was," Leonard said, turning back to the table as the game of darts he'd been watching broke up and the participants sauntered over to the bar. "Buck was always teasing Howie."

"He was always picking on someone," Josh said. "And this day we'd had to run the mile for Phys Ed. Poor Howie was so overweight he could barely walk a mile, let alone run one, and Buck was all over him about it, saying the only person he knew with more rolls was the Michelin Tire Man, crap like that."

Leonard nodded. "I remember."

Josh focused on Mary and Candace. "Rebecca heard what Buck was saying to Howie and decided she'd had enough. She threw down her books, marched up to Buck and told him to keep his big fat mouth shut or she was going to shut it for him."

"She *did?*" Candace said. "Buck was one of the strongest kids in school."

"He went through puberty in the sixth grade, but she

didn't care," Josh said. "She told him he'd better quit teasing Howie or she'd make him pay."

Mary pulled her chair closer to the table. "What'd he do?"

"Started shoving her, telling her to mind her own business before he taught her how."

"And she…"

"Shoved him right back. Pretty soon they started swinging at each other and all the kids gathered around."

Mary laughed. "You've got to be kidding. Did she come out of it okay?"

"No." Josh took another drink of his beer. "She got her ass kicked. For Fat Howie."

"Why?" Candace wanted to know. "Were they friends?"

"Not that I know of. Fat Howie didn't have any friends."

"Why didn't she try to get away when she could see that Buck had the best of her?" Leonard asked. "All she had to do was go crying for the principal."

"Rebecca wouldn't give up. She just kept swinging." Josh shook his head. "Damnedest thing I ever saw."

"How'd it end?" Mary asked.

"The yard duty finally came and broke it up."

"Did Buck get suspended?"

"They both did." He sighed as he toyed with the condensation on his glass, watched a drop roll from the rim to the base. "I've always been ashamed of myself because of that day," he admitted.

Mary's brows gathered above her wide blue eyes. "Why? What did *you* do?"

"Nothing," he said. "That's just it. I stood by and let a girl defend Howie."

"No one else jumped in," Leonard said. "We were only

twelve, just out of grade school, and pretty surprised by the whole thing.''

Josh had been more than surprised; he'd been shocked. And even though he remembered it in slow motion, it had actually happened very fast. Still, he should've done something. He'd felt worse when he realized that because of her reputation for being a difficult child, Rebecca was going to get into as much trouble as Buck.

Shoving away from the table, Josh left Mary and her friends and strode over to the jukebox. If he'd thought he had any chance of getting Mary to leave, he would've headed home at that moment. But she loved hanging out at the Honky Tonk, socializing with all her old friends, and generally insisted they stay until well after midnight. Sometimes he wondered if she realized they weren't in high school anymore.

He stared down at the songs listed on the jukebox, forcing himself to focus on the titles in an effort to block out the mental picture of how Rebecca had looked after she'd fought Buck. Blouse torn and dirty, nose bleeding and hair mussed, she'd shaken her fist at Buck as the yard duty was dragging them both away, and shouted, ''You leave him alone, you hear?''

There was no one like Rebecca, he decided. No one.

He glanced over at Mary, and suddenly saw her as rather plain. She liked tailored, conservative clothes, the same kind all her friends wore. Which had suited him just fine—until this moment. Now he wanted her to get a tattoo. Probably because he knew she'd never do it. But, if not that, *something* to prove she could step out of line and dare to be different, to be an individual, instead of a compilation of all the traits and beliefs that were patently approved by the masses. God, he was dating someone who was completely...*homogenized.*

He jammed his hands in his pockets. No, that wasn't kind or fair. He was only reacting to this day, this moment. Because of Doyle Wilson and his little truce, Rebecca Wells had been tossed back into his orbit, and he hadn't yet adjusted. After not seeing her for months, other than brushing elbows occasionally on the street, he'd sat in her chair at the salon for half an hour this morning, her breasts at eye level, while she ran her fingers through his hair. And now, here she was at the Honky Tonk, looking like a wet dream. The tattoo was daring, and sexy because it was daring, and made him remember a year ago last summer and wish he could finally have the satisfaction of making love to Rebecca.

But it was only a competitive thing, a desire to conquer at last. That was all. He wanted to win the one woman who'd gotten away.

Mary was petite and attractive and nice and...and a good parent to Ricky—although, like tonight, her mother often took care of him. He was a lucky man to have Mary, Josh reminded himself. He knew at least a dozen other guys who'd gladly take his place.

So why couldn't he seem to stop staring at Rebecca?

REBECCA HAD BEEN RIGHT to get out. She felt better than she had in months—freer, more light-hearted. The music pounded in her ears, tempting her to move to the rhythm. Her margarita was taking the edge off the tension that had been dragging her down. And it no longer seemed terribly important that she marry and leave town right away. Buddy seemed distant and not likely to come any closer, and Booker was the perfect companion for her mood. He danced, he talked, he laughed; he looked at life simply.

Before Delaney and Conner had arrived, she'd told him about Buddy postponing their wedding and he'd given her the same answer he gave for everything. "Tell him to go to hell."

Well, tonight Rebecca was telling the whole world to go to hell, and she was having a great time doing it.

"Let's dance again," she said, pulling him to his feet.

He took a quick sip of his beer before leaving it on the table with Delaney and Conner and letting her lead him onto the dance floor. She could see Josh sitting with Mary and Mary's friend Candace, along with some guy Delaney didn't recognize, off to the left. But his presence didn't bother her. At least, not the way it normally did. His hair looked damn good—she was pretty proud of that. But then, what else was new? Josh always looked good.

"In case you're interested, Josh Hill is sitting over there," she told Booker.

"Why would I be interested?"

"It's been a while since you've seen him."

He swung her around to take a look. "Hasn't changed much."

"I guess that makes three of us, huh?"

He chuckled. "Who's the chick? His wife?"

"Which one?"

"The brunette."

"That's Mary. Don't you recognize her?"

"Oh, yeah," he said. "She used to be captain of the cheer squad for your high school, didn't she?"

"That's her. She and Josh have been dating for several months."

"He'll be sorry if he marries her."

"Why?"

"I used to sit on the front row of the bleachers while the cheerleaders were practicing, so I could make a big deal about looking under Mary's skirt when her stunt partner tossed her into the—''

''If this is supposed to impress me, you can save your breath,'' Rebecca interrupted. ''I already know you're a pervert.''

''I wasn't getting any kind of thrill out of it,'' he said. ''I just liked messing with her. Every few minutes, she'd march over to the fence and rattle off a lecture about school spirit and respect and how I'd never amount to anything.''

''What would you do?''

''Shrug and say, 'You want me and you know it.'''

''Really?''

''That drove her nuts.''

''I'll bet. So she's probably thrilled to see you're back in town, hmm?''

''I don't care if she is. She can go to—''

''I know. She can go to hell. It's a rather simplistic motto, but effective,'' she said.

He turned and bent her over his arm in a dramatic dip. ''Now you're catching on, babe. What they think can only bother you if you let it.''

Rebecca certainly liked Booker's philosophy. She just wasn't sure he was the best person to emulate. Fortunately Delaney's presence seemed to check her wilder tendencies. To Delaney, Booker was the big bad wolf. She wasn't about to let Rebecca become his first little pig. Which was why she wouldn't leave, even though she was exhausted and Conner was bored stiff.

''So if Josh is dating Mary, why does he keep looking over here?'' Booker asked.

''What?'' Rebecca replied.

''I want to know why Josh keeps staring at you.''

''I don't know. I didn't realize he was.''

''Anything ever happen between you two?''

"A lot's happened between us."

"I mean, did you ever get together, hook up?"

"No," she lied, thinking a year ago last summer was such a small exception it wasn't worth mentioning.

"Well, he wants you, babe. He wants you bad."

Rebecca rolled her eyes and started laughing. "No, he doesn't. He *hates* me. I used to put gum in his hair."

"I'm just telling you what I see. You don't have to believe me if you don't want to."

Booker had to be wrong. He was confusing all the bad blood between her and Josh with something else. Or Josh wasn't staring at her at all. More likely he was staring at Booker. Except for Rebecca, no one was particularly happy about his return.

"How do you like Conner?" she asked, catching sight of Delaney's husband quietly conferring with her over at the table. He was probably begging her to give up her vigil and go home and, in a way, Rebecca wished she would. Having Delaney there grounded her, and she appreciated that. It was the whole reason she'd taken the precaution of inviting her. But Rebecca had discovered that she didn't want to be grounded at this particular moment. Not when she was telling the whole world to go to hell.

"He's okay, I guess," Booker said. "Delaney's still hot. Too bad she's married."

"Sometimes I think so, too," Rebecca admitted. "I'm happy for her, but I miss having someone to live with. And now that my lease is up, I'm going to have to move into a new house alone, *if* I can find one. There aren't a lot of rentals in Dundee."

"Don't move into a house alone," he said. "Come out to Granny's and live with us."

Rebecca pulled back to see his face. "What? I can't do that."

"Why not? There's plenty of room and Granny would love it because she'd have another pair of hands she could put to work."

"Doing what?"

"Weeding the garden, washing her old Buick, making a meal or two."

"I wouldn't mind helping," Rebecca said. "I think it'd be fun to be around people again. It's been me and my phone for the past five months."

"I'll talk to Granny and give you a call."

"Great." Rebecca smiled at finding a possible solution. The Hatfield place seemed like the perfect stopgap. Maybe her luck had changed.

Or maybe—she looked up at Booker—maybe she was selling her soul to the devil for a roof over her head.

CHAPTER SIX

TODAY WAS A DAY for change; Rebecca could feel it. Booker had called to tell her Granny Hatfield had no problem with her moving in, so she had a new place to live. Provided she performed a short list of chores each day, Hatty wasn't even going to charge her rent. Her current landlord had agreed to let her out of her lease so she could move right away—actually, he'd practically wept in relief that his son, daughter-in-law and grandkids would now be able to have their own place. And Rebecca had gone the entire day yesterday without a cigarette. Surely she was making great strides toward solving the problems in her life.

Now she just needed to pack and borrow a truck. Booker had offered to help using Hatty's Buick, but if they had only the Buick and her Firebird, they'd make a dozen trips, at least, and still have no way of getting her furniture into storage.

Rebecca was contemplating whose truck to borrow when the phone rang. She thought it was probably Buddy, but instead of hesitating, she snatched up the receiver because she no longer felt any need to avoid his calls. She could be positive and cheerful because she was *feeling* positive and cheerful. No man would be afraid to marry her if he talked to her right now. "Hello?" she said brightly.

"Becky?"

A little of Rebecca's exuberance faded. It was her sister. "Hi, Greta."

"Mom wanted me to call and see if you can come to dinner today."

"Why doesn't she ever invite me herself?"

"It's nothing personal, Beck. I just phoned her to share a great soufflé recipe, and she mentioned that it'd be nice to get the whole family together this afternoon to finish making plans for your wedding. I told her I'd follow up on it."

So much for making great strides toward solving the problems in her life. There were still two weeks until the anniversary party—two weeks during which she had to keep her plans a secret. In addition to that, she knew her family wasn't going to be happy about her moving in with Booker, even if it was only temporary. And depending on how badly her sister annoyed her, she doubted she'd get through this conversation without a cigarette. "Um, I don't know. I'm pretty busy today, Greta."

"Why? What are you doing?"

"I thought I'd move a few things into storage."

"It's Sunday and you have the day off tomorrow. Can't you do the storage thing later? We really need to finalize a few details if we're going to pull this wedding off in six weeks, Beck. I've worked too hard to let anything slip through the cracks."

Rebecca heard the accusation in her sister's voice, the "after everything I've done for you, you'd have the nerve to refuse me?" and felt trapped. She hadn't *asked* Greta to do anything special for her wedding. She'd wanted to keep it simple, and she'd said so from the beginning. But Greta was a stay-at-home mom with three small boys, and Rebecca suspected her older sister was a little bored. She'd embraced this event as though she was Jennifer Lopez in *The Wedding Planner.*

Regardless, Rebecca knew better than to suggest Greta had involved herself because she needed a diversion. Her sister had baked and decorated five hundred sugar cookies. She'd spent countless hours using special food coloring to paint wedding bells on each one, and she'd filled the freezer of almost every friend the Wells family had ever had. After effort like that, no one was going to care whether Rebecca had asked for her help or not.

"When do you want me there?" she asked in resignation.

"At three."

"Okay. Can I borrow Randy's truck later tonight, then?"

"Sure. We picked up the wedding arch from the Porters' house yesterday and we're delivering it to Mom and Dad's tonight, so it'll be there in the living room for the anniversary party. Once we get it unloaded, you can take the truck."

"Thanks. Is there anything I can do for Mom and Dad's big celebration?"

"Let's see…the house is basically ready. I'm having the food catered except for a few extra dishes I'm making myself. Mom's made out the guest list, and Delia and Hillary have already created the invitations using a program I found at the computer store in Boise. It's amazing what you can do with a home printer these days, isn't it? So I think we're fine. Unless… You don't know how to do calligraphy, do you?"

"If you mean that fancy scroll-like writing, no."

"It's not that difficult, Beck."

Rebecca could feel her sister's irritation through the phone. "I thought you were just marveling at the modern miracle of desktop publishing."

"I think addressing them by hand will add a personal touch."

"Why don't I take charge of cleaning up after the party?" Rebecca asked before her sister could suggest she sign up for a class in calligraphy.

"Perfect," Greta said, which was probably what she'd been hoping for all along, and hung up.

Rebecca waited for a dial tone, then called her fiancé.

"There you are," he said the moment he heard her voice. "What's going on? Are you mad at me?"

"Of course not." She was making such progress with patience.

"Then why haven't I heard from you?"

"I was super-busy at work yesterday."

"And last night?"

"An old friend's moved back to town. We went out for a drink."

"Oh." A pause. "So everything's okay between us?"

"Of course."

"Great. You had me worried. What are you doing today?"

"Packing. I've found another house."

"You're moving?"

"I have to. I couldn't extend my lease."

"But you still have another six weeks before your lease ends."

"This other place will be a lot cheaper."

"And your current landlord doesn't mind? Good for you. See? Postponing the wedding might turn out to be the best thing for both of us."

Rebecca hardly considered two thousand dollars worth the wait, considering the abuse she was going to suffer when she told her family those cookies of Greta's would have to remain in the freezer for an extra two and a half months. "I'm thrilled it's turning out so well," she said.

Fortunately, he missed the slightly sarcastic tone to her voice. "We'll be set up, babe."

"Life is good."

"I miss you."

"Miss you, too."

"I still have the plane ticket I bought for the wedding, so we'll get to see each other soon."

"My mother and father are having an anniversary party in a couple of weeks. Can you change your flight and come for that?" she asked.

"Maybe. Let's see about the cost. We wouldn't want to waste any of what you're saving in rent."

As far as Rebecca was concerned, her moving early meant they'd have money to burn. But then, she was impulsive. Impulsive people weren't typically big savers. Which was just another of the many reasons Buddy would be good for her. He was so levelheaded.

"Let me know what you find out," she said.

"Are you in a hurry to get off the phone?"

"I promised myself I'd start a workout regimen today. I was about to go jogging."

"You? Jogging?"

"You say that as though you can't imagine it."

"Because I can't. Why bother? You're already skinny and you smoke. What good's it going to do?"

"I don't smoke anymore," she said, thinking positively. "And I want to tone up. Something wrong with that?"

"No, it's just—" a brief silence "—you don't have to do it for me."

Rebecca couldn't say why she suddenly felt the desire to get in shape, but she was pretty confident Buddy wasn't part of the equation. It worried her, now that he'd pointed it out. The last time she'd shown any interest in diet and exercise had been right after her night with Josh Hill—a funny coincidence, considering he was now front and center in her life again.

"I appreciate that," she said.

"I love you just the way you are."

Which was why she'd had to wait two days since their last conversation before she could safely call him back. "Have *you* ever thought about giving up cigarettes and losing some weight?" she asked.

"Not really. I've never been the athletic type. But you've known that from the beginning," he added, a defensive note in his voice.

Rebecca ignored his slight bristling. She wasn't trying to make him feel bad. She wasn't even trying to get him to lose weight. She was trying to understand why he didn't feel he needed to change something that was obviously less than ideal. "So you're saying, 'I am what I am.'"

He seemed to clue in to the fact that she wasn't belittling him. "I guess. Why?"

"A friend of mine said the same thing about himself last night."

"So?"

"He's sort of a thug."

"And?"

"I like the concept. 'Take me or leave me' is right up my alley. But on the other hand…"

"Yes?"

"It sounds like a cop-out."

"Rebecca, what are you talking about? No more smoking. Workout regimens. Take me or leave me. What's going on with you?"

Rebecca wasn't sure, but she hoped to hell it had nothing to do with Josh Hill.

MAYBE JOGGING over to her parents' house hadn't been such a good idea.

Rebecca wiped the sweat off her forehead and squinted down the highway to the next bend in the road, trying to count how many more of those bends there'd be until she reached the turnoff to her parents' neighborhood. Doyle and Fiona Wells lived on the outskirts of town, only about five miles from Rebecca's rental house. But those five miles had to be the longest she'd ever traveled. To add to her misery, the weather was cool enough that she hadn't thought to carry water, and now she was so parched she felt as though she might pass out.

Leaning against a yellow road sign that signaled a curve, she put her head between her knees and tried to catch her breath. Lots of runners ran five miles—and they did it in less than an *hour*. She'd been out nearly forty-five minutes and was barely halfway.

But those runners probably hadn't been smoking since they were sixteen.

Rebecca noticed the sound of an engine, which gave her enough adrenaline to get going again. A painful cramp gnawed at her side, and her tongue felt like sandpaper against the roof of her mouth. But just before she'd left home, she'd called Greta to say she might be a little late, that she was jogging over, and her sister and her sister's husband, Randy, had immediately laughed her to scorn.

Rebecca had stupidly responded, ''You'll see.'' After ''you'll see,'' she *couldn't* let a member of her family find her sucking wind on the side of the road.

Keeping her head high, she put a bounce in her step through willpower alone and prayed that whoever was com-

ing up from behind would pass quickly so she could col-
lapse. But the vehicle didn't pass her at all. Slowing, it
drew even with her. When she looked over, she saw Josh
Hill sitting behind the wheel of a new Ford Excursion,
wearing a pair of sunglasses and a forest-green T-shirt that
stretched taut across his muscular chest.

His window lowered smoothly. "Something happen to
your car?" he hollered.

Rebecca was so out of breath she wasn't sure she could
speak. "No," she managed to respond.

"You need a ride?"

God, did she ever. Her lungs felt like they were about to
burst. She glanced longingly at his leather interior, heard
the country music playing on his stereo and could already
feel her tired body sinking into his passenger seat. She was
desperate enough to agree—until she saw the amused smile
playing around his lips. He didn't think she had what it
took to be a jogger; he stood with Greta and Randy.

"I'm fine," she said, trudging doggedly on.

To her horror, he didn't speed up. "You going out to
your parents' house?"

"Yeah."

"That's what I thought. I'll drop you off."

She didn't answer. It took all her focus to put one foot
in front of the other.

"What are you trying to do?" he asked, his voice flat.

She cast him another glance from the corner of her eye.
"What...does it...look..."—here she had to break off so
she could gasp for air—"...like?" she finally finished.

"Are you sure you want to know? Because it looks like
you're about to faint. I've never seen anyone so red in the
face."

That had to be attractive. Plus she'd started her workout
regimen before she'd had the chance to shop for some of
those cute little outfits. She doubted her torn T-shirt and

cutoffs were making much of an impression—a positive impression, anyway. "I'm just out...for a...jog," she insisted.

She thought her response had done the trick. He sped up, but only so he could cut her off by pulling to the side of the road.

He got out and met her, his smile gone, as she tried to go around his vehicle. "Get in the car," he said.

"No." She stopped, secretly thankful for the excuse, and propped her hands on her knees, her chest heaving. "I'll...take a little...rest and—"

He walked over and opened the passenger door. "And what? Start off again? Quit being so damn stubborn and get in. You're obviously long past done."

She shook her head, straightened, and tried to start again, but he easily intercepted her. "Dammit, Rebecca," he said, taking her by the shoulders and glowering into her face. "You know what's wrong with you?"

Did he want the long list or the short one? If he wanted the long list, he should probably ask her father.

"You don't know what's good for you," he continued before she could summon the energy to tell him not to bother. "If I were Booker, you'd jump right in. As if Booker's some kind of wonderful guy. But because it's me, you'd rather faint on the side of the road."

"There's nothing...wrong with...Booker."

"Then why don't you explain what's wrong with me?"

She blinked up at him, surprised by his frankness. How could her opinion possibly make enough difference for him to even ask? He had the unequivocal admiration of almost everyone in town. "There's nothing...wrong with you. Ask anyone."

"Right," he said. "Get in."

"No! I'm—"

"Get in or I'm going to put you in."

"You wouldn't dare."

"Watch me." Sweeping her into his arms, he strode to the truck and deposited her in the passenger seat with such quick, powerful movements she knew better than to struggle. He'd made up his mind he was getting her that far, and she had no strength with which to fight him. She could have gotten out again, though. He couldn't force her to stay inside once he walked away. Except that her legs felt like rubber, and she was afraid she'd fall on her face.

She caught a whiff of his cologne as he climbed into the driver's seat, and feared she smelled like a locker room. But if he noticed, he gave no indication. Revving the engine, he popped it into drive and peeled out onto the highway.

He drove the next two miles in silence, looking tense and angry and keeping his eyes on the road.

By the time Rebecca's heart rate had slowed enough to speak normally, he was making the turn into their old neighborhood. "You want to explain your little burst of temper back there?" she asked.

He scowled and jammed a hand through his hair. "I don't think I could if I tried."

He dropped her off at her parents' house without saying another word.

She watched him continue down the street and park in front of the redbrick house where he'd grown up. When he got out, he stared at her for a few seconds, then shook his head and went inside.

And people told her *she* was temperamental, Rebecca thought.

"YOU LOOK LIKE HELL," Greta said as soon as Rebecca entered the house.

Rebecca heard Randy chuckle from where he was sitting

in the living room, reading the paper. "Shut up, Randy, or I'll invite another hundred people to my wedding. Then you'll be helping Greta bake cookies for the next three weeks," she said as she went to the fridge for a much-needed drink.

"If Buddy gets to know you very well, there won't be a wedding," he retorted.

Greta tried to hide her smile, but Rebecca caught it anyway and was glad someone seemed entertained by her and Randy's constant barbs. They generally didn't take each other too seriously, but sometimes they got carried away. Which was what her mother was constantly trying to avoid by saying, "Come on, you two."

"Could we have some peace in this household for a change?" Fiona said today, as she put some garlic bread in the oven next to what looked like a pan of lasagna.

Rebecca guzzled a big glass of cranberry juice, feeling as though she might die in relief. "Talk to Randy," she said. "Or better yet, ask him to go visit his old pal, Josh. He's down at his parents' house. I'm sure he'd love to have Randy over to spend the entire afternoon."

"Nice try," Randy said.

Rebecca poured herself some more juice. "Next time I see Josh, I'll have to tell him you weren't interested in his invitation."

Doyle ducked through the French doors that opened to the patio. "Thought I'd better turn those sprinklers off," he said to no one in particular. "We don't want it muddy back there, or we'll have a mess when we try to move that wedding arch inside. These doors are probably the only way in for something that big."

"Where're Delia and everyone else?" Rebecca asked, taking a chair at the kitchen table as far away from Randy as she could manage in the open kitchen/dining area/family room.

"Delia and Brad took the kids to Boise for the weekend to see his parents," her mother answered. "And little Joey has the flu, so Hillary and Carey won't be coming."

"What about the girls? They're not dropping Tasha and Sydney off?"

"I told them not to," Greta piped up. "They could be carrying whatever Joey's got, and I don't want my three to be up all night, tossing their cookies."

"Would that be so bad?" Rebecca asked. "You could always make cold compresses that look like bunnies or freeze Pepto-Bismol and cut it into shapes."

"Cute," Greta said.

"So it's just us?" Rebecca had been counting on the noise and constant confusion created by her nieces and nephews to offer some distraction while she slogged through whatever discussion Greta wanted to have about the wedding. But even Greta's boys were completely entertained by the Sony PlayStation Grandpa and Grandma had bought a few weeks ago.

"It's just us," Randy said. "Which was perfect until you arrived."

"Randy—" Fiona warned.

"Oh, boy. How are we going to get the wedding arch into the house?" Greta interrupted. Fiona's constant admonishments were mere background noise after so many years. "We need more hands than yours and Randy's, Dad."

"Especially when Randy's about as good as a little girl," Rebecca added.

"Rebecca, that's enough." It was her father this time, so Rebecca closed her mouth and her eyes and attempted to enjoy her respite from not having to move.

"Nice jogging outfit," Randy said. "What were you doing jogging over here, anyway? Trying to give yourself a heart attack?"

Rebecca cracked open one eye. "Being a couch potato yourself, I know this is probably a foreign concept to you, but it's called health and fitness."

His newspaper rattled as he turned the page. "That's pretty funny, considering you smoke like a chimney."

"I don't smoke anymore."

"You don't?" her mother said, setting the timer for the bread. "Good for you, Beck."

"Smoking's a filthy habit," her father muttered.

Rebecca tossed the hand towel she'd been using as a cool compress into the sink. "Thanks for the encouragement, Dad."

"Let's get that wedding arch unloaded," he said, ignoring her.

Rebecca didn't think she could get up without a winch. "We can't. There's only you, me and Randy, and we need more hands than that. We wouldn't want Greta to break a nail. She might decide to sculpt something out of it."

Greta's jaw dropped. "Ow! Leave me out of your little spats, okay? What's gotten into you today?"

It wasn't "what" had gotten into her. It was "who." She was still trying to figure out what had happened with Josh Hill. Why had he been so upset? Because she didn't want to ride with him? What was it to him if she fainted by the side of the road?

"I wasn't joking about Josh being at his parents' house. I ran into him earlier," she said, as if that was explanation enough for her bad mood. Unfortunately, it was the wrong excuse to use today.

"That shouldn't make any difference," Doyle said. "You two called a truce, remember?"

"Yeah, well, talk to Josh," Rebecca grumbled. "I think he must've forgotten about that."

Her father shifted onto the balls of his feet. "Damned if he did. You go down there and tell him we need his help unloading this wedding arch."

Rebecca jerked upright. "Randy's his best friend. Have him go."

Her father gave her "the look," the one that indicated he meant business. "I asked *you*."

"He admitted to me just yesterday that his mother doesn't like me," Rebecca said.

"After all the trouble you and Josh had growing up, can you blame her?"

"Considering you still like him, yes."

"Go on over there," her father said. "I want to get that arch off the truck before the neighborhood kids start climbing on it. The last thing we need is for someone to get hurt."

"If I go down to Josh's parents' house, *I* have a good chance of being hurt," she argued.

"Don't worry, I'll make you a butterfly bandage," Greta said sweetly.

Rebecca rolled her eyes. "Good one, Greta. Now I know why you want to stay out of the line of fire. You're only packing a pellet gun."

"Hurry," her father said, cutting off any rejoinder Greta might have made. "Let's get this over with."

"If I do this, can we have our little wedding meeting during dinner, instead of after?" Rebecca asked.

"Why?" Greta wanted to know.

"Because I have to move some things into storage, remember?"

"Okay. You go get Josh. And we'll keep the meeting short."

"Fine." She turned to her mother. "I need to change my shirt. Can I borrow something?"

CHAPTER SEVEN

AFTER HER EXUBERANT ATTEMPT to get fit in one day, Rebecca could barely walk. And she'd seen all of Josh Hill she wanted to see. But if fetching him meant she could go home, move her furniture into storage and shower that much sooner, she was determined to do what had to be done.

Her family, except her mother, who stayed to watch over dinner, spilled out of the house behind her and milled around Randy's Chevy pickup as she hobbled down the street. She could feel her brother-in-law's interest, knew he was laughing at her, and wished she had the energy to turn and flip him off. But, in her bid for self-improvement, she was currently stifling such tendencies. And her father was standing right there, which helped a great deal with the old self-control. She doubted Doyle would buy the ''I am what I am'' routine. The one thing she *didn't* want was to start him off on another of his ''What's this world coming to?'' tirades.

Josh's house had once looked huge, or at least daunting. Rebecca recalled sneaking over there as a child, her heart pounding with the anticipation of whatever mischief she was planning. She also remembered being caught a time or two by the formidable Mrs. Hill. Those memories loomed large in her mind.

But Josh's mother had to be in her early sixties, Rebecca

reminded herself. Surely, even gimpy, she could outrun her by now.

"Rebecca, get Mike, too, if he's there," her father called.

Rebecca threw a glance over her shoulder and nodded in acknowledgment. Randy was standing at the curb. He taunted her with a grin and a wave, so she threw back her shoulders and marched, as best she could, through the Wellses' neatly tended yard, past an American flag, up the two steps of the green porch, and right to the front door.

Staring at a beautiful autumn wreath hanging at eye level, Rebecca punched the doorbell.

Josh's father answered a moment later. "Well, if it isn't the little girl from down the street. We haven't seen you around our place for a few years—thank God," he added under his breath, as though he thought she wouldn't be able to hear him.

Rebecca raised her chin. "My father was wondering if Josh and Mike might be willing to help us lift something from the back of Randy's truck."

Larry Hill poked his head out of the house and looked down the street as though confirming what she'd said. Her father waved; he waved back. "Mike's out of town on business for the weekend," he said. "But I'll help, and I'll get Josh."

"Who is it?" Mrs. Hill asked, coming up behind her husband as he moved away and left the door ajar.

Rebecca heard Larry say her name.

"Well, for heaven's sake, don't leave her unattended. You never know what she might do," she snapped and promptly appeared in the doorway.

Rebecca cleared her throat and attempted polite conversation. "Hello, Mrs. Hill. The weather's sure been beautiful this fall, hasn't it?"

"What happened to you?" she responded, eyeing the dirt on Rebecca's sweat-streaked legs. "You look like hell."

REBECCA AGAIN. Josh couldn't believe it. After several years of relative tranquility, she'd burst back into his life, and now she seemed to be around every corner.

He and his father followed her down to her parents' house without speaking, Josh determined to remain more aloof during this encounter. He'd embarrassed himself by letting her know how badly she was getting to him when he dumped her in his truck; he wasn't about to regress to the point where the frustration he felt in her presence boiled out of him again.

Fortunately, the moment he reached Doyle's yard, Randy clapped him on the back and drew him into a conversation about the University of Utah and the potential of their football team this year. Josh thought he'd be able to ignore Rebecca completely, but then he caught sight of something that kicked his gut into his throat. She'd changed out of her sweaty T-shirt and into a long-sleeved white shirt she'd probably borrowed from her mother, judging by its size. The ends were tied an inch or so above her navel, revealing not only her butterfly tattoo but a wide swath of flat tan tummy. And when she turned right, he could tell she wasn't wearing a bra. Her nipples were standing erect, probably stimulated by the light chafing of the fabric when she moved.

Josh felt his throat go dry. Mary had a compact body with large, full breasts and was certainly more amenable to sharing. But just now, her breasts seemed far less appealing....

"Josh? Are you going to answer me?" Randy asked.

Josh jerked his attention away from Rebecca's blouse and searched his recent memory for a fragment of what

Randy had asked him. When he came up blank, he said, "Sorry, my mom wants us to hurry back for dinner. We'd better get to that wedding arch."

"Are you feeling okay, buddy?" Randy asked.

Josh shrugged. "Sure. Why?"

His friend's eyebrows knitted as he nodded at Rebecca, who was standing by her sister. "Is it Rebecca? She just went jogging," he explained. "That's why she looks so bad."

Problem was, she didn't look bad. Not to Josh. She looked better than an ice-cold beer in the worst summer heat, despite her sweaty hair, lack of makeup, their history, everything.

"Can we get this thing unloaded?" Rebecca asked everyone, her voice tinged with impatience. "I have a lot to do today."

"Just what are you planning to move into storage?" Greta asked her as they all converged on Randy's truck.

"My furniture."

"Already? The wedding's still six weeks away."

Rebecca didn't answer.

"Who's going to help you?" Greta asked.

Rebecca's gaze slid quickly past Josh and fixed on Randy. "Randy's got to be good for something."

"Sorry, sweetcakes, I'm good for a lot of things. But I can't help you today." He put down the tailgate of his pickup. "After we leave here, I've got a Scout meeting."

"He's the den leader," Greta added, as though that designated him a pretty important person.

Rebecca looked like she was about to make some type of comment, but Doyle diverted her attention.

"You shouldn't be moving anything this early, Rebecca," he said. "You'll end up packing things you need. Wait a few weeks."

Rebecca hoisted herself into the bed of the truck. Briefly Josh wondered why she was even trying to help them unload. Greta certainly felt no similar compulsion. Rebecca's sister took charge, telling them what to do and how to do it, but she didn't come within ten feet of the wedding arch. Now that they had five men, Josh didn't think they needed Rebecca, either. But this was Doyle's show, not his.

"I don't want to wait a few weeks," Rebecca said.

"If you try to do too much by yourself, you'll end up hurting your back," her father warned.

Then why don't you go over and help her out? Josh wanted to ask. *Support her a little?* But it was none of his business. Getting involved detracted from his primary objective. So did that blouse Rebecca was wearing, but there were some things that couldn't be helped.

"I'll only lift the light stuff," Rebecca said.

WAS THAT A COUCH she was trying to wrestle through the door?

Josh slowed and craned his neck to get a better look. It was difficult to see very well. The sun had set, and the light inside Rebecca's small house provided only a backdrop. But after a few moments he could tell that she was indeed shoving her couch outside, an inch at a time. What she planned to do once she got it on the sagging porch, he had no idea, because there wasn't any way she could load it into the truck waiting in her drive. At least not by herself.

With a sigh of resignation, he parked in front and cut the engine. He'd come by her place in spite of the many times he'd told himself he wasn't going to. And now that he knew she needed him as much as he'd suspected she might, he wouldn't be able to talk himself into going home until he'd moved the heavy stuff.

Climbing out of his Excursion, he slammed the door and

started up the walk. "Hang on," he said. "I'll get this end."

She hadn't changed clothes since she'd left her parents' house. Which wasn't a good thing. That blouse, or rather the strip of bare skin beneath it, tended to make him forget some pretty important realities. First, that she was engaged. Second, that she was trouble with a capital "T." Third, that he sort of had a girlfriend, though there'd been no promises spoken between them. And last but not least, that Rebecca had made it abundantly clear she'd never found him appealing.

"What are you doing here?" she asked, blinking at him as though he'd just beamed down from another planet.

"I was on my way home. Thought maybe you could use a hand."

She arched a skeptical brow. "You came over to *help* me?"

"Isn't that what people typically do once they've decided to be friends?"

"Calling a truce doesn't make us friends," she said.

"So? Would it be so bad," he asked, "if we became friends?"

She propped a knee on the arm of the couch, which was mostly out of the house, and leaned against the open doorway. "We're not really cut out for friendship."

"Who said?"

"You're a Scorpio."

"Your birthday's the day after mine. Doesn't that make you a Scorpio, too?"

"Exactly. Scorpio is an extreme sign. We're all-or-nothing people, far too intense to ever get along."

"I didn't know you were into astrology."

"I'm not, but I know that much."

"We *can* get along," he said. "We've just never tried."

"We lived across the street from each other for years."

"We don't live across the street from each other anymore. Maybe that was the problem. Maybe now it'll be easier."

"Somehow I don't think so."

"Why not?"

"I don't think friends force friends into their cars, for one," she said.

"They do if it's in the friend's best interest, right? If one friend's drunk. Or, as in your case, if she's about to pass out."

"I wasn't about to pass out."

He smiled at her denial. She pulled on her tied shirttails in what seemed to be a self-conscious movement. "Besides, we don't even like each other."

"Yes, we do." Circling the couch, he purposefully invaded her space. He wondered if she'd retreat inside, maybe even tell him to get off her property, but he should've known better. Rebecca Wells didn't back away from anything. She stayed right where she was and watched him with a certain wariness in her eyes.

"Are you sure?" she asked.

He nodded. "Positive."

"You did trust me to cut your hair," she said, nibbling on her bottom lip. "Maybe we could give friendship a trial run. But I think we should define the term."

He leaned against the same doorjamb she was leaning against, just inches away. "Okay, define it."

Her eyes flicked downward, as though noting this further encroachment. But she still didn't move. "First and foremost, it doesn't mean that we ever have to hang out together."

"So we're not *close* friends."

"Right." She stood up straight. A subtle move to ease

away without appearing to be the first to withdraw? "Second, we agree to forget our past sins."

"Hallelujah. Now we're making progress," he said, "especially since I'm not really sure what my past sins are. At least the ones you can't forgive."

She glossed over his words by continuing, "And third, whether or not we've become friends is nobody's business but our own. We say nothing about each other to anyone. There's plenty of talk in this town as it is."

"Done." He folded his arms. "Anything else?"

She frowned at his arms, now almost brushing her breasts. "Not that I can think of."

"Well, if it makes you feel better, I won't ask you to sign in blood. We can amend the arrangement as we go."

She nodded as though she should've thought of that herself. "Then it's a deal."

He reached out to shake on it and knew he'd made a mistake as soon as she slipped her hand in his. Her touch had the same effect on him as her bare midriff—it immediately brought him back to that night a year ago last summer.

"Isn't it getting a little chilly for that outfit?" he asked, immediately pulling away and putting some distance between them.

She glanced down as though she'd forgotten what she had on. "It's cooling off, but there's no point in dirtying another set of clothes. I want to move a few things before I shower."

Her rationale made sense but, as far as Josh was concerned, she couldn't change soon enough. A pair of flannel pajamas might help remind him of the limitations of their new friendship. But if he knew Rebecca, she'd never settle for sleepwear half as bland as he needed it to be. The night he'd taken her home from the Honky Tonk she'd been wearing a sexy white thong and matching lace bra that had looked beautiful against her smooth tan skin....

Maybe if she'd give him just one night, he could get her out of his system. But he doubted their fledging friendship could survive a fling. Besides, he'd have to break it off with Mary first, and Rebecca was engaged, anyway.

"So what made you drop by?" she asked.

Josh thought about what had happened when Doyle came to the salon and decided to test out a theory that had been forming in his mind. "Your father wanted me to see if you needed a hand."

Her eyes widened. "Really?"

The hope in her voice made Josh wish her father *had* asked him to check on her. He would've felt a lot better toward Doyle Wells if that had been the case. "Yeah, he thought it would be nice," he lied.

She smiled as though he'd just given her a wonderful gift, and the fact that such small proof of fatherly concern could elicit that kind of reaction from jaded Rebecca Wells pricked Josh's heart. Despite the eye-rolling and resentment and arguing between them, Rebecca loved her father much more than she ever let on. He wondered if Doyle Wells knew how she felt, and doubted it. He was too busy complaining about all the trouble she caused him.

"Well, it's a good thing he didn't come himself," she said as they bent to lift the couch. "He'd want to know why I'm moving all this stuff."

"Why *are* you moving all this stuff?" Josh asked as they started across the small yard with the couch. "You're not getting married for another six weeks."

"Yeah, but—" she shrugged "—it's better to be prepared."

"By moving your furniture outside? What were you going to do once you got it out here?"

"Booker's stopping by later. I was planning to have him help me load it."

Josh felt a rush of intense dislike. "Oh. How does your fiancé feel about you hanging out with Booker?" he asked as they loaded the couch onto the truck.

"He knows we're only friends. Anyway, Buddy's not the jealous type."

Josh had never been the jealous type, either. Yet he hated the memory of Booker dancing with Rebecca the way he'd danced with her last night, hated the thought of him coming over here so late. As if that made any sense. He was supposed to be jealous over Mary, not a woman who was engaged to someone else. "What's next?"

"The kitchen table, I guess. But first I need to get out some blankets we can use as padding."

The inside of Rebecca's house was certainly different than Josh had expected. Because she came off as rather unconcerned about domestic things, he'd assumed her place would be messy. But it wasn't. There was no clutter, no dusty corners or blinds, no dirty dishes in the sink, no crumbs on the counters or floors. Even the dishrag had been folded neatly across the faucet. Some of the furniture was obviously old and mismatched, but there was evidence of creativity—an antique icebox that doubled as a sideboard, a tile mosaic that hung above it, a braided rug beneath the kitchen table. One whole wall of the dining room was covered with shelves that had been made using simple planks and cinderblock, but the collection of blue, green and yellow jars displayed there, and the assortment of wonderful-smelling candles, somehow made them look trendy. If he had to pick a word to describe Rebecca's home, it would have to be…unique, he decided. Like her.

"If you store your kitchen table, where are you going to

eat until the wedding?'' Josh asked as Rebecca came into the living room carrying a stack of blankets.

''At my new place.''

''What new place?''

She dropped the blankets on a recliner that faced an entertainment center made of distressed pine. ''I'm moving to another house until I get married.''

''Why would you do that?''

She went into the kitchen, and he followed.

''It's a long story,'' she said, pulling the chairs away from the table.

''Where is this other house?'' he asked, helping her.

''Out in the boonies.'' She grabbed one of the kitchen chairs and walked outside with it, and he brought two more.

''Just put them on the lawn,'' he told her. ''We've got to get the table on the truck first.''

''Where's Mary tonight?'' she asked as they headed inside.

''I think she's home with her mother and her son.'' Actually, he knew she was. She'd just called him at his folks' house and invited him over. He'd told her he was too tired because he'd thought he was. But, strangely enough, since he'd arrived at Rebecca's, his energy had apparently revived.

Rebecca moved the quart jar filled with fresh flowers that had stood on the kitchen table to the counter. ''Do you think you two will be getting married soon?'' she asked, positioning herself on the far side of the table.

He glanced up at her, instead of taking hold of his end, surprised by the personal nature of her question.

''Friends ask friends those kinds of things,'' she said defensively.

''Right. Well…I don't know.'' He leaned, palms down, on the table. ''Do you think we should?''

"You're asking *me?*"

"Friends ask friends those kinds of questions," he said.

She thought for a minute, then obviously tried to sidestep giving him a direct answer. "Everyone says you two are perfect for each other. You know, golden boy marries golden girl. Cheerleading captain marries football captain."

He made a face. "Golden boy? Don't call me that. Anyway, that cheerleading captain, football captain stuff is pretty superficial. Is that the best you can do? As a *friend?*"

She propped her own hands on the table and leaned forward just enough that Josh was distracted by what her blouse threatened to reveal. Working to keep his eyes from straying, he waited for her response.

"You want the truth?"

He wasn't really sure, but he nodded.

"Okay, as a *friend,* I'd have to tell you that Mary's an opportunist," she said. "She's only interested in what makes her look good. If you were ever down and out, really down and out, I suspect she'd walk away without a backward glance, move on to more promising opportunities."

Her answer made him blanch. "I'd say that's a definite no."

"I'm not finished. If you were anyone *else,* I'd tell you to stay the heck away from her. But you're not. You're Josh Hill."

"Why do I get the impression that means you think we deserve each other?"

She shrugged. "I'm not saying you deserve each other. I'm saying you're always on top, so what do you have to worry about? Chances are, you'll never see the worst of Mary."

"I had to ask," he grumbled.

She started to lift her end. "Ready?"

He was about to help her, then changed his mind. "No, I'm not ready. I think I'm offended by what you just said."

"Why?"

"I work as hard as anyone else for what comes my way."

She didn't answer.

"Rebecca? You don't believe I've earned what's mine?"

"I don't know," she said. "You asked me what I thought about Mary, and I told you, okay? Can we get this table loaded?"

Josh had the feeling they'd just scratched the surface of what had always stood between them, but he wasn't sure he wanted to pursue it any further. Rebecca was leaving in a few weeks. They'd finally managed to form a friend-ship—or some semblance of one. Probably best to leave well enough alone.

They fit the table and all four chairs on the truck, along with a small end table, a bench and several lamps, and padded everything with blankets before tying it down. Then they jumped in the cab of the truck to make their first trip to the Store & Lock. "Can I tell you what I think of Buddy?" Josh asked as he started the engine, still annoyed by what she'd said earlier about him and Mary.

Rebecca fastened her seat belt. "You don't know Buddy."

"I've heard a few things."

She folded her arms and braced herself against the door. "Like what?"

Josh checked for oncoming traffic and pulled out when he saw, as he'd expected, nothing. Rebecca lived on a short street that dead-ended into a trailer park. Not exactly a high traffic area. "That he's too young for you."

"Who told you that? My dad?"

Josh checked both mirrors to make sure the furniture wasn't going anywhere as he accelerated and didn't answer.

"Of course it was my dad," she said. "He's so weird about the age difference. Buddy's twenty-six. That's hardly robbing the cradle."

Twenty-six was better than Josh had figured, after what Doyle had said, but he was still convinced Buddy wasn't the right man for her. "It's not just his age," he said. "From all accounts, he's pretty mild-mannered."

"From my father's account, you mean." She kicked off her shoes and adjusted her seat belt so she could put her feet up on the dash. "What's wrong with being mild-mannered? Isn't that exactly what I need?"

He turned onto Main Street. "No."

"How do you know?"

"Because you need someone who understands your nature. Someone who can fulfill you without giving you too much rope, on one hand, or breaking your spirit, on the other."

"I'm not one of your horses, Josh."

"The concept is the same. You won't be able to respect Buddy if he doesn't stand up to you."

"You don't know that he won't stand up to me. He's put the wedding off…er…a couple of times already. I certainly wasn't happy about that."

"He isn't corralled yet."

"Horses again?"

He ignored her in favor of making his point. "It'll be different once he feels he's committed."

"And you know all this because—"

"I know you."

She gave him an incredulous look. "We weren't even friends until an hour ago."

› He slung an arm over the steering wheel. "You asked me what I thought."

"No, I didn't," she said. "You just wanted to tell me."

"What do you see in him, anyway?"

"Besides the fact that he's going to take me five hundred miles away from here?" she asked, twirling a section of hair around her finger.

"Yeah, besides that."

Her hand dropped into her lap and she turned to stare out the window. He could barely hear her when she spoke. "Maybe I like the fact that we get to start in the present."

"What does that mean?"

"Nothing," she said.

CHAPTER EIGHT

FRIENDS. She and Josh were now *friends*. He was actually sitting in her living room on the only chair she had left—a recliner that belonged to Delaney and had to go out to the ranch—waiting for her to make him something to eat in exchange for all his hard work. Booker had canceled a few hours earlier, when he found out she already had help, which left her and Josh to move everything into the little cubicle she'd rented from the Store & Lock at the far end of town. Now it was after midnight and they were finished, but they were both hungry and exhausted.

"How about some macaroni and cheese?" Rebecca called from her small kitchen.

"Is that all you've got?" he asked, hardly exuberant.

"Unless you want cold cereal. My mother sent home some garlic bread I can warm in the oven, if that helps."

"Sounds good," he said. She could hear him flipping through the channels on her television. Rebecca had decided to leave the TV for last, knowing she could always fit it in the passenger seat of her car. She wanted to finish moving tomorrow, because she had the day off, but the house was too quiet to go without television for even twenty-four hours.

"Who'll be around to help you tomorrow?" he asked.

"I'm sure Randy will come by. I've got his truck."

"Is all your other stuff going with you to your new place?"

"No, my new place is furnished. Once I get packed, a lot of boxes will have to go into storage—all the kitchen stuff and my summer clothes. Which reminds me. I need that key I gave you to my storage unit."

"I left it in my ashtray when I took that last load of small stuff you didn't want rolling around in the back of Randy's truck. I'll give it to you when I leave."

"What if you forget?"

"You've got another one, haven't you?"

"Yeah, but that isn't any reason to lose my duplicate."

"I'm tired. And it's not going anywhere."

"Anyway," she continued, "I can handle the boxes. Randy will only need to help me with my bedroom furniture."

"Good thing we've only just become friends," he said. "If we were old friends, I'd have to come back."

Good thing was right, Rebecca thought. Despite their agreement, she wasn't sure she wanted to be even casual friends with Josh Hill. He unsettled her, made her think about possibilities she was better off not thinking about—possibilities that weren't very reassuring for someone who was engaged. But she had to admit he'd been a godsend tonight.

As she started cooking, he settled on a movie that sounded a lot like *Terminator*. He'd offered to help her in the kitchen but she'd declined. She felt indebted after all the work he'd done and hoped to relieve at least some of that sense of obligation. She certainly couldn't walk around town feeling beholden to Josh Hill. It wasn't natural.

The macaroni and cheese took Rebecca longer than she'd thought it would. By the time she'd boiled the noodles, added the Velveeta, brown sugar, milk and seasonings and taken the garlic bread from the oven, twenty minutes had disappeared. Josh hadn't spoken for a while, but she could hear Arnold Schwarzenegger's relentless pursuit of Linda Hamilton. Soon she and Josh would eat, she'd thank him, and that'd be the end of entertaining him. As before, they'd occasionally pass on the street, nod and that would be that.

"Dinner's ready," she said, setting everything on the counter that separated the dining area from the kitchen, since she no longer had a table.

He didn't respond, so she filled a plate and carried it over. She figured there wasn't any need to make him move. He already had the only seat in the house. "Josh?"

Again no response.

Rebecca leaned closer so she could see his face in the flickering light of the television. Sure enough, his eyes were closed. He'd fallen asleep.

"Josh." She shook his arm. "Are you still hungry? Do you want to eat?"

His eyes fluttered open and he mumbled something unintelligible, then dropped off again.

Now what? She couldn't let him sleep in Delaney's recliner. His truck was parked in front of her house. If he stayed, it would be all over town in the morning that they'd had an affair. Maybe her father deserved that for pushing them together, but she didn't think Buddy would be especially happy about it.

Of course, she *was* moving in with Booker. Rumors were bound to rage about the two of them. But Buddy was the reason she'd had to come up with other living arrangements in the first place, which made it okay. More importantly, Rebecca didn't want to have sex with Booker.

Josh was a different story entirely.

Putting his plate on the floor, she shook him harder. "Josh, you'd better wake up. You wouldn't want Mary thinking you spent the night with me, would you?"

"Stop it," he growled and knocked her hands away. She

doubted he even knew who she was, but she definitely got the point that he didn't want to be bothered.

"Well, damn," she said. "What am I going to do now?"

She stepped back and stared at him for another few seconds before coming to a decision. She'd just move his truck. She'd seen him drop his keys on the counter earlier, when they were struggling to drag Delaney's old bed outside. She might not be able to remove him from her living room, but she could certainly remove his truck from in front of her house.

Problem solved. Until morning. She wasn't sure what it would feel like to face Josh Hill upon waking. But she was too tired to deal with that prospect right now. Maybe she'd wake up and he'd be gone—provided he was smart enough to figure out she'd moved his truck and that it hadn't been stolen.

Before going out, she picked at the macaroni and cheese she'd made, polished off two pieces of garlic bread, cleaned the dishes and put the extra food away, thinking he might wake up after he'd had a little nap. But he didn't.

"Josh?" she said again as she left the kitchen, just to be sure.

He didn't answer, so she scooped his keys off the counter and parked his truck in a far corner of the trailer park.

He was still sleeping like the dead when she returned. Taking one of the blankets from her bed, she threw it over him and turned off the television. Then she showered, towel-dried her hair, pulled on a big T-shirt and fell into bed.

SHE'D POISONED HIM. That had to be it, Josh thought. He'd never felt sicker in his life, even that time she'd duped him with the laxative. Chills wracked his entire body, he could hardly open his eyes for the pain lancing through his head, and nausea roiled in his stomach. She must've put something in his food again—but he didn't remember eating anything before falling asleep.

"Rebecca?" he called.

No answer.

The house was completely dark. She'd been kind enough to provide him with a quilt, but it wasn't nearly enough to keep him warm. Not right now. He longed for some Tylenol, a hot water bottle, a big feather comforter and his own bed. He had to get home.

Except he didn't think he was capable of driving.

Forcing himself up and out of the recliner, he stumbled around the unfamiliar living room, searching for his keys. He could have sworn he'd left them on the counter, but he patted the top of it for a full five minutes without finding anything. Finally he sought a switch on the wall and flooded the room with light.

He winced against the sudden brightness and put his head down so he wouldn't pass out from dizziness. When he could look up, he found his keys next to the telephone. Dragging them off the counter, he used the wall to keep himself upright until he could stumble to the front door. But when he gazed outside, he could only stare in silent wonder. The road was empty; his truck was gone.

"Dammit, Rebecca," he muttered, sliding down the wall. He didn't have the energy to shut the door, even though the air was far colder outside than in.

He was shivering uncontrollably by the time he heard some noise coming from the back of the house.

"Josh?" Rebecca asked, standing in the hallway, blinking. It looked as though she wasn't wearing anything except an oversized T-shirt. But she could've been standing there stark naked; he was too sick to care.

"What are you doing?" she asked when her eyes adjusted and she saw him sitting on the floor. "Why's the door open?"

"My truck's gone."

"No, I just moved it. It's at the trailer park. Is something else wrong?"

"Tell me you didn't do this to me," he said.

She hurried forward and shut the door. "What do you mean? I didn't do anything."

"I'm sick."

"In what way?"

It took a moment to catch his breath. "Chills. Aches. My head feels like it's going to explode. And you might want to bring me a pan."

"Oh, it's just the flu," she said. "My nephew has it right now."

"*Just* the flu?" he mumbled. "You gotta take me home."

"I can't take you home when you're this sick. Your dad said your brother's out of town. There won't be anyone to look after you."

"Then…" He tried to think of a good alternative. "I guess you can take me to my parents' house."

"I can't do that, either," she said. "They're going to think what you did—that I did this to you. And even if I'm able to convince them I'm not to blame, they're going to wonder why you were with me in the middle of the night. It's nearly three o'clock."

Despite the flu, what she said made sense. His mother wouldn't be particularly happy to think he'd been spending the night with Rebecca. Come to think of it, neither would Mary.

"Here," she said. "I know what to do. We'll get you fixed up."

Josh thought it was a sad day when he had to rely on

Rebecca Wells to take care of him. "That's okay. I'm not sure I trust you *that* much."

"Oh, quit being such a baby," she said, scowling at him. "I promise you'll like what I'm going to do."

Two days earlier, before the truce, he would've made it out of her house if he'd had to crawl. But he didn't want to miss anything he might like—especially since she seemed so definite about it. And she'd done a good job on his hair....

"Just get me warm," he said.

"I can do better than that. Come on." She was next to him then, helping him stand, and the softness and warmth of her body felt so good he wasn't sure he'd be able to let her go.

She guided him through the living room, down a short hall and into her bedroom, which was the only room he hadn't visited while they were moving her furniture. The blinds were pulled, so he could scarcely see it even now. But he thought he could identify the outline of a double bed, a nightstand, a dresser and something low and square—a steamer trunk?—off to one side. He couldn't tell whether the room was decorated in the same offbeat way as the rest of the house. But he knew one thing: it smelled like heaven.

"First let's get your boots off," she said as he sank gratefully onto her bed.

She bent down and removed his boots. He heard them clunk against the wall as she tossed them out of the way. Then she pulled off his shirt.

"Okay, now take off your jeans and crawl under the covers," she said.

He stared up at her. "Take off my jeans? You're kidding, right?"

"Do you want to feel better or not?"

She left the room, obviously bent on some errand, and he tried to think clearly enough to decide what to do. He already felt pretty vulnerable. He wasn't sure he wanted to make himself any more vulnerable by sacrificing what remained of his clothes.

"You haven't moved," she said when she came back into the room carrying a pan in one hand and a glass of water in the other.

"I think I'm better off with my pants on. Just in case."

"In case of what?" she asked.

"In case you're going to throw them outside and leave me to find my way home."

She smiled. "Would I do something like that?"

"There was definitely a time when you would've done exactly that."

She handed him a couple of Tylenol and put the pan within easy reach. "Then play it safe," she said.

He wasn't sure he'd be able to keep the pills down, but he swallowed them anyway and curled up on the bed. "You got a hot water bottle?"

"Here, cover up at least," she said, helping him get beneath the blankets. "I've got a heating pad and a few other things. Just wait, okay?"

She lit a couple of candles on the nightstand, and he recognized the slightly floral scent as the one that had been lingering in her room. Then she turned on some low, wordless music, and went to her closet. A few minutes later, he heard her by the bed again and opened his eyes to see her rummaging through a square case. She withdrew what looked like a big bottle of hand lotion, wrapped the heating pad around it and plugged the cord in at the wall.

"I thought that heating pad was for me," he complained, shivering.

"You'll be warm in a minute."

He tried to be patient. The candles, the music and the heating pad promised good things. "What are you doing?"

"I'm going to give you a massage. It'll help your body rid itself of the toxins that are making you sick and ease the aching in your muscles."

Years ago Josh had heard something about Rebecca attending Carlson's School of Massage Therapy in Iowa. She'd been there part of the time he was attending the U of U. But when he graduated and returned home, she'd already changed her focus to hair care.

She disappeared into her closet again. When she emerged, she carried a big vinyl-covered headrest, which she positioned on the bed beside him.

"Put your face in the opening," she told him as she situated the heating pad between his chest and the mattress.

He did as she said and immediately felt the wonderful heat from the pad seeping through his skin. He was about to tell her to pull up the covers and just let him sleep. He felt too miserable to be around anyone. But then she poured warm oil on his back and began to rub, and he knew she was right—this would help. As the candles scented the air and the music played softly in the background, her fingers seemed to find every sore spot on his back. Gently yet firmly, she worked each muscle. She moved up his spine to his neck and then massaged his head, soothing away his aches and pains until he scarcely felt them anymore. Finally, his eyelids lowered, blocking out the dim light, and he drifted off to sleep.

REBECCA CONSIDERED massage to be very therapeutic. She believed the right kind of touch could heal people on more than one level. She also knew that touching some people affected her differently than touching others—and touching Josh Hill seemed to have the greatest impact of all.

Drawing a bolstering breath, she gazed down at his smooth bare skin, gleaming with oil in the candlelight, and wondered how it had come to this. Just two days earlier, she hadn't spoken to him in ages—other than that August 16th and an occasional "how do you do." Now he was in her bed, and the massage she performed so mechanically on others felt more like a labor of love. Her hands actually shook with the desire to explore the rest of him....

Buddy. Think of Buddy. He was a kind, gentle lover. A good man. So what if they'd never enjoyed the same type of mind-blowing sex she'd almost had with Josh? So what if during those few unguarded minutes in Josh's arms last summer, she'd fancied herself so deeply in love with him she thought she'd drown? She'd been dazed, confused, drunk. Tonight her body's response stemmed from the music and the candles.

Or maybe she was as flawed as everyone said she was.

Wiping the oil from Josh's back, she got up and put her things away. She was stupid to have agreed to this friendship. All it did was shine a bright light on her weak character. She was engaged and yet, when she came into contact with Josh Hill, she lost sight of the small, neat house she imagined sharing with Buddy.

Fortunately nothing had happened that she needed to be ashamed of. She hadn't been disloyal or unfaithful to Buddy or anyone else. All she had to do was stay on the straight and narrow course that would lead her to marital bliss and not moral ruin. And that shouldn't be too hard, she reasoned—not if she kept her perspective. If Josh wanted her at all, he wanted her for only one thing. It wasn't as though he could ever fall in love with her or marry her, as Buddy was willing to do. She wasn't about to destroy her engagement for a cheap, unfulfilling fling, despite the desire that dogged her so tenaciously. She was better than that, smarter than that.

In the morning, she'd tell Josh that she didn't want anything more to do with him, that he was to leave her alone beginning immediately—

"Rebecca?" he murmured.

She froze at the entrance to her closet. "Hmm?"

"I'm sorry I didn't trust you," he said. "I should have taken off my pants."

Rebecca's shoulders slumped as she dragged a blanket out to the living room. Cutting him off wasn't going to be easy. As much as she wanted to believe that what she felt for him was strictly a physical response, the one he inspired in most women, she knew she was starting to really like Josh Hill.

"I DON'T WANT to be friends anymore," Rebecca announced as soon as Josh stumbled out of her bedroom the next morning. She'd been up for several hours already, scrounging boxes from various businesses in town and packing. She'd just finished telling herself that she was going to wait for the right time to spring her change of heart on Josh. But there didn't seem to be a good time to wreck a friendship. And when her first glimpse of him made her heart pound and her body grow warm, even when he was looking sleepy and unshaven, she knew sooner was better than later.

"What?" Obviously not quite coherent yet, he scratched his head and glanced around as though trying to find his bearings.

"I said I don't want to be friends with you anymore."

He was still wearing only his blue jeans, which were zipped but not buttoned. Yawning, he walked toward her. "Was it just last night we loaded up all your furniture?"

he asked, sprawling on the floor a few feet from where she was packing dishes. "It seems like eons ago. What time is it?"

"Nearly noon. Didn't you hear me?" she asked.

He propped himself up on his hands. "Yeah, I heard you. You don't want to be my friend. I assumed you were joking, of course."

She gathered what she could of her remaining nerve. "Well, I wasn't."

He met this statement with several seconds of wary silence. "I don't understand," he said finally.

Rebecca wrapped newspaper around a plate and put it in with the other dishes she'd already packed. "It's simple. I want to call off the deal we made last night."

His eyebrows shot up. "Why?"

"Because I don't like the change, that's why. I don't want your help moving. I don't want your truck in front of my house. I don't want you spending the night." She hesitated. "How are you feeling? Can I get you a glass of juice?"

He shook his head. "You don't want to be my friend *and* how am I feeling? God, you're confusing. What did I miss between last night and this morning? I'm sorry I got sick while I was here, if that's what has your panties in a bunch."

"It has nothing to do with you getting sick. I just want things to go back to the way they were."

"What's so appealing about being enemies?"

"Nothing. It's just more appealing than being friends."

"That doesn't make any sense."

She kept packing so she wouldn't have to look at him. "It does to me. We made a mistake trying to turn our relationship into something it can't be."

He sat up and crossed his legs. "Do you mind telling

me how I'm supposed to react here? Because I'm at a complete loss. I've never had anyone decide they don't want to be my friend anymore, at least not out of the clear blue and without a reason.''

''Can't we just pretend the past two days never happened?'' she asked. ''Then you can say goodbye and go, and after another hour or two, I can pat myself on the back for doing the right thing.''

''How can you say that's the right thing? You're being mean to me!''

''I'm engaged!''

''I know that. But we're only friends. We haven't done anything wrong. I mean, there was last summer, which was—'' he let his breath go all at once ''—crazy good, I'll admit. But that was before Buddy and you—''

''I don't want to talk about it,'' she interrupted, taping up the box she'd filled.

He sat without moving and watched her search for the marker she'd been using to label everything, and Rebecca thought if he didn't leave soon the butterflies in her stomach might make her lose the donut she'd had for breakfast. ''Well?'' she said.

''You really want me to leave?''

She swallowed hard, wondering why, if this was the right thing to do, it was hurting like some kind of breakup. ''Yes.''

He stood. ''Then come over here and tell me that.''

She looked up at him from where she knelt by the box on which she was writing *kitchen*. ''You've got the flu. I wouldn't want to catch it.''

''I'm better now.''

''You can't be completely better.''

''I'm mostly better. Come here.''

''Why?''

"Because. I've never seen you scared of anything in your life. But I think you're scared of me."

"I'm not scared of you," she said, capping the marker. "That's silly. Why would I be scared of you?"

"That's what I want to find out."

She rose, dusted off her low-cut jeans and cap-sleeved T-shirt and moved closer, telling herself she'd stare him in the eye without flinching and repeat everything she'd just said. Then maybe he'd believe her. She wasn't going to be anything less than what Buddy deserved her to be, wasn't going to settle for "I am what I am." She wanted to be so much more.

She stopped a few feet away from him.

"Is that the best you can do?" he taunted.

"You borrowed my toothbrush!" she accused, catching the scent of toothpaste on his breath. "When did you do that?"

"I woke up this morning while you were gone."

"So you helped yourself to my toothbrush?"

"I had to. I'm a real clean freak when it comes to teeth."

"Good for you. But that's sort of a personal thing to do, don't you think?"

"I think you're stalling."

She stepped closer, determined not to let him know how deeply he affected her.

When they stood only a foot apart, she stared into his eyes—the gray-green eyes that had always tormented her in some strange way—and felt the strongest magnetic pull she'd ever experienced. She'd moved too close to the sun. It was going to pull her in and burn her up. Or simply cause her to instantaneously combust.

She wasn't sure whether she closed the gap or he did, but a moment later they were standing so close the tips of her breasts tingled as they grazed his bare chest through her shirt. His lips hovered near her own. She could feel his breath fanning her cheek and smell the oil she'd used on his skin the night before and, for a fleeting second, imagined his mouth on hers in one of those hungry, passion-filled kisses she remembered so well from last summer....

She was hovering only inches away from complete ruin, hanging on by her fingertips, she realized dully.

And then everything that hung in the balance—her self-respect, her engagement, her escape from Dundee, her refusal to become another of Josh's conquests—suddenly came into sharp focus, and she jumped back.

He must've felt something, too, because his head snapped up and he stepped away at almost the same time.

"You're right," he said gruffly. "Forget the damn truce, forget the friendship, forget it all." Grabbing his boots and his keys, he left without even bothering to pick up his shirt.

CHAPTER NINE

SITTING ON THE FLOOR, her face buried in her hands while she tried to make some sense out of what had just happened, Rebecca didn't realize that Randy had entered the house until he spoke.

"Tell me that wasn't my best friend I just passed on the street," he said, standing in the open doorway.

She jerked her head up. Her brother-in-law's company was the last thing she needed right now. She had no emotional reserves left, no energy to spar with him. "I don't know. I wasn't there."

His eyes narrowed as he gave her a searching look. "He was tall, blond and driving like a bat out of hell. And he didn't seem to be wearing clothes. That ring any bells?"

"No."

"Rebecca, he didn't even recognize me. Only a man who'd just encountered *you* could be that crazed."

Rebecca counted silently to ten and found her feet. "Randy, I don't want to argue with you today. Maybe Josh has a new girlfriend. Maybe she lives at the trailer park. How should I know?"

"Come on. The only women in that trailer park have a houseful of kids or they're over seventy. What did you do to him?"

"I didn't do anything to him!" She waved a hand at the boxes and newspapers and tape. "Can't you see I'm working here? I'm trying to get moved. Are you going to help me or not?''

He didn't look completely convinced, but Rebecca could see him wavering.

''Randy, I'm fully dressed. I'm obviously in the middle of packing. And I'm engaged. Can't you cut me a little slack?''

Finally he nodded. ''Yeah, you want to get married too badly to screw it up. You wouldn't get involved with another guy right now.''

''Try never,'' she said.

''Okay. I'm with you. So, where does everything go?''

''This box here needs to—''

A rap on the open door caught both their attention. ''Hey, babe,'' Booker said, sauntering inside. ''You still moving in with me today?''

Randy straightened, instead of picking up the box he'd been about to lift, and his eyes went immediately to her. ''You were saying?'' he muttered.

Rebecca felt her stomach drop. ''Your timing is impeccable,'' she told Booker.

''HEY, GUESS WHAT I just heard? You're gonna love this one.''

Startled by his brother's intrusion into the otherwise quiet stable, Josh jumped up and accidentally knocked over the bucket he'd been sitting on while brushing Sheza Beaut. ''What'd you hear?'' he asked, kicking it out of the way.

The mare stomped and nickered at the disturbance. ''Whoa, girl, it's okay,'' Josh murmured, stroking the mare's neck.

Mike, older by three years, paused at the front of the stall to lean on the gate. ''Rebecca Wells is moving in with Booker Robinson.''

"What?" Josh felt as though his brother had just slugged him in the stomach. He hadn't completely recovered from last night's flu but until that moment, he'd been feeling much better. "Where did you hear that?"

"I stopped by the diner on my way into town just a few minutes ago. Judy said Booker and Rebecca had been in with Hatty. She heard them talking about the move." He chuckled and rubbed his neck with one hand. "Only Rebecca would shack up with another guy when she's supposed to be getting married in six weeks. Doyle's probably going to have a coronary when he learns, if he doesn't know already. Can you imagine? Having a daughter who…"

Mike kept talking about the rumors that were flying around town. He mentioned that some folks were speculating Booker had served time in prison during the past fifteen years. But Josh couldn't concentrate on his brother's words. He was too busy remembering snatches of conversation with Rebecca last night, remembering all the opportunities she'd had to tell him she was moving in with Booker. He'd even asked her where she was going—and she'd said, "Out in the boonies."

"That can't be true," he said, interrupting a list Mike was giving of Booker's possible offenses against the law.

"'Course it's true. Sounds just like her—wild as ever." Mike kicked a clod of dirt off the back of his left boot. "I pity the guy stupid enough to tie the knot with her."

Josh flinched. He pitied Rebecca's prospective husband, too—in a way. He also felt something else, something he knew would surprise his brother almost as much as it surprised him—a sort of gut-roiling jealousy that a man was going to possess her and it wasn't going to be him. She'd give her husband hell. But Josh liked his women and his horses with ample spirit, and there wasn't a more spirited woman around than Rebecca Wells. Sure, she'd be hard to handle, but no one could make a man feel more like a man simply by closing her eyes and surrendering to his touch. He remembered the excitement he'd experienced with her, an excitement he'd never felt with anyone else—ever. Certainly not with Mary, who seemed to think of sex as a party favor to be doled out at the end of each date. There'd been no artifice in Rebecca's reactions to him, no coyness, just a raw physical passion that had held him absolutely spellbound—until Mike had come in, of course.

"Something wrong?" Mike asked. "I thought you'd be surprised, but..."

Josh dropped his brush. Whether he and Rebecca were calling a truce or not, he didn't want her living with Booker Robinson. He didn't want her anywhere near Booker. And he sure as hell wasn't going to be the stupid fool who helped her move in.

"Come on," he said. "There's something we have to do."

"YOU JUST *HAD* TO MENTION that I was staying here to my brother-in-law," Rebecca complained to Booker. They were lounging on the couch at his grandmother's house watching television, exhausted from their long day of moving.

"How was I supposed to know it was a secret?" he asked. "Were you just gonna disappear without a forwarding address?"

Rebecca punched the pillow she'd brought out of the upstairs room Hatty had designated as hers and curled into a more comfortable position. She hadn't yet unpacked the clothing she'd carted over in a suitcase, but everything else was where it should be. Only a few things remained at her old place—her telephone and answering machine, her television, which she was planning to put in her bedroom, and some plants. She needed to pick them up tonight and do some last-minute cleaning so she could get her deposit back. But with all the progress she'd made in only two days, she figured she could allow herself a few minutes to rest.

"It wasn't a secret exactly," she said. "I was going to tell them in a couple of days."

"I saved you the trouble," he said with a shrug.

She rolled her eyes. "Thanks. Your grandmother said my father's called four times already."

"If you'd talk to him, he might quit calling."

Rebecca wasn't ready to talk to her father. She'd had enough distressing encounters today. First Josh, then Randy...

"Did Buddy get hold of you?" Booker asked.

"I've talked to him a couple of times this afternoon. Why?"

"He called here a little while ago. Seemed surprised to find I had such a deep voice."

"He didn't seem upset when I talked to him."

Booker fiddled with the remote, surfing channels. "Did you tell him I'm gay or something?"

"I didn't lie to him. He wasn't pleased that we'll be living together, but he handled it just fine."

"What's just fine?"

"He said a lot of things like, 'In the future I hope you'll discuss your plans with me, Rebecca,' and 'communication is key in any relationship.'"

Booker scratched his head. "Does this guy have any testosterone at all?"

"He's not the macho type. He's low-key and sweet, and he's going to bring more emotional balance into my life."

"The kind of emotional balance that comes from being afraid of commitment?"

"He's not afraid of commitment."

"He's put the wedding off three times, Rebecca. Doesn't take a psychology degree to see he's dragging his feet."

"It's not that. He's just really close to his family and wants them all to be there."

"Which could indicate something worse."

"What's that supposed to mean?"

"Maybe he's a mommy's boy."

Rebecca sat up. "Quit being so negative, Booker. You're going to like him," she said, even though she doubted he would.

"Tell me again why you want to marry this guy," he said, settling on VH-1.

"Besides being a very fine person, he's gentle and consistent. I admire that."

"To hell with gentle and consistent," he said. "What about passion?"

"I have enough passion for both of us. I'm looking for other things. How many men do you know who'd go along with their fiancée moving in with a male friend? Now, *that's* trust."

"Or stupidity," he muttered.

"What's stupid about saving two months' rent?"

"So he's tight-fisted as well as stupid? Where'd you find this lemon?"

"Quit it!" she said. "You don't even know him."

He fell silent through a Janet Jackson video. "When's the wedding?" he asked when the VJ returned to the screen. "Did Buddy say?"

"January 25th, but you'll meet him before that. He's flying out for my parents' anniversary party a week from Friday." She purposefully didn't mention the only tense moment in her whole conversation with Buddy—when he'd told her it would cost as much as a new ticket to change his travel itinerary, and she told him she didn't care. She doubted these details would reflect well on Buddy, considering Booker's earlier comment about his being tight-fisted.

"You've invited me to the wedding, but you haven't said anything about taking me to your parents' big celebration."

Rebecca felt a flicker of apprehension. "You don't really want to go to that, do you?"

"Why not? Half the town will be there, including that cute little Katie from your salon, right?"

"Er...yeah. Probably," Rebecca responded.

"Then I'm in."

She shook her head. "I don't know about that."

"Aw, come on. You can get me an invite, can't you?"

"Rebecca, your father's on the telephone again," Booker's grandmother called.

For a little old lady barely five feet two with wispy gray hair, translucent skin and brittle bones, she had quite a voice. Rebecca scrambled off the couch. "I'm just on my way out, Hatty. Could you tell him I had to go to my old place to finish up a few things?"

"But it's almost ten o'clock, dear. Are you sure you want to go back tonight?"

Yes! Rebecca wanted to wash her hands of the old and concentrate on the new. She also wanted to sleep late in the morning. She didn't have to work until ten. "This stuff is important, I'm afraid," she called. "Tell him I'll stop by his office tomorrow at lunch."

Hatty said nothing more. Rebecca nudged Booker with her knee. "Want to go with me?"

His eyes flicked away from the television screen. "Not especially. I'm beat."

Now that she had a roommate again, she hated the

thought of going alone. "What would it take to convince you?"

He considered for a moment. "Is A&W open this time of night?"

"Not during the week."

"Then I guess you're out of luck." A half smile curled his lips as he went back to watching television.

"What about a rain check?" she asked. "I'll take you out for ice cream tomorrow."

He made a big deal about turning off the television, tossing the remote aside and getting to his feet. "I didn't know you were going to be such a pain in the ass when I said you could move in here," he grumbled.

She gave him a sweet smile. "You'd be bored stiff without me."

"Don't get cocky just because you're the only person in this town I can tolerate—besides that cute little Katie."

"Katie's only twenty-three."

"She's older than eighteen," he said, trailing her through the front door, down the porch steps and to her car.

"I don't think she'd be very responsive," Rebecca said. "She's had a thing for Josh Hill's older brother as far back as I can remember."

"*Older* brother? I thought you said she's only twenty-three."

Rebecca unlocked the doors, took the driver's seat and reached into the back for a sweatshirt. "She is."

"How old is Josh's brother?" he asked, climbing in beside her.

"Let's see…" Her radio blasted through her speakers as soon as she started the car. She turned it down before throwing the car into reverse. "He was a senior when Josh was a sophomore and I was a freshman, so he's got to be thirty-six."

"If they didn't go to school together, how'd she get to know him?"

"Her family owns Don and Tami's bakery. Tami is Josh's mother's best friend."

"Thirteen-year age difference. She must like father figures," he said. "I can be a father figure."

Rebecca couldn't help laughing. "Good luck."

They spent the next fifteen minutes fighting over which radio station to listen to—country western or acid rock. Booker was still trying to find something suitably repulsive when Rebecca pulled into the drive of her old rental house and cut the engine. "I don't believe it," she murmured, staring at her yard in astonishment.

"Now this...this is music," Booker said, as loud screeching guitars and someone screaming into a microphone made the whole car vibrate.

"My key. I should've insisted he give back my key."

"What are you talking about?" He finally looked up, then blinked in surprise. "What's all this?"

"My furniture," she said numbly. "Everything Josh helped me move into storage. He had the duplicate key to my unit—he must've gone in there and brought everything back."

IT WAS LATE, but Rebecca couldn't sleep. She was in a new place with different sounds and smells and textures. She was worried about her furniture, which was still sitting on the lawn of her old rental house because she and Booker had been too exhausted to deal with moving it again tonight. And she was angry.

"You'll get yours, Josh Hill," she muttered for the hundredth time.

Fortunately Booker and his grandmother were both asleep, so she was alone with her thoughts. Booker had stayed up for a while, drinking a beer and watching television, but Rebecca couldn't get interested in any of the sitcoms he preferred. She'd needed a more physical outlet and began to pace, silently cursing Josh Hill, and Booker had eventually dragged himself off to bed.

"Who does Josh think he is?" she said aloud, pivoting at the end of the family room and coming back for another pass. Just because she didn't want to be his friend didn't mean he had to turn on her.

Finally, she sat down at the small built-in desk in the corner of the room to call Buddy, hoping his calmness would soothe her. He wouldn't like her spending so much money on long-distance calls, instead of e-mailing, but she needed to hear his voice.

"Hi, honey," Buddy said.

"You're not sleeping?" she asked.

"No, I'm surfing the net." He surprised her by not saying anything about the money she'd owe Hatty for this call.

"What are you looking for?"

"Just checking out some new games, stuff like that."

"Find anything fun?"

"Actually I did. I was visiting an astrology page my mother told me about and read something I was going to e-mail you. Now that you're on the phone, I'll just read it."

"What is it?" she asked.

"Proof that we're meant to be together."

"Really?" That sounded good. Exactly what Rebecca needed at the moment.

"Here it is—'What Attracts the Scorpio Woman...' Just a sec, I'm pulling it up."

Rebecca waited, hoping to hear that she was wildly attracted to a mild-mannered sweet man who would never cause her angst or fear, never make her see red, never leave her furniture out on the lawn—

"The type of man who attracts you seems inscrutable and has a kind of magnetic charisma that hints at smoldering sexuality and passion," Buddy read.

Smoldering sexuality? "Go on," Rebecca said, feeling a slight glitch in her enthusiasm. Obviously, he hadn't gotten to the part that talked about him.

"You're strong-willed and possessive," he continued, "and like the same in a mate, for you have a deep-felt need to be wanted. A subtle power struggle may be a seductive aspect of the attraction. Men who seem mysterious or brooding or have 'deep dark secrets' could intrigue and entice you. You are often attracted to men who seem powerful or dangerous—"

"Powerful?" she said.

"Well, I interpret powerful to mean confident. And I'm confident, right?"

"Right. That *could* be you," she said, because she didn't know what else to say. So far none of Buddy's stronger characteristics had been mentioned.

"I thought the first part was a little more applicable, but I suppose some women might say I'm a man of secrets," Buddy said. "Still waters run deep and all that, you know?"

Sometimes still waters were simply what they appeared to be—still waters. Rebecca had realized that with Buddy. But she certainly didn't want to make him feel bad if he imagined himself as enigmatic. "Um...you're—" she cleared her throat "—sort of mysterious, I guess. I wouldn't call you brooding, exactly."

"Wait till you hear this. 'If you have Mars in Scorpio, you will have extra-strong passions and sexual magnetism that is sensed by others, especially Scorpio types.'"

"Why would you read me that?" she said, her voice slightly shrill. "You're not a Scorpio." Rebecca wasn't sure whether she had Mars in Scorpio or not, but Josh Hill was the only male Scorpio she knew. Not that she'd ever share that information with Buddy. Her fiancé wasn't the type to understand illicit attraction—or lifelong feuds. And she was definitely leaving her past behind when she moved to Nebraska.

"You interrupted before I got to the good part," he said. "This is the good part: 'You are the ultimate seductress and may be especially aroused by the raw sexual energy of a passionate man.'"

Rebecca sat staring at nothing. Had she called the right number? Was this Josh and not Buddy, playing some kind of cruel joke?

"Hello? Rebecca?"

"I'm here."

"What do you think of that? You're a seductress."

"And...you're the man with the raw sexual energy?"

"Of course."

Then why had she conjured up Josh's face when Buddy was spouting that silly horoscope?

"After a reading like that, the extra money we're spending for me to come for your party should be money well spent, huh?"

Rebecca took a deep breath and tried to gain some perspective. It was just a horoscope. It didn't mean anything. "I'm looking forward to seeing you, Buddy," she said numbly. "But I'm exhausted. I'd better talk to you tomorrow."

"Goodbye, my little seductress."

She shook her head and hung up. Whatever had possessed Buddy to read her that? Didn't he know there probably wasn't a woman on earth who'd classify him as sexually intense? As dark and brooding? He had plenty of strengths; he was going to make a great husband. But sexual intensity wasn't one of those strengths. Neither were any of the other things he'd read her.

It was Josh's fault. If he hadn't gotten sick last night and made her feel obligated to give him that massage, she wouldn't be picturing him at every mention of sexual desire....

Grabbing the telephone book, she looked up his number at the ranch he owned with his brother. She didn't appreciate what he'd done to her furniture, and she wanted to let him know it.

The phone rang twelve times before someone answered, but Rebecca knew it was Josh and not Mike. She recognized the voice.

"Hello?"

She opened her mouth to say something about the furniture, but what was really on her mind was that stupid horoscope. *If you have Mars in Scorpio, you will have extra-strong passions and sexual magnetism that is sensed by others, especially Scorpio types.*

"Hello? Is anyone there?"

Rebecca hesitated. Even sleepy, Josh sounded sexy. The slight rasp to his voice seemed to spiral through her, making her long to close her eyes and just listen to him talk...

But she wouldn't give in to his appeal. No way in hell.

"You have no sexual energy," she blurted. "None. You're not strong-willed or possessive—well, maybe you *are* strong-willed and possessive—but you're not seductive and you don't entice me. As a matter of fact—"

"Rebecca?"

"What?"

"I don't know about any of that other stuff, but I have plenty of sexual energy," he said. "Anytime you want to let that fiancé of yours off the hook and find out how much, come on over.''

Anger and frustration combined to make her clench her fists. ''I wouldn't sleep with you if you were the last man on earth!'' she cried and hung up.

''WHO WAS THAT?'' Mike said, coming to stand in the doorway of Josh's room, his hair sticking up on one side.

Josh chuckled and set the phone back on its cradle. ''Just Rebecca thanking us for helping her move.''

CHAPTER TEN

CITY HALL SAT on a large shady lot next to the post office only a block away from the salon. Rebecca finished her eleven o'clock color for Mrs. Dobbins, told Katie she was going out to grab a sandwich and walked to her father's office, frowning at the sky. Dark clouds were forming overhead and the wind was picking up, which concerned her. She and Booker wouldn't be able to move her furniture inside until after she got off work. But the people from the trailer park at the end of the street would probably have carted it all away by then, so she wasn't sure why she was bothering to worry about rain.

Josh Hill... Rebecca felt her mood darken. To think she'd even *considered* becoming his friend.

Ignoring the elevator in the lobby, she took the stairs to the second floor and slipped through the double doors of the mayor's office. Ruth, the receptionist, immediately glanced up from behind the tall mahogany desk that shielded most of her birdlike body. "Your father will be available in a moment, Rebecca," she said stiffly.

"If he's busy, I can come back later."

Ruth shoved her glasses higher up on her nose. "No. I think he'd rather you waited."

Somehow Rebecca had known Ruth would say that. Sinking into one of four burgundy upholstered chairs arranged around a small coffee table, she selected a women's magazine from the pile at her disposal and started thumbing through it. She noticed right away that it featured a horo-scope, but she purposely flipped past it. She'd heard enough about her Zodiac sign. She was marrying Buddy whether he had strong passions or not.

She read the latest Hollywood gossip, pulled out a per-fume sample and rubbed it on her arm—lightly floral, pretty—and studied the hairstyles. Then she came across an article titled: "Long Distance Relationships: How To Make Them Work."

The phone rang. Rebecca looked up as Ruth answered, heard her say, "Of course, Mr. Balough, I'll put you right through," and figured it might be a while before her father was free. So she settled back to read.

The article talked about the growing incidence of divorce and cited the Internet as one of the possible causes. People were meeting and marrying without really knowing each other, it said. But she knew Buddy. They'd been engaged for several months and, while they hadn't spent much time in each other's presence, they'd certainly communicated a lot over the phone and through e-mail.

Still… Rebecca bit her lip and glared at the discourag-ingly high divorce rate. She'd been so intently focused on getting married and moving away, she'd never thought much about what might happen if her marriage to Buddy failed. She'd always told herself they'd make it work some-how.

What if she was wrong? What if his mother drove her crazy and he always took his mother's side? Or he clung more tightly to a dollar than she could tolerate? She'd seen suggestions that they were significantly different in such areas, but that didn't necessarily mean these differences would ever develop into serious marital problems…

A compatibility quiz followed the article but, after last night, Rebecca was almost afraid to take it. How dependable could it be? What if it told her she and Buddy were *in*compatible and steered her toward someone tall and blond and confident—someone with enough sexual energy to light up the entire east coast?

The door of her father's office opened and he stepped out.

Rebecca quickly set the magazine aside. She and Buddy didn't need a compatibility test. She already knew they were perfect for each other.

"Come on in," he said and moved out of the way so she could pass him.

Ruth studied them over the rim of her glasses, probably as surprised by the formal note in his voice as Rebecca was, but she didn't say anything.

Rebecca followed her father inside, and he shut the door before crossing to his desk. "Have a seat."

She glanced at her watch, wishing now that she hadn't waited for him. His strange calm didn't bode well. It promised to make her regret coming here. She should've gone to lunch, instead. "I only have another ten minutes or so. Fanny Partridge is coming for a perm at one," she said, preparing her escape before sitting on the edge of a burgundy-upholstered chair.

He didn't answer. He claimed his tufted leather chair behind his desk, steepled his fingers and stared at her.

She waited for whatever it was he had to say, feeling uncomfortable beneath his unswerving gaze. "What?" she finally said.

"You're an adult now, Rebecca." His voice was still surprisingly calm. "I can no longer tell you what to do."

"I realize that," she said. She thought *he'd* taken a little long to arrive at that conclusion, however.

"But I *can* tell you that getting involved with Booker Robinson is a mistake."

"Booker and I are only friends, Dad."

"He's a bad seed. He's always been a bad seed."

Rebecca tucked her hair behind her ears, and wondered if the perfume she'd put on in the lobby was making her sick. It suddenly seemed cloying, overpowering. "Not to worry. I'm getting married soon."

"Does Buddy know about your new living arrangement?"

"Of course."

"And he's okay with what you're doing?"

"Yes. It's only temporary."

Her father rolled away from his desk and stood. Placing one hand against the large window that flooded his office with sunlight, he looked out, presumably at the carefully manicured grounds below. "I tell you, Rebecca, you've just about been the death of me. I don't know how much more I can take."

She made no comment.

"It's always something, isn't it?" he went on. "Your sisters were easy to raise. Even the other kids on the street, Josh and his brother, have turned out to be responsible, dependable adults." He sighed and shook his head. "I don't know where we went wrong with you. We certainly tried to teach you the right things."

Rebecca squeezed her hands together in her lap. "Maybe I'm like Booker," she said. "Maybe I'm just a bad seed."

Straightening, he sighed. "Maybe so. In any case, your mother's really counting on this wedding. She thinks, once you're married, everything'll be fine. So don't do anything to screw it up, okay? Can you do us this one favor, Rebecca?"

Rebecca thought of Buddy's postponement and felt a stab of foreboding. Her parents would blame her because she'd moved in with Booker. Or they'd say it was her temper that had caused Buddy to shy away.

She opened her mouth to tell her father and get it over with, but she remembered their anniversary party and hesitated. If she told him now, she'd start a ripple effect that would ruin the whole celebration.

She couldn't do that. What difference would twelve days make, anyway? They could blame her after the party as easily as before.

"I'll do my best," she said and walked out.

WHEN REBECCA RETURNED to Hair And Now, Katie handed her a key.

"Josh Hill dropped this by."

Rebecca stared at her palm. It was the extra key to her storage unit. After what he'd done, she'd never dreamed Josh would dare show his face at the salon today. She'd assumed he'd mail her the key, give it to her parents or wait for her to show up and demand it. The fact that he'd risked a face-to-face confrontation showed her just how brazen he was.

"He has some nerve," she replied.

Momentarily between clients, Katie was busy sweeping up hair clippings. "He can have all the nerve he wants," she said. "There isn't a better-looking man within a hundred miles of here. Except his brother, of course."

The buzzer over the door squawked, and Mary Thornton stepped inside. "Hi, everyone."

Mona, who worked only half a day on Tuesday, did Mary's nails every other week. She'd arrived sometime while Rebecca was gone and was now busy setting up her station. Erma, the owner of Hair And Now, took Tuesdays off, and they rotated to be sure there'd always be someone available to close the salon at night.

"Hi, Mary. I'm almost ready," Mona said. "Come on over and have a seat."

"We were just talking about your boyfriend," Katie volunteered.

Mary pulled off her sunglasses and slipped them into her purse, along with her car keys. "What were you saying about Josh?"

"Just that he's handsome as the devil."

"And rich, too, which certainly doesn't hurt," Mary said, smiling proudly.

Rebecca gritted her teeth and headed purposefully to her own station. She wasn't going to get involved, wasn't going to say anything.

"When do you think you two will be getting married?" Katie asked.

Mary sauntered over to Mona's chair and settled in for her appointment. "I'm thinking December might be nice. I'd like to give Ricky a father for Christmas. Wouldn't that be fun?"

Great, she really *would* be the last in her group of peers to marry, Rebecca thought. "I didn't realize the two of you were engaged," she said, unable to keep her silence any longer.

Mary twisted to look at her. "Well, it's not official or anything, but everyone knows it's just a matter of time. We've been together for six months."

Rebecca remembered Josh's answer when she'd asked him if they'd be getting married soon. *I don't know. Do you think we should?* He'd sounded almost flippant, definitely not as certain as Mary. And there'd been other moments when he'd seemed less than committed. Just before he stormed out of Rebecca's house was one of them. And then, on the telephone he'd said, "Anytime you want to let

that fiancé of yours off the hook and come on out here…"
He hadn't even mentioned Mary.

Probably because he was all talk, Rebecca decided. He'd made that offer assuming she'd never take him up on it. But he still seemed far from devoted….

"Well, money isn't everything, you know," Rebecca said.

Mary laughed and shook her head. "Only you would say something like that. Everyone else knows Josh has it all."

Rebecca knew it, too. She'd heard it her whole life. Most often from her own father. But she wasn't about to admit—to anyone—that, deep down, she agreed.

"What's his brother doing these days?" Katie asked Mary. "Is he still seeing that woman from McCall?"

Rebecca knew Katie was trying to make the question sound nonchalant. She failed miserably, but Mary was so caught up in flaunting her plan to become the wife of the most admired man in town, she didn't notice. "I think so," she said absently. "I suspect he'll be getting married soon, too."

A sad expression flickered over Katie's face, but Mona had already started Mary's manicure, so Rebecca was the only one watching. Catching the younger woman's eye in the mirror, she said, "You never know about those things, Katie. A wedding's not a done deal till both parties say 'I do.'"

Katie smiled gratefully, but it was Mary who answered.

"Oh, it's pretty much a done deal for me and Josh," she said. "All we have to do now is set the date."

REBECCA CLOSED HER EYES, took her first sip of coffee and told herself she could relax at last. She was at Jerry's Diner. Grandmother Hatfield couldn't bother her here.

"I thought you told me she'd have a *few* chores for me,

nothing too arduous,'' she complained to Booker, who sat in the booth opposite her.

Booker still wasn't quite awake. She'd gotten him up before dawn and dragged him out to breakfast, hoping for a reprieve—anything to stop Hatty from banging on her door at seven o'clock to ask for some new favor. They'd lived together for a week now, plenty long enough for Rebecca to learn that Booker's grandmother was no one's fool. She came off as fragile and elderly, but she knew what she wanted and how to get it. Rebecca had already spent as many hours helping the old woman make raspberry jelly, varnish the kitchen cupboards and label the shelves in the cellar as she'd spent at the salon. Now she understood why Hatty had been so agreeable about letting her move in. She was actually getting the better end of the bargain. Especially because she kept Booker as busy as Rebecca. He'd already changed her oil, rotated her tires, fixed a few broken sprinklers, organized the shed and was now in the process of cleaning out the garage—which hadn't been done since Mr. Hatfield died twenty years earlier.

''She takes that saying, the one about idle hands being the devil's workshop, seriously,'' he said. He rested one arm over the back of the booth, letting his black leather jacket gape open to reveal the white T-shirt beneath.

''No kidding,'' Rebecca grumbled. ''So how did you manage to get into so much trouble when you were a kid?''

Judy delivered his breakfast, a big plate of eggs, bacon, hash browns and pancakes, and he started right in. ''Like any other self-respecting punk,'' he said between bites. ''I'd sneak out.''

''Sort of like we're doing now?''

He poured ketchup over his hash browns, then added half a bottle of Tabasco sauce. ''Exactly, babe. You learn fast.

But don't worry. Granny'll chill out once she feels caught up.''

Rebecca suspected Hatty would never feel "caught up." She was the kind who believed in spring-cleaning—all year round. Rebecca had never met such a clean freak in her life, and she'd always thought she and her own mother were pretty scrupulous in that area. But she didn't want to disabuse Booker of his pleasant illusions. With her luck, he'd bail out and leave town, and she'd be left alone with Hatty until her wedding in January.

"I used to look forward to my day off," she said, stirring another packet of Sweet-'N Low into her coffee. "I used to sleep in and do laundry and go grocery shopping and—" She dropped her spoon. "Oh God," she said. "Can my luck get any worse?"

"What are you talking about?" Booker wanted to know.

"Don't turn around now, but Josh Hill just walked in."

Without bothering to put down his fork, Booker immediately twisted in his seat to stare at Josh.

"Booker! I told you not to turn around," Rebecca whispered harshly. "I don't want him to see me. I've had enough of him *and* his girlfriend." But it was too late. Josh had spotted her and Booker, had obviously noticed Booker's less-than-friendly glare and was busy returning it, with interest.

"Hi, Josh, just one today?" Rebecca heard Peggy, the other waitress, say.

"Two," he said, but he didn't break eye contact with Booker.

"Just ignore him and eat your food," Rebecca muttered.

Booker listened about as well as he had the first time. He smiled, rather malevolently, at Josh as the hostess began to lead him to a table.

With Booker working so hard to attract Josh's attention,

Rebecca couldn't exactly cower in her seat and hope to go unnoticed. Folding her arms, she lifted her chin and watched her nemesis draw closer.

As she should have expected, he recognized the challenge in her eyes (or maybe it was Booker's glare that did the trick) because he stopped as soon as he reached their table. With a tip of his black cowboy hat, he even had the audacity to flash her that crooked grin of his—the one that showed the dimple in his right cheek—as though he hadn't left her furniture sitting out, unprotected, on the lawn. It had taken her and Booker two evenings to put it all back.

"How'd the move go?" he asked.

"Great. Thanks to my friend *Booker*." Spine rigid, Rebecca forced a taunting smile of her own, irritated that the sight of Josh always seemed to kick up her pulse. But it had been that way for so long, she doubted it was likely to change—another reason she was glad to be leaving Dundee.

"You get your key?" he asked.

"Katie gave it to me."

"Your table's the one over there," Peggy said, briefly interrupting to point Josh in the right direction.

Josh nodded to acknowledge her words and she hurried off to take care of the customers still crowding the entrance. "Well, next time you want to wake me up at night, don't bother calling, Rebecca. Just come on out," he said. Then he winked at her, grinned at Booker and took his seat in the booth across the aisle.

"What was that all about?" Booker asked.

"Nothing. Josh has some sort of problem, but I don't know what it is."

Booker downed one piece of bacon and then the other. "I already told you what it is."

"What?"

"He wants you."

"He left my furniture on the lawn!"

"So?"

"You have an amazingly simplistic view of life," she said.

"You've mentioned that."

"I suppose you think I should tell him to go to hell."

"That's exactly what I think."

For once, Rebecca tended to agree, but she wasn't about to say anything right now. Mary Thornton had arrived and was giving them a condescending smile as she passed their table on her way to join Josh.

"Too bad she's so uptight," Booker said, shaking his head and staring after her. "She's got a nice ass."

Judy brought them their check, and Rebecca quickly threw down her credit card. Suddenly Hatty's house didn't seem like such a bad place to be. Canning pickle relish was certainly preferable to watching Josh and Mary eat. "I really don't want to hear about Mary's ass," she said once the waitress moved away.

"Okay." He shoveled another mouthful of food into his mouth. "Can we talk about Katie's?"

Rebecca arched an eyebrow at him. "To think I once had a place of my own."

"Did you get me a ticket to your parents' big bash yet?" he asked after swallowing.

"I can't begin to imagine why you'd want to come. You know my father hates you. He's told the chief of police to keep an eye on you."

"Barney Fife can follow me around all he wants. He'll get damn bored after a while, though. It's not that exciting watching me clean out the garage."

Rebecca laughed in spite of herself. Regardless of what others said about Booker, she found him rather endearing.

"I'll call my father when we get home. The worst he can say is no."

"That's the attitude," he said. "You want the rest of my pancakes?"

"No." Rebecca tried to keep her attention on Booker and her own coffee, but she couldn't help listening for Josh's voice.

"What would you like?" she heard him ask Mary.

"I'll have whatever you're having," Mary responded, and Rebecca ground her teeth. Couldn't that woman have an opinion of her own?

She glanced back at the two of them, curious to see the expression on Josh's face, but his menu was in the way. All she could see was the adoration in Mary's eyes, the solicitous hand on his arm—and thought she might be sick. Let Josh marry Dundee High's old cheerleading captain and have a passel of brats as empty-headed as their mother. Rebecca was getting out of town, anyway.

"Rebecca?"

She turned back to Booker. "Hmm?"

"You want to tell me what suddenly has you so preoccupied?"

"Nothing," she said, fiddling with the sugar substitute because she could no longer meet his eyes. "I'm just ready to go."

He said nothing for a moment. When she thought it was safe, she looked up, but he was still watching her closely. "You're scaring me, babe," he said.

She took a sip of her coffee, even though it had grown far too cold. "What's that supposed to mean?"

He leaned closer. "For a minute there, I thought you wanted Josh Hill right back."

"No way," she said, "That's crazy."

He chuckled and didn't pursue the subject, but she knew he didn't believe her for a minute. And she couldn't blame him.

LYING ON HER BED, feet dangling over the side, Rebecca stared at the message Hatty had handed her as she came in.

"Buddy can't make it next week. Something came up. Says not to worry about the airfare, though—he never purchased his plane ticket. Give him a call."

Rebecca crumpled the paper and tossed it at the waste-paper basket in the corner of her room, then rolled onto her back to stare at the ceiling. Damn! How could Buddy miss her parents' anniversary party? She'd told him how important it was to her, how badly she needed to see him. Shortly after the party, she'd have to announce that he'd postponed the wedding; in order to avoid the inevitable skepticism, she needed Buddy to smile and hug her and let everyone know that he still wanted her. If he didn't show up, all the murmuring and knowing glances were going to be much worse. And now that Josh was apparently on the verge of getting engaged, and Delaney was so close to the end of her pregnancy, Rebecca felt like the whole world was passing her by while Hatty took full advantage of her free labor. She could easily imagine standing in the kitchen labeling jars of dill pickles when she was fifty-five....

"Rebecca?" Hatty called up the stairs. "Rebecca, would you mind coming down here for a minute? I want you to run to the grocery store for a few things, dear. It won't take long."

Rebecca plugged her ears in an effort to shut out the sound of her name on Hatty's lips. It was eight o'clock on Monday night, the very end of her day off, and she'd still had no time to herself.

"Beck, I can go," Booker called. He'd been outside

most of the day, ever since they'd returned from Jerry's Diner, trying to chop down a dead tree at the edge of the property. Hatty was determined that he turn it into firewood, but it was really a job for one of those tree services with big equipment. Rebecca knew he had to be twice as tired as she was, so she dragged herself off the bed.

"No, I'll go, Booker," she hollered. "I'm coming." She glanced at the telephone and considered making a quick call to Buddy. She wanted to tell him that he simply had to come. She needed a change in luck, something that would put a little wind at her back. But she doubted she could convince him. He probably hadn't planned on coming in the first place. Otherwise, he would've already bought the darn plane ticket.

"What's wrong?" Booker asked as soon as she descended the stairs.

"Buddy's not coming for the anniversary party," she said.

She thought he'd make some wisecrack like, "And that's bad news?" but he didn't. He actually gave her a sympathetic smile and went for his coat. "I'll go to the store with you."

"You're both going?" Hatty sounded disappointed. "I was hoping you'd take a look under the sink in my bathroom, Booker. I think I have a leak."

"Sorry, Granny." He dropped a quick kiss on her cheek. "I'll check it out in the morning, okay? Where's the grocery list?"

She pulled a notepad from a purse the size of a suitcase. "Here you go. Just have them put it on my account. But don't forget to ask the manager if he has any loose bananas. They sell them a lot cheaper that way, you know. Only they don't put them on the table. You have to ask, and they bring them out from the back. That's how you get the deal.

And pick me up one of those flyers that says what's going to be on sale next week. I'm hoping it'll be pot roast. They haven't had a sale on pot roast for a long time, and I'd really like one.''

"How much could you save by waiting?" Rebecca asked.

"As much as three dollars," Hatty reported proudly.

Rebecca didn't get it. *Three* dollars? Was it worth three bucks to wait week after week, month after month, for a sale on pot roast?

"Do you think Buddy will expect me to follow those sale flyers as closely as your grandmother does?" she asked Booker as they walked out to her car. "Do you think he'll expect me to ask the manager for loose bananas?"

Booker shrugged. "Depends. Did he say why he's not coming for the party?"

"Something cropped up at work."

"So it wasn't because of the plane fare?"

Rebecca thought the plane fare might've been part of it. Which was probably why she was so irritated with Hatty for trying to save a couple of bucks on pot roast. Suddenly everyone in the world seemed cheap. "I don't know. He never did buy his ticket, even though I made it crystal clear I wanted him to come."

"Doesn't say a lot for his intent," Booker said.

She nodded. Neither did a third postponement of their wedding.

Booker grabbed her purse and the shopping list and headed back inside.

"What are you doing?" she asked.

"We're not buying groceries tonight." He jerked his head in the direction of his motorcycle. "We're going for a ride on my bike."

"What about your grandma?"

"She'll get her loose bananas in the morning."

CHAPTER ELEVEN

REBECCA HAD INTENDED to call and ask her father if she could bring Booker to the anniversary party. She'd meant to do it a week ago. But since their meeting in his office, she hadn't heard from him or anyone else in her family—except Greta, who'd phoned to try and talk her into changing the color scheme of her wedding from periwinkle and turquoise ("Beck, they're just so *unusual*") to something more classic and timeless ("ivory and green would be perfect, don't you think?"). In addition to a general lack of contact, Rebecca had been busy, what with Hatty lining up project after project. And, if she was being perfectly honest, she'd have to admit there was never a good time to approach her father about something he wasn't going to like. So she'd procrastinated—and now it was too late.

She parked her Firebird behind a large black pickup and saw so many cars lining the street she almost lost her nerve. She'd known it wouldn't be wise to bring Booker along under any circumstances. But without express permission...

Still, she couldn't see how his presence would hurt anything. What was one more among so many? She couldn't tell him he wasn't welcome. Not after he'd been so good to her. It was Booker who'd given her a place to stay, Booker who'd helped her move, Booker who'd been there for her when Buddy let her down.

Besides, Rebecca knew what it was like to bear the brunt of everyone's disapproval. She wasn't about to distance herself from Booker just because the other folks in Dundee found him unacceptable. Booker was her friend, and she was going to stand behind him.

She just wished standing behind him didn't have such potential for causing a scene.

"Would you mind carrying the salad?" she asked, getting out of the car.

"No problem," he said.

Greta hadn't asked Rebecca to bring any food, but she'd whipped up a chicken salad from a recipe she'd seen in a magazine, as sort of a peace offering. Maybe if Booker was busy finding a place for the salad when they first arrived, he'd be too preoccupied to hear anyone gasp.

She opened the trunk. He removed the large bowl of salad and she retrieved the gift she'd bought her parents—a hammock for their back porch she thought they might enjoy next summer.

"If we don't like it, we don't have to stay," she said, preparing him, and herself, just in case. "I need to put in an appearance, that's all."

He shrugged. "Whatever."

Whatever? She wished he'd seemed that nonchalant about the party before they'd left home. Maybe she wouldn't have been so quick to let him come.

"What's wrong?" he asked when she hesitated.

She considered telling him he might not be welcome, then decided against it. Certainly her family would treat him graciously. They might disown her after the party, but they'd never make themselves look bad by mistreating a guest. Especially one who might be eligible to vote in the next election.

At least he'd cleaned up for the party. He'd shaved, which was something he didn't bother to do every day.

He'd also changed into a pair of khaki pants and a polo shirt that almost made up for his rough edges.

Straightening her own lightweight sweater to conceal her tattoo, which would embarrass her father if she revealed it in public, she dusted off her black slacks and pressed forward. Her father didn't like some of her more trendy clothes—the hip-huggers, the six-inch heels, the midriffs and animal prints—but she'd dressed in an admirably conservative fashion tonight. She looked almost like one of her sisters; she had food and she had a gift. So what if she also had an uninvited guest?

The weather was chilly and the smell of ham drifted clear into the street. A live band played "Boogie Woogie Bugle Boy" somewhere in the house. Judging by the voices babbling just beyond the front door of her parents' home, everyone seemed to be having a good time, so when Rebecca and Booker stepped inside, she hoped it was only her imagination that a hush fell over the crowd.

Slowly everyone turned to stare, including her own family. Her mother held a hand to her heart, her sisters covered their mouths, and her father went so red in the face he looked like Elmer Fudd in a Bugs Bunny cartoon. A few people like Mary Thornton, started whispering, while others, like Josh's parents, chuckled outright.

Rebecca realized immediately that bringing Booker was a bigger mistake than she'd thought, but she'd already committed herself and had no choice except to soldier on. Upping the wattage of her smile, she slipped an arm through his, wishing they'd waited until later to appear, closer to the time she expected Delaney and Conner, so they'd at least have an ally.

"Why don't we put the chicken salad in the kitchen?" she said as if fifty pairs of eyes weren't riveted on them like magnets to steel.

Booker looked from her to the stunned crowd and back again. Before he could say anything, however, her mother came forward and kissed Rebecca's cheek. "Hello, glad you could both join us," she said, using the cordial voice that told Rebecca she was on her best behavior. "Please help yourself to the food in the kitchen. It's buffet style, of course, and the champagne is on the dining room table."

Rebecca might have been a mere acquaintance for all her mother's warmth, but at least *someone* had greeted them.

"Thanks," Booker said, and Fiona nodded stiffly before moving on.

Greta approached next and swept Rebecca into a brief hug. "Are you insane?" she hissed in her ear. "Everyone thinks you two are having an affair. What are you *doing* bringing him here?" But when she pulled away, she was smiling as though she'd said nothing unpleasant and immediately introduced herself to Booker.

Rebecca glanced over her sister's head to see her father. Evidently no one had clued him in that he was supposed to play along and save his rage for later. He was standing next to the punch bowl, glowering at her and Booker, and making no attempt to hide it.

"I can see your father's happy we're here," Booker said under his breath.

Rebecca tightened her hand on his arm. "Don't worry about him."

They were just heading toward the buffet when Rebecca felt someone catch her by the elbow. Josh Hill. She hadn't seen him until that moment. Surprisingly enough, he was smiling.

"Booker, glad you could make it," he said.

Booker nodded once, then Josh's smoky green eyes focused on her. He was wearing jeans and boots with a button-down solid red shirt that wasn't a far cry from his usual jeans and T-shirt. But he looked good in anything and the shirt somehow dressed him up enough that he blended beautifully with the crowd. Maybe it was the solid color, which brought out the blond in his hair and the lightness of his eyes. "You look great as always, Rebecca."

Rebecca felt pretty sure his compliment came from no real admiration. He was only making a statement, and it wasn't that she looked nice. He was publicly including her and Booker in his circle of friends, lending them his support in front of the others. But she resented the fact that he felt it necessary to rescue her among her own family and in her old home. It was the ultimate humiliation, the ultimate contrast between their respective positions in the community— even in her father's esteem. Besides, she wasn't about to forgive him so easily for what he'd done to her furniture.

"Go away," she muttered. "I don't need you."

At that his smile grew genuine. "I'm fine," he said loudly. "Thanks for asking."

"Wonderful. Maybe you wouldn't mind taking this wherever it needs to go." She handed him her parents' gift and pivoted so fast she nearly ran into Katie, who'd arrived just behind them.

Booker steadied the younger woman, then winked at Rebecca as though she'd purposely thrown Katie into his arms.

Trying to pretend she was happy to be where she was, Rebecca introduced them. Booker suggested they get a glass of champagne and drew Katie away. Then Rebecca was standing in the middle of the party alone.

WHY COULDN'T *HE* be Rebecca's friend?

Josh watched her chalk her pool cue in the basement of her parents' home. What made him so different? She was obviously good friends with Billy Joe and Bobby West.

And Perry Paris. And Booker, of course. Sometimes Josh wondered if there wasn't potential for something more to exist between her and Booker, but neither of them acted like it tonight. Booker had spent most of his time hustling Katie; Rebecca had spent most of her time hustling pool. And she was taking all comers. When had she gotten so good?

"There you are," Mary said, coming up behind him and slipping her arms around his waist. "I wasn't sure where you'd wandered off to."

Josh took another sip of his beer and wished Mary would leave him alone for fifteen minutes. He wanted to see this game, and he wanted to do it without a commentator.

Rebecca studied the table, leaned low and banked the nine ball off the side into the left corner pocket. It was a tough shot, but she made it look easy, and now only two striped balls remained. Billy Joe, who had twenty bucks riding on the game, still had four solids.

"What's up, man? You're getting your butt whupped by a girl," his brother taunted.

"Shut up," Billy Joe snapped. "She's gonna whup you next."

"No, she ain't," Bobby replied. "I got fifty bucks says I'm gonna take her."

"You getting the itch to play?" Mary asked, her fingers moving in irritatingly small circles on his abdomen.

"Yeah."

"You're not thinking about playing Rebecca, though, are you?"

"Actually I am." Stepping away from her, he put his quarter on the side of the table behind Bobby West's to save his place in line. He hadn't played Rebecca since they were in high school. It used to be that he could beat her easily enough. But she'd obviously improved a great deal, and these days he played only occasionally.

If Rebecca saw that he was there, she gave no indication. He hadn't been able to get her to acknowledge him since she'd shoved that damn gift in his face and walked away.

"We could stop by the Honky Tonk and play a game if you'd rather," Mary offered, slipping her arms around him again. "Then we could go on over to your place."

He heard the innuendo in her voice, but for some reason the thought of winding up at his place with Mary didn't tempt him tonight—at least not as much as playing pool with Rebecca. He missed the challenge she provided, wondered if he could still best her. "Not right now," he said, intent on the game. "It'll be my turn soon."

Billy Joe scratched and had to bring out another ball. Rebecca sank one of the two remaining stripes, and Billy Joe knocked down two solids before Rebecca made her last shot. But she missed the eight ball. Billy Joe missed the five, and it was Rebecca's turn with another chance at the eight. She studied the angles, took the shot and smiled as the eight ball fell neatly into the side pocket.

"Darn!" Billy Joe said, shaking his head. "You beat me every time!"

Rebecca laughed and pocketed the money. "You think your brother can do any better?"

"You bet I can, honey," Bobby said and racked the balls. When he took his brother's cue stick, Rebecca told him he could break. Balls scattered everywhere from the power of his shot, but amazingly nothing fell.

Rebecca ended up with stripes again. Then she systematically destroyed Bobby like she had his brother and shoved another wad of bills into her pocket when the game was done.

Josh removed Mary's arms from around his waist and

forged through the crowd of onlookers. Rebecca arched a brow when she saw him.

"You ready for some *real* competition?" he asked, teasing Billy Joe and Bobby.

"She's better than you think, man," Billy Joe said.

Rebecca propped a hand on her hip. "How much?" she asked him.

Josh considered what he had in his pocket. "A hundred bucks says I'll win."

"Make that two hundred, and you've got a game."

"Ooee, she's feeling it tonight," Billy Joe cut in, putting another quarter on the table.

"Maybe it's time to humble her," Josh said, but he knew, even if he won, there was no humbling Rebecca Wells.

"Talking trash already?" she asked.

"Two hundred dollars." He grinned. "Ladies first."

Rebecca sank two solids but missed the third.

"Nice start," he said, chalking up. He eyed the table from several angles, went after the thirteen and sent it into the far corner pocket. Then he buried the ten, but he also knocked down Rebecca's five.

"Thanks for the help," she said, smiling.

Mary came up beside him. "You can take her," she said, her words almost fierce.

Josh glanced up for a second and noticed that they were attracting quite a few new spectators. His brother had come downstairs and was among the crowd, standing toward the back. Booker and Katie had joined them, too.

Josh watched Rebecca take aim. He hadn't left her much of a shot, but she was good enough to work with what she had. She sent the seven flying with just the right amount of power to bounce it off three sides before nearly sinking it in the closest corner.

"Darn," she said, stepping back when it didn't fall.

He walked around the table, considering what was open to him. The twelve was in a pretty good position. But if he hit the twelve, he might leave her with the perfect opportunity to drop two more of her own balls.

"Try the nine," Mike said, suddenly at his elbow.

"The twelve's looking pretty," Josh said. "Dangerous but pretty. I think I'm going to have to take the twelve."

He aimed and fired, the twelve fell, and then they were three to three.

"What did you leave me?" Rebecca muttered, frowning.

Fortunately not as much as he'd thought he would. But she managed to bury the one ball on a trick shot that should never have worked. That opened her up for an easy shot along the left side, which took care of the three. Next she attempted to tap in the six, but to his relief she scratched.

"Aw, that's too bad," he said, grinning as he removed her penalty ball—the three.

They were even again, but not for long. He placed the white ball in front of the fourteen and pointed to the left corner pocket. "It's going there," he said and, a solid click later, proved himself right.

At that point, Booker stepped up and whispered something to Rebecca.

Josh tried not to be annoyed by this evidence of their mutual esteem, but the fact that he'd lost his "friend" status so quickly, while Booker seemed to be hanging on to his, rankled. What did he have that Josh didn't? A few tattoos, maybe.

As Rebecca moved past him, he caught a subtle whiff of her perfume, reminding him of that night she'd massaged him at her house. He'd smelled the same scent on her sheets and pillows. It was mingled with the whole experience— the candles, the warm oil, Rebecca's hands sliding over his body. He'd thought a lot about that night. He'd thought even more about the next morning, when they'd stood so close he could have licked *her* lips without moving. In that moment, it had been all he could do to remember that she had a fiancé and he had a girlfriend, and that she was the worst woman in the world for him to want—

"Go, man," Mike said, nudging him. "It's your turn."

Josh blinked. Rebecca had pocketed the three again. If he wasn't careful how he finished this game, she'd walk away with his money.

Bending, he smacked the nine, decisively burying it in the right corner pocket. Then he sank the eleven in the side and set himself up for the fifteen. It was two solids to one stripe; he finally had the advantage.

Glancing up, he saw her worrying her bottom lip. She leaned over and said something to Booker, who whispered something back.

Josh tried not to let it bother him. He certainly didn't care about Booker—he just didn't like the fact that he and Rebecca had become so close, didn't like the implied trust because that kind of trust was so far from what he'd ever been able to achieve with her.

Frowning, he shot, but the distraction of their whispering took its toll. He missed, leaving himself wide open for Rebecca to take the lead.

She chalked her cue, gave Booker a small smile and dropped the seven into the side pocket.

"I told you," Booker said to her, chuckling. "Now bank the four off here—" He motioned to one side of the table.

"No, the eight ball's in the way," she complained.

She went for the corner, instead, and missed.

"You should've done what I told you," Booker said. "Next time—"

"Hey, am I playing her or you?" Josh snapped.

They both looked up in surprise. "You have a problem with Booker giving me his opinion?" she asked.

"No," he said, instantly feeling a little foolish for the outburst.

She waved Booker back. "I can beat you on my own," she said. "I don't need anyone else."

Josh knew he'd already said too much and didn't respond. He shot the fifteen into the nearest corner and aimed for the final ball—the eight. In one stroke the game could be over. He sent the eight toward the side pocket, but accidentally smacked Rebecca's four, putting it in, instead.

"Too bad," Rebecca said, her voice laced with false sympathy as she prepared for the easy kill. "Say goodbye to your money."

The eight went down, and the game was over. Everyone patted Rebecca on the back, murmuring about how good she'd gotten.

She smiled broadly. "You want to write me a check?" she asked.

"I can't believe she beat you," Mary said, obviously stunned.

Josh stared at the empty table and rubbed his chin. He couldn't believe it, either. He wanted another chance.

"Double or nothing," he said.

"Josh, that's four hundred dollars!" Mary cried.

He ignored her. "What do you say, Rebecca?"

Rebecca's eyes widened, but she seemed tempted. "There are people in line ahead of you."

"That's okay," Perry volunteered. "I'm next. He can have my turn."

This met with murmurs of general approval. Most folks had taken an interest in his and Rebecca's running feud. And rarely did anyone in Dundee see a four-hundred-dollar bet, at least on a game of pool.

"Looks like we're in the clear," he told Rebecca. "You interested?"

"Four hundred dollars?" she said.

"Losing your nerve?"

She turned to Booker. "Go for it," he said. "You can take him again."

She nodded. "Okay."

CHAPTER TWELVE

SHE'D BEATEN HIM. She'd beaten Josh Hill. And it felt great. Those few hard-won victories always did. So why was she giving him another chance? Why was she risking four hundred dollars?

Because it wasn't enough to beat him once, she realized. She wanted to beat him again and again until she knew she was better at something than he was. Until she could establish her own little niche and quit feeling that anything she could do, he could do better.

"You first this time," she said, feeling generous.

His smile told her he took the gesture as it was intended—to let him know she had every confidence in the world of doubling her money.

This game went much like the previous one, with Rebecca maintaining a small lead. She was close to winning—they were down to just a few balls—when her father walked into the room. Rebecca was aware that the band had stopped playing some time ago and the caterers were talking to each other upstairs, obviously clearing away what was left of the food. She knew her mother and sisters would be expecting her to start cleaning up and had probably sent her father to get her.

"Does Mom need me?" she asked as he parted the group that had been watching the game and emerged at her elbow.

"When you're through."

"Tell her I'll be right there," she said, but he didn't go.

He rested his knuckles on the edge of the table and studied the game. "Who's winning?"

Rebecca had been about to shoot, but now she hesitated. She didn't want to play Josh in front of her father. She could play anyone else without a problem, but she remembered her father looking on too many times when Josh bested her at something. Doyle always smiled at the outcome, as though he'd expected it all along. Sometimes he'd even slap Josh on the back, as though he'd been rooting for *him.*

"She is," Josh said.

Her father seemed a little surprised. "No kidding?"

Rebecca stretched her neck, chalked her cue stick again and studied the angles. She was far too tense to make an accurate shot. But everyone was waiting and watching her expectantly. She had to finish. Four hundred dollars depended on the outcome.

Taking a deep breath, she wiped her palms on her slacks and positioned herself. Then she shot—and missed.

"How'd you miss that?" Doyle demanded. "That was a give-me if ever I've seen one."

Rebecca didn't know how she'd missed it. That shot was one she could make ninety-nine times out of a hundred. But she was suddenly so nervous.

She blinked, nodded and tucked her hair behind her ears, staring intently at the table.

Josh braced his cue stick and, leaning low, deftly managed to bury the six ball off a ricochet. Rebecca's heart sank when the ball landed snugly in the pocket. She'd blown it. He had only the eight ball left. If she hadn't choked on her last turn, she could've put him away. Instead, the opposite was about to happen.

"He's got you," Doyle said, sounding disgusted. "I've told you and told you that you need to keep your hand steady. You're never going to win a game of pool if you play like that."

She didn't answer. It didn't matter that she'd won the last game. That she'd won almost every game tonight. This was the game her father was watching, which meant this was the only game that mattered.

Josh sized up his next shot, which was pretty clean. One bank off the far left edge and the eight ball would land in the right corner pocket. Easy. Game over. She was history.

He glanced up at her and her father before sending the eight ball rolling. It banked off the far left edge, just like it was supposed to, and traveled in a straight line for the corner pocket. Rebecca was so sure it was going to drop, she almost set her stick down and started getting out her money. But it didn't. It slowed and came to a stop at the very edge of the pocket.

Mary groaned and Billy Joe murmured, "I thought he had her. Jeez, that was close!"

It was close. But not close enough. She had a reprieve.

Booker caught her eye and smiled. *Now's your chance,* his look said. *You can do it.*

Giving him a slight nod, she sent her stripe flying decisively into the side pocket. Now only the eight ball remained for her, too—and it was already hovering an inch from where she needed it to go. Telling herself to forget that her father was watching, to forget he was even there, she tapped the white ball so that it barely kissed the eight. The eight slipped over the edge, making a satisfying *thunk,* and the game was over.

"I won," she said, feeling a rush of relief and hope as she looked to her father. "I just beat Josh."

"Yeah, well, your mother needs you," he said and walked off.

"CAN YOU BELIEVE Rebecca brought Booker to her parents' anniversary party?" Mary asked as Josh drove her home from the party.

Mary had been talking nonstop since they'd gotten into his Excursion. He'd only been half listening, for the most part. He wasn't interested in a recap of the compliments she'd received on her new jacket. But he heard her mention Booker and Rebecca. "They're friends," he said.

Mary adjusted her seat belt. "Friends *and* lovers, probably."

Josh scowled. "Would you give up on that? Booker was hitting on Katie all night. I hardly think he and Rebecca are lovers."

She turned to face him, using the door as her backrest. "You never know. Rebecca strikes me as a little kinky. She might like a ménage à trois once in a while."

"I don't think so," he said sharply. Josh suspected her sexual experience fell far short of her reputation. Some of the things he'd said in the past were probably to blame for why people like Mary considered Rebecca kinky, and he hadn't had a damn clue about her sex life when he'd made those statements. It was just part of the smear campaign they'd waged against each other.

"She ran away with that biker," Mary pointed out.

Josh stopped for a light. Johnny Red. Even a Hells Angel hadn't been able to handle Rebecca—strong evidence that Josh was lucky she didn't seem as drawn to him as he sometimes was to her. But logic and evidence didn't always help. Not at moments like that one in her house…

"So she had a fling," he said, starting through the intersection as the light turned green. "I think most of us are guilty of poor judgment on occasion."

"Poor judgment *on occasion?* What do you call moving in with Booker when she's engaged to another man?" Mary turned up the heater, although Josh was already tempted to roll down the window. "And what about bringing Booker to the party tonight? Did you see the look on Doyle's face? I thought he was going to have a stroke."

Josh had been more concerned about the look on Doyle's face when Rebecca had beaten him at pool. There hadn't been a hint of the pleasure or pride he'd expected when he'd purposely missed his last shot. He'd paid four hundred dollars to see Rebecca's father give her a shred of praise for a change, and it hadn't netted him so much as a smile or a "good game." Worse, it had confused him even more about how he felt toward Rebecca. There were times when fear that she'd be hurt made him do the damnedest things—like trying to make her feel welcome in her own parents' home or losing a four-hundred-dollar bet.

Part of him wanted to be her friend. All of him wanted to be her lover. And whatever sanity he had left still tried to warn him that he'd be a fool to become, either.

"I can't believe she's taking advantage of Hatty the way she is," Mary was saying. "I mean, it's bad enough that Booker's living off her. But now Rebecca, too? I don't blame her father for being upset. That would make me—"

"Wait a second," Josh interrupted, feeling the irritation that occasionally haunted him when he was with Mary. "How do you know she's taking advantage of Hatty?"

"You don't think she and Booker are actually paying rent, do you?"

They passed the drive-in, the library and Dundee's two historic buildings, one of which was now a bed-and-breakfast. "I don't know that they're not," he said, turning the blasting heater vents away from him. "Besides, it doesn't matter. Rebecca's only going to be living there for another—what, four weeks?"

Josh was relieved to think Rebecca would be marrying

so soon. Surely that would finally put an end to this strange attraction. Not only would she be completely unavailable, she'd be living in Nebraska. Whatever had happened between them in the past would have to be forgotten, the good—like that night a year ago last summer—along with the bad.

Maybe after she was gone, he'd be able to make a commitment to Mary....

"What?" he said when he realized Mary had stopped talking and was watching him a little too closely.

"Why are you suddenly sticking up for her?" she asked. "You two have never gotten along."

Josh couldn't tolerate the heater any longer. "I'm not sticking up for her," he said, flipping it off. "I just don't think what's going on in her life is any of our business, okay? She gets enough of that kind of thing already."

"Then I guess you don't want to hear what I learned tonight at the party," Mary said.

He drove into Mary's neighborhood and pulled up in front of her parents' house, where she'd been living since the divorce. "Not if it's more conjecture about Rebecca's sex life," he said.

"It's not. It's about her wedding."

After the way he'd criticized Mary's gossiping, he could hardly show interest, but she definitely had him with that statement. "I don't want to know," he lied.

"Fine." She leaned over and kissed him before getting out of the truck. "Night."

"Night." He felt a welcome rush of cold air as she stepped out—he could finally breathe again.

"Call me later," she said.

"I'll call you tomorrow." He rolled down his window and drove away. But he made it only to the edge of town before using his cell to phone her. "Okay, what about Rebecca's wedding?" he asked as soon as she answered.

"I thought you didn't want to gossip," she said, sounding smug.

"You've piqued my curiosity."

She laughed, prolonging the suspense. "It's been postponed again."

Oh, boy. "How do you know?"

"Candace heard Delaney talking to Conner about it tonight while they were dancing."

"Why?"

"Because she was dancing right next to them."

Josh sighed impatiently. "No, why has the wedding been postponed?"

"I don't know," she said. "From what Candace could gather, what's going on is pretty hush-hush. Delaney said something about Rebecca waiting until after the party to tell her parents."

He remembered what Doyle had told him in the hair salon and knew Rebecca's father wouldn't be happy about this turn of events. He saw Buddy as Rebecca's only wedding ticket, his release from further obligation to his difficult fourth daughter.

"When's the new date?" he asked, wondering how much longer he'd have to deal with running into Rebecca everywhere he went.

"Candace didn't say." She paused. "You want to come back here? Watch a movie?"

"Not tonight," he said. "I'm pretty tired."

"Tomorrow then?"

"Okay." He hung up and, suddenly feeling a chill, rolled up his window. What was going on with Rebecca's engagement? Three postponements? Didn't Buddy *want* to marry her?

Maybe her fiancé had figured out what everyone in Dundee already knew—that he'd never be able to handle her on a full-time basis. Doyle said Buddy was too mild-mannered for Rebecca. Maybe he'd seen something in her that had tipped him off.

But Buddy *had* to marry Rebecca. Josh needed him to make their marriage final so he could move on with his own life. And he needed him to do it as soon as possible, before Josh lost all perspective and did the absolute worst thing he could do—and started dating her himself.

Picking up his cell, he called Katie Rogers.

"It's Josh," he said. His mother was close to Katie's mom and used to baby-sit Katie after school. She was a little like a kid sister to him, but he didn't call her often and he knew his request was going to sound pretty strange.

"Hi, Josh. What's up?" she said.

"Is there any chance you could get me Buddy's phone number?" he asked.

"Buddy's?"

"Rebecca's fiancé."

"Mona and I have both taken messages for Rebecca at the salon. I'm sure it's on the duplicate copy of the message pad. Why?"

He slowed and pulled off the road. "Do you have a key to the salon?"

"Yeah. We all have a key. We take turns opening. What's up?"

"Nothing. Would you mind meeting me there?"

"Right *now?*"

He flipped on the overhead and glanced at his watch. It was almost midnight. "If you can."

"I can," she said, "but I'm not going anywhere until you tell me what you're doing to Rebecca *this* time."

"It doesn't have anything to do with Rebecca. Someone

at the party tonight told me Buddy might be in the market to breed a mare. I thought I'd give him a call.''

"Oh, okay.'' She seemed slightly disappointed that there wasn't more fun in what he was doing. "I can be there in five minutes,'' she said. "Where are you?''

His tires ground on the gravel at the side of the road as he turned around. "It'll take me ten, but I'm on my way.''

"You are who?'' Buddy said, sounding groggy even though it was nearly noon.

"Josh Hill. Rebecca might have mentioned me,'' Josh said, standing inside the door of his largest stable and propping the telephone against his ear with one shoulder so he could remove his leather gloves. He usually took things easier on Sunday, but he'd already been working for six hours, trying to get the place ready for the mares that would start arriving in November. And he'd been tempted to call Buddy since dawn. But he knew not everyone kept the same kind of hours he did, so he'd made himself wait. Obviously he hadn't waited long enough.

"I don't think so,'' Buddy said. "I don't recognize your name.''

That was a little deflating to his ego, but Josh thought it could only help. Now Buddy would have no reason to suspect his motives.

"We're old friends,'' he said, slapping his gloves against one dust-covered leg to distract himself from the guilt twisting in his gut for meddling in something that was none of his business.

"You're not the fellow she's living with,'' Buddy said.

Josh frowned and tried not to let his voice reveal his displeasure with that situation. "No, that's Booker.''

"Oh.'' He sounded a bit more interested. "What can I do for you, Josh?''

"Rebecca's birthday is coming up in a few weeks and some of us are hoping to throw her a surprise party," he said, using the only excuse he'd been able to think of that would be plausible enough to contact Buddy. "We were wondering if you might be here for it."

"When is it?" he said. "We were supposed to be on our honeymoon for her birthday, but now that we're not getting married until January, we need to make other plans. Do you have a date?"

Josh had thought so much about his main objective—removing Rebecca from his circle of acquaintances as soon as possible—that he hadn't spent much time perfecting his cover. "Uh…we were thinking the first Friday in November might be good," he said off the top of his head.

"That's a week before the Saturday Rebecca and I were supposed to get married," Buddy responded. "I already have a plane ticket, but I don't fly in until the following Wednesday."

"Maybe you could change your flight and come out a little early."

"I don't think so. My mother will be here."

"She could come with you."

"No, that wouldn't be a good idea." He chuckled uncomfortably. "She's a little resistant to the idea of me getting married."

Evidently Buddy's mother had already encountered Rebecca. "Rebecca's the type of girl who grows on you," Josh began. "Maybe with a little more exposure—"

"It's not that," he said. "My mom lives out of state and hasn't had a chance to meet Rebecca. She's just not sure I'm ready for marriage."

"Oh." Josh straightened in surprise. How old was this guy? Hadn't Rebecca said he was twenty-six? "In that case, you're probably right to spend some time alone with her.'' If Buddy's mother hadn't come face to face with Rebecca yet, he certainly didn't see any advantage in muddying the waters. ''We'll just have it the next weekend, then, since you'll already be here.''

''That would work.''

''Good.'' Josh stared at the trees between the stable and the house, watching as a single yellow leaf swirled to the ground. He'd reached the point in the conversation where he should promise to get back in touch and finish the call. But he hadn't made any headway in convincing Buddy to remove Rebecca from his life as soon as possible—thereby saving him from his own personal Delilah. ''So your mother's worried you might be making a mistake, huh?'' he said, looking for some way to draw Buddy out.

''You know how moms are.''

Josh knew how *his* mother was—strong-willed and sometimes overbearing. But he was just as strong-willed and, while he loved Laurel Hill tremendously, he'd never let her stand between him and the woman he wanted to marry. If he ever found the woman he wanted to marry… ''She's pretty protective?''

''You got it. She keeps going on and on about the permanence of marriage and how you never really know a person until you live with her. The scary thing is, she's usually right about stuff like that.'' An uncertain pause. ''Not that I'm particularly worried, of course. That isn't the reason I postponed the wedding. I just thought it would be smarter to save a little more money. And my great-aunt really wants to come. That had a lot to do with it. She can't make it until after the first of the year.''

''Your great-aunt?'' Josh repeated.

''Yeah, she's never been to Idaho and thought it would be nice to see the state.''

''Oh.''

Buddy segued from a discussion of his aunt to the importance of being fiscally conservative at this point in his career. Then he talked about rent savings and vacation days and giving his mother time to adjust. But each new excuse began to sound flimsier than the last.

Josh tried to reclaim the sense of purpose with which he'd originally phoned Buddy. He even made an attempt to say Rebecca would make him an excellent wife. But he couldn't bring himself to put any conviction, real or fabricated, behind those words. The more he listened, the more convinced he became that Doyle Wells was right. Buddy *wasn't* a good match for Rebecca. Rebecca was a spirited, sleek mare, Buddy a plodding workhorse without enough spunk to muster anything beyond a walk. He couldn't see Rebecca with someone so…neutral. She'd be bored within a year.

"You know, I hate to say this because Rebecca and I have been friends for ages," he said. (Buddy wouldn't know any better, anyway.) "But I think your mother's probably right. Maybe you should give your relationship some time, get to know Rebecca a little."

Had those words really come out of his mouth? If Buddy waited, he might not marry Rebecca. If he didn't marry Rebecca, Josh might end up pursuing her himself. If he pursued her, he could end up falling in love with her. And if he fell in love with her, God help him. Then she'd finally have real power over him. He'd be handing his heart to the one woman in the world who'd promptly stomp on it and hand it back.

But he simply couldn't see her with this guy.

"Why do you say that?" Buddy asked, instantly alert.

"Rebecca is…" Josh searched for the correct word "…unusual. You have to know how to handle her."

Apparently the frank honesty in his voice came through, because Buddy quit trying to pretend he wasn't worried.

"What do you mean by that?"

"She's temperamental. You've probably heard what she was like growing up."

"No, actually I haven't. She's never said much about her past."

Josh smiled, recognizing the incredible opportunity that had just fallen into his lap. "You don't know about the time she nearly burned down the high school?"

"…No."

"Or the time she broke Gilbert Tripp's nose?"

"She broke someone's nose? A *man's* nose?"

Biting back a laugh at the memory of the purple bruise that had marred Gilbert's face for the next three weeks, Josh proceeded to enlighten Buddy. Once he started on Rebecca's past, he couldn't seem to stop. He related every crazy thing she'd ever done—and he knew more than most people. Then he enumerated all the reasons someone like Buddy would never be happy with someone like Rebecca and, when he was finished, he felt a definite sense of satisfaction that had nothing to do with his original agenda and everything to do with serving some deeper purpose. He'd called to talk Buddy *into* a wedding, not out of one. But anyone who *could* be talked out of marrying Rebecca didn't stand a chance with her in the first place.

"HEY, YOU FINALLY DONE?"

Rebecca glanced up from the salon door she was locking to see Booker leaning against his motorcycle. It had been busy for a Sunday, but more so in the morning. Afternoons always slowed a bit, both in appointments and walk-in business. During the last hour, Rebecca had only one cut—for a ten-year-old boy.

"What are you doing here?" she asked, surprised to see him waiting for her.

"I ran into Katie down at the diner. She said you were closing tonight, so I decided I'd come by."

"You ran into Katie? Or you followed her?"

He grinned. "I think it came off looking accidental enough."

Rebecca couldn't help laughing. "She interested in going out with you?"

"Of course not. But then she doesn't know me very well."

"That's the spirit." She selected the key to her Firebird. "I thought you were supposed to be painting the garage for Granny Hatfield."

"I painted earlier. I'm taking the night off. I was hoping you'd want to spend some of the money you won at the anniversary party on a few drinks at the Honky Tonk."

Rebecca would've been excited about the money she'd won last night—especially Josh's money—except that her father's reaction had soured the whole experience. "I'll give you twenty bucks, but I think I'm going home to bed. I'm pretty tired."

"Come on. It's only seven o'clock. If we have a drink together, you can tell me what your family said when you told them the wedding's been postponed. I couldn't hear very well from the living room."

Rebecca arched a brow at him. "You were listening?"

"I was trying to. Your father made it easy. Your mother did not."

"You could've asked me what happened while we were on our way home," she pointed out. "We rode together, remember?"

"I could tell it hadn't gone well when Greta stormed

past me before you came out. Besides, you wouldn't have wanted to hear what I had to say."

Rebecca wasn't sure she was ready to hear what anyone had to say. Not yet. "Word will have spread to the Honky Tonk about the wedding," she said, considering her options. "I think I'll give it another week before I face everyone there."

"No one cares about the postponement, babe."

That might be, but she still ran the risk of running into Josh, and she wasn't about to take that chance. She might have beaten him at pool last night, but it was only a game. She felt foolish for having cared so much. The money was nice, of course, but one or two games of pool were never going to change anything. Her father still had a way of making her feel inferior to Josh—to almost everyone.

"No, thanks. I'm going home," she said.

"That's boring," he complained.

"For you, maybe."

He gave her an endearing smile. "Does anyone else matter?"

She shook her head and started around the building to the small gravel lot where she'd parked her car.

"Okay, I've got it," he called after her. "Let's stop by the diner and grab a bite to eat."

"I'm not hungry," she replied.

"Let's go for a ride on my bike."

"No, thanks."

"So you're not in the mood to go out? Let's rent a movie."

There was no getting rid of him, Rebecca decided, chuckling. "Okay," she said. "Follow me to the store."

CHAPTER THIRTEEN

As soon as they reached Granny Hatfield's, Rebecca told Booker to get the popcorn ready and headed upstairs to change into something more comfortable. Tossing her coat on the bed, she set her purse on her desk next to a slip of paper that turned out to be a telephone message.

Buddy needs to talk to you, Hatty had written. *It's sort of an emergency.*

What now? "I'll be down in a minute," she called to Booker. Then she quickly pulled her shirt over her head, slipped into some sweats and picked up the phone.

Buddy answered on the second ring.

"I got your message," she said. "What's the emergency? What's wrong?"

A significant moment of silence followed this question. "I don't know for sure," he finally responded.

"You leave me a message that there's an emergency, and you don't know what it is?"

"It's not that kind of emergency. I just wanted to catch you before…before you told your family the new date for our wedding." He said the last part of the sentence fast, as though he wanted to fit it all in one breath.

A sickening feeling invaded Rebecca's stomach and started radiating outward. "Why? What do you mean?"

"I've been doing a lot of thinking, and…well, I'm not sure we know each other well enough for marriage."

"You're not?"

"No."

"Why is that?"

"I…I talked to a friend of yours today, and he got me thinking."

Rebecca grew still. *He?* "What friend?"

"I'd rather not say."

"Why?"

"He told me some things that have me pretty concerned."

"Like what?"

"Like some of the stuff you've done. To be honest, I was more than a little surprised. What kind of girl nearly sets the high school on fire?"

"I can explain that," she said. "I was only trying to burn the mascot into the field for homecoming, and it got a little out of con—"

"Or dyes someone's hair blue," he said, cutting her off.

"Some people want their hair blue," she replied.

"Did Mrs. Reese?"

He had her there. "No, but I can explain that, too. See, she told her son that his father would fire him from his job at the bank if he kept dating me. Byron and I were both twenty-five at the time, way too old for her to be interfering and—"

"But why wouldn't she want her son to date you in the first place?"

Rebecca could hear Booker calling her from the bottom of the stairs, but she was too panicked to answer. Who had paraded her sins in front of Buddy? Her father?

"That's all in the past," she said, grappling for something to say that might minimize the damage. "Everyone makes mistakes once in a while. Haven't you ever done anything you regret?"

"I've never set a football field on fire."

The creaking of the stairs told her Booker was coming up, but she didn't even look at him when he knocked briefly and opened the door. She had to convince Buddy that she wasn't as bad as he now believed, or it would be over for good.

"Who is it?" Booker asked.

She ignored him, focusing on her racing thoughts. "Like...I don't know. Like shaving someone's head while he was sleeping. Or putting bugs in someone's locker."

"Is it Buddy?" Booker asked.

Rebecca nodded, her cheeks feeling warm, her heart pounding.

"I've never shaved anyone's head," Buddy said. "I've never even wanted to."

"Oh, so you've always been a saint, right? I'm the only one with a temper here."

"Most women don't have a temper bad enough to make them break a man's nose."

"Are you talking about Gilbert? I wouldn't have hit him if he'd owned up to damaging Delaney's car."

"Still, those stories frighten me. Maybe it would be different if there were just one or two instances, but...I've never met a woman who's done anything remotely like a whole *bunch* of the things you've done."

Anger began to replace Rebecca's panic. She'd tried so hard to please Buddy. She'd patiently allowed him to make her look like a fool when he kept shifting their wedding date. She'd let him off the hook when he disappointed her and didn't show up for her parents' anniversary party. She'd held her temper in check for him like she hadn't for anyone else. And he was still backing away.

"Maybe we should just forget the whole thing," she said, glancing up in time to see Booker's eyebrows shoot up.

"I'm not saying that," Buddy said. "I'm just saying maybe we shouldn't rush into marriage, that's all. Why don't we let things roll along for a while and not worry so much about setting a date?"

She'd just told her parents that they were *for sure* getting married on January 25th. She'd already bought her dress and given her notice at work. Greta had five hundred cookies waiting in half the freezers of Dundee. And now he was telling her he didn't even want to set a date? How did she go back to her family a fourth time? How did she tell them the money they'd spent might be wasted?

"Who told you all these things?" she asked.

"Why? What difference does it make?"

"I want to know. I have a right to know. Were you checking up on me?"

"I'd never do that," he said.

"You had to get the dirt from somewhere."

"I told you, I received a phone call."

"It was my father, wasn't it?"

"No. But he called me once before. And that's what has me worried, babe. It isn't only one person telling me to handle you with kid gloves. There are several people who are concerned about us."

"They're not concerned. They just don't like me," Rebecca said. "Don't *you* have any enemies?"

"We're not talking about enemies. We're talking about your own father."

"He's the worst of the bunch," she said. "He's been angry ever since I was born."

"Why would he be?"

"Because I was the last of four girls. When I arrived, he knew he wasn't getting a boy. "

"That's crazy."

"Exactly. What kind of man holds his daughter responsible for not having a penis?"

"Rebecca, whether you believe it or not, your father loves you," Buddy insisted.

Rebecca remembered Doyle turning away when she'd won the game last night. "Is that why he always mutters, 'God have mercy' whenever I'm around? Because he loves me?" she asked.

"I don't know why he says what he says. I don't really know him. He told me he loves you, though."

"So it *was* my father."

"No, it wasn't. Not this time."

"Who then?"

"I don't want to say," Buddy responded. "He seemed to have my best interests at heart."

"What?" she nearly shouted. "Why would a complete stranger have *your* best interests at heart?"

"Maybe he's a nice guy."

"Or maybe he wants to start trouble. Ever think of that?"

"He warned me about you. He said you need a strong hand and not to give you too much rein. But he also said, if we got married, I'd better not break your spirit or I'll have to answer to him."

Too much *rein?* Break her *spirit?* It sounded as though Buddy's caller was talking about a—

Suddenly Rebecca knew exactly who had phoned him. "Josh Hill! It was Josh who told you all those terrible things, wasn't it? He's the one who called you."

Silence. Then he said, "Beck, I don't want to get anyone in trouble. Look—"

"Just tell me the truth," she said, and to Booker, "Who else, besides Delaney, knows so much about me?"

Booker rubbed the stubble on his chin. "Makes sense to me."

"He probably didn't like losing all that money in front of everyone last night," Rebecca muttered.

"I don't think it's about the money—" Booker started to say, but she turned her attention back to the phone.

"Is it him?" she demanded. "Is it Josh Hill?"

Buddy's lack of denial confirmed her suspicion. "He said he's a good friend and that he means well."

Rebecca set her jaw, her body now filling with resolve. "I'll talk to you later," she said. "There's something I have to do."

"Wait! Rebecca—"

She hung up, grabbed her coat and keys and tried to brush past Booker.

"Where are you going?" he asked.

"To Josh Hill's house."

"That can't be good," he said. "I'd better go with you."

"SO WHAT ARE YOU GOING TO DO?" Booker asked as they sat in her Firebird across the road from Josh's ranch.

Rebecca considered Josh's large, rustic, two-story cabin-like house with the hammock hanging on the front porch. Then she studied the circular drive, the split-rail fence enclosing the property, and the row of shade trees along the right side, and felt her resentment grow. *Of course* Josh's ranch would be a cut above everyone else's. Trucks and SUVs clogged the drive, along with a small tractor, and several horse trailers and Quad-runners sat lined up on one side of the road that led around back. Brand-new stables and corrals had been built behind the house for the mares Josh and his brother owned, and the studs—a couple of which had cost over a million dollars.

Josh and Mike ran a lucrative business. They'd achieved

a level of success Rebecca could only imagine. Even if she and Buddy eventually got married, she doubted they'd ever be rich.

But she hadn't asked for rich. She'd asked only for a fresh start with a simple man who loved her.

And Josh wouldn't leave her even that much.

"Are we going to the door?" Booker asked when she didn't respond to his earlier question.

A light glimmered toward the back of the house, but Rebecca's rage had already burned itself out. She no longer felt the fierce need to hit something. Now doing anything at all seemed rather pointless. The damage was done.

Climbing out of the car, she strode up to Josh's Excursion. She was driving a car older than most people's houses while he drove one of the nicest SUVs on the market. Why did he have to have it all?

She heard the crunch of footsteps on gravel as Booker came up behind her. "Are you ever going to say anything?" he asked.

"These SUVs cost thirty-five thousand dollars," she responded.

He glanced at the maroon Excursion. "They're nice."

"Everything Josh has is nice." Rebecca opened the door and sat in the passenger seat, letting her legs dangle out the side. She wasn't surprised to find the vehicle unlocked. There wasn't any crime in Dundee to speak of, especially out in the hills where the next property was five or more miles away.

The inside of the SUV smelled of leather and Armor All—and Josh. Rebecca noticed the scent of his cologne right away and wondered why, after everything they'd been through, she still liked it.

More irony, she supposed. Josh had blighted her whole existence, and she still couldn't help admiring him.

"How would it be to drive something like this?" she asked, running a hand over the simulated wood grain on the door panel.

Booker lit up a cigarette, his face momentarily glowing in the little blue flame of his lighter.

A cold breeze fanned the smoke toward her and she breathed deeply, craving the taste and savoring the smell. She hadn't had a cigarette for almost two weeks, but she suddenly saw little point in denying herself. She couldn't change. She wasn't going anywhere.

Reaching out, she caught Booker before he could shove the pack into the pocket of his coat.

"You quit, remember?" he said.

"That was yesterday."

He hesitated briefly before relinquishing the cigarettes. "What the hell. If smoking's the worst thing you do, go for it."

Rebecca lit up and enjoyed her first drag. Booker leaned against the car and tilted his face toward the sky. "So what are we doing here?" he asked after a few moments of silence.

What *were* they doing? Rebecca longed for some type of revenge. She owed Josh for more than sabotaging her engagement. What about all the love and attention he'd cost her over the years?

I've told you and told you that you need to keep your hand steady. You're never going to win a game of pool if you play like that... her father had said. *Your sisters were easy to raise...Josh and his brother have turned out to be responsible, dependable adults...I don't know where we went wrong with you...wrong with you...wrong with you...*

But she was too old for the kind of high school pranks she and Josh used to pull on each other. And regardless of what the community thought of her temper, she'd never done anything seriously wrong. Bottom line, there wasn't anything she *could* do that would counteract Josh's incredible appeal. She couldn't *make* him be anything less than he was. Part of her didn't even want to. That was what made her the craziest. Deep down, she appreciated his good looks and abilities as much as everyone else—even while she resented how easily he'd stolen her father's heart.

Flicking away the butt of her cigarette, she got out of the Excursion and shut the door.

"Nothing," she said. "We're not going to do anything."

"Cool." Booker gave her a rare smile. "Let's go get a cup of coffee at the diner."

JOSH HAD BEEN lying in bed wearing nothing but a pair of boxers, watching television for more than an hour. But he wasn't paying much attention to any of the programs that flashed past the screen as he clicked his remote. He couldn't stop thinking about his conversation with Buddy earlier in the day and how quickly what he'd been trying to do had turned around on him. He'd meant his call to *help* Rebecca. She wanted to get married, and he wanted to forget about her. Their goals seemed compatible enough. But once he'd gotten Buddy on the phone, he'd purposely told him every unappealing thing he could think of to scare the poor guy away from Rebecca.

He shifted in bed, trying to conjure up the humiliation he'd suffered when Rebecca had bought a child-sized jock and bandied it around school, claiming she'd stolen it from his locker. If there was going to be some kind of negative fallout from his call, it was no more than she deserved after that stunt and all the others like it, he tried to tell himself. But somehow the satisfaction he'd felt earlier had withered away and now he was afflicted with a variety of other emotions—guilt for meddling in something that was clearly none of his business mingled with the stubborn hope that Buddy *would* break off the relationship and disappear from Rebecca's life.

Flipping through a few more channels, he settled on CNN because news seemed to fit his mood more than the canned laughter of the sitcoms. Rebecca might have pulled a few pranks on him in the past, but he'd done similar things to her. And interfering with personal relationships wasn't quite the same as hoisting her panties up the flagpole. He shouldn't have involved himself in something that had the potential to be so hurtful.

So what did he do about it?

For a moment, he considered calling Buddy to apologize, to see if he could fix any damage he might have caused. But he doubted he could explain the complex emotions that had motivated his first call. There were some realities he'd rather not face. Besides, he was still convinced Rebecca would be better off, in the long run anyway, if Buddy terminated the engagement. The man was still sleeping when Josh had called—at slightly past noon, for crying out loud—which spelled lazy, even if it was a Sunday. And Buddy obviously wasn't the brightest bulb in the pack. He'd never questioned Josh's motivations, never doubted his veracity. Instead, he'd gone on and on about the quiet, peaceful life he wanted to live.

If Buddy wanted peace and quiet, what the hell was he doing even *thinking* about marrying Rebecca? Only if a man was serious about increasing his daily angst to never-a-dull-moment, frustrated-to-the-point-of-wanting-to-break-something intensity should he consider Rebecca Wells.

Maybe it was only obvious to Josh, but Rebecca needed a man with more backbone than Buddy. She needed someone who understood her tempestuous nature. Someone capable of riding out the emotional storms. Someone who could soothe the ache Josh sensed inside her—the ache that made him think of her at odd hours during the night and unexpected moments during the day ever since they were kids. She needed—

"Josh, I think you'd better get out here! Fast!"

At the urgency in his brother's voice, Josh jumped out of bed. The remote clattered to the hardwood floor, but he ignored it as he hurried into the kitchen to find his brother standing in a pair of pajama bottoms and a sweatshirt, looking stunned. Through the wide front window, Josh could tell that something in the drive was on fire.

"What the hell is that?" he cried.

"Your Excursion," his brother answered, his voice full of awe.

"That ball of fire is my ride?" Running for the door, Josh charged into the cold night air to find his brand-new Ford Excursion engulfed in flames. Torn between dashing forward to save what was left and turning away because he couldn't bear the sight, he finally sank onto the porch steps, too shocked to do anything. "Not my Excursion," he said. "Not my new SUV."

"I'm calling the fire department," Mike said, a cordless phone pressed to his ear. "Start hosing it down."

Josh resisted the little shove his brother gave him. For all he knew, the Excursion was about to explode. And it was too late, anyway. Even if it didn't explode, by the time they extinguished the flames, the vehicle would be nothing more than a charred wreck.

"I searched for that truck for months," he complained aloud, even though Mike was now talking to the fire department and wasn't able to respond. "It was in cherry condition: custom rims, tan leather interior, every upgrade in the book...."

Mike hung up and went for the garden hose. But he

didn't dare get close enough to do any good. When he realized he was wasting his time, he turned off the water, stomped back to the house and sat next to Josh. Together they stared in silent wonder at the fiery spectacle.

"Think it was kids?" Mike asked at last.

They could hear the shrill siren of a fire truck in the distance. Josh wrinkled his nose at the acrid smell of the smoke billowing into the black sky above them and rubbed his bare arms against the cold, which he was just beginning to feel. "We've never had any trouble with kids, not way the heck out here. And what reason would they have to destroy my SUV and not your truck? You're parked even closer to the road."

"But if it wasn't kids," Mike said, "who did it?"

Josh couldn't imagine. Who would purposely single out his vehicle and burn it to the ground? Who would—

Realization dawned suddenly and, once it did, he knew there could be no mistake. Who would single him out? The same girl who'd tormented him since he was eight years old. Rebecca Wells. He'd called Buddy, and this was her revenge.

He shook his head, unable to believe she'd go so far. So what if he'd told her fiancé a few of the juicier details from her past? Did she think she could hide her true nature from him forever? He might have slanted his stories a bit, but she didn't have to torch his Excursion.

Briefly, he thought of calling Ned Parks at the sheriff's office to file a complaint. Destruction of private property. That would cause Rebecca some serious problems, some *well-deserved* problems.

But even as he watched his Excursion burn, in his heart Josh knew he'd never make that call. The war that raged between him and Rebecca had gone on a long time. They'd both done some pretty stupid things, but they'd never ratted on each other to anyone in authority. In the first place, he had no proof that she was the one who set the fire. He couldn't call and tell Ned to arrest the mayor's daughter simply because she was the only person who'd ever had it in for him.

Besides, if he brought Ned into the mess, she'd tell everyone that he'd tried to sabotage her marriage. Buddy might back her up, and then Mary would want to know why he cared enough to involve himself at all. He'd have to deny that he cared about Rebecca, pretend that ache he sensed inside her didn't bother him. And...

Dammit! Why'd his family ever have to move into the house across the street from Rebecca Wells?

CHAPTER FOURTEEN

REBECCA STUDIED BOOKER over her coffee cup. It was well past midnight, but she still wasn't ready to head home. "So what are *your* plans?" she asked so she wouldn't have to think about her own. At this point, she wasn't sure whether she and Buddy would ever get married, and envisioning herself living with Hatty for an indefinite period of time wasn't cheering her.

He shrugged. "Finish painting the garage."

"And after that?"

"I'm sure Granny will have something else for me to do."

"You can't work for her forever. You're going to have to get a job eventually, aren't you?"

"Eventually." He leaned back as Judy came around to fill his cup.

"What kind of job would you like?" she asked.

"I'd like my own repair shop someday. I'm pretty good with engines. I was about to buy out the place where I worked in Milwaukee, but—" He shrugged.

"What?" Rebecca pressed.

"Granny said she wasn't feeling well and—" he grinned "—I fell for it."

"Somehow I get the impression you don't mind."

"She's getting old. Someone needs to look after her."

"What about your parents?"

"They're too busy with their own lives."

So Booker had postponed his dreams and come to Dundee to do the job. Rebecca had no doubt that would surprise a few people—like her father. "That's why you're so patient with her. You *want* to be doing what you're doing."

He didn't say anything.

"And when she dies, will you go back to Milwaukee?" Rebecca asked.

"I don't know. Maybe I'll open a shop right here. There's only Lionel and his son doing auto repair, and they don't know shit."

"Where'd you learn so much?"

He set his cup in its saucer and leaned back, leveling his gaze at her. "In prison."

Rebecca toyed with the handle of her cup. "I've wondered about that," she said. "What did you do?"

The bell went off over the door, and Rebecca looked up to see Greta's husband, Randy, step into the diner, along with Jeffrey Stevens, the second of Dundee's two firefighters. Their faces were streaked with sweat, and they were both wearing a good bit of their firefighting regalia, but she didn't want to hear about the latest brush fire.

She averted her face, hoping Randy wouldn't notice her as Booker said, "Federal drug charges. I got busted for selling crack when I was twenty. I was pretty messed up in those days."

"But you've changed."

"I don't do drugs. I don't hang out with other people who do them. I'm not angry anymore."

Rebecca stirred another packet of sugar into her coffee because it gave her a way to occupy her hands. "What was it like in prison?"

"Bad enough that I don't want to go back."

Rarely did Booker embellish his statements with any detail. Rebecca would have questioned him further, however, if she hadn't heard Jeff say something to Judy and Rick, the late-night cook, that caught her attention. Something about a car fire.

"That thing is toast, man. You should see it," Randy said, sitting at the bar in front of the cooler that contained the pies the owner of the restaurant made daily.

"No one's going to be driving *that* charred heap," Jeff concurred.

"Does Josh know what happened?" Judy wanted to know.

"He knows his Excursion's destroyed. He doesn't know how it happened, though."

"A vehicle doesn't just burst into flames for no reason," the cook said.

"What vehicle?" Rebecca asked, forgetting that she didn't want Randy to notice her.

Her brother-in-law swiveled to face her. His expression turned to a glower when he saw Booker with her, but he answered. "Josh Hill's Excursion just burned to cinders."

Rebecca felt a chill go down her spine. The same vehicle she'd been sitting in only a couple of hours earlier? The same vehicle she'd been *smoking* in?

"How'd the fire get started?" she asked, scarcely able to breathe.

Randy shrugged. "Don't know. There was a gas can in back. Josh had just filled it for the Quad Runners and forgotten to take it out. We think that had something to do with it."

"So you're saying the Excursion…what? Spontaneously combusted?" she asked, her voice sounding reedy, even to her own ears.

"Not in this cool weather," Jeff said, his voice as skeptical as his words. "It would've taken a spark of some kind."

Rebecca tried to recall what she'd done with the butt of her cigarette. She'd been sitting in the truck smoking, talking to Booker. They'd decided they were wasting their time, and she'd flicked her cigarette away. But it had fallen on the damp ground, hadn't it? She couldn't remember. She'd been so preoccupied with what Buddy had said, and what Josh had done to make Buddy say what he'd said, and what she was or wasn't going to do in response, that she hadn't been paying attention. Maybe she'd flicked the butt into his Excursion by accident. Or maybe she hadn't done it by accident at all. Maybe her subconscious had *wanted* to destroy Josh's fancy SUV....

The "bad seed" stuff her father had mentioned echoed in Rebecca's mind. It was too much of a coincidence that she'd been smoking in Josh's truck the same night it burst into flame, wasn't it? Had *she* provided the spark?

Oh, God... She opened her mouth to ask if a cigarette butt could have started the fire, but Booker interrupted her by squeezing her hand.

"We're sorry to hear that," he said to Randy and Jeff, taking over the conversation. "But Rebecca and I better get going. It's late, and we've already been here for ages. Isn't that right, Judy?"

"Huh?" the middle-aged waitress said, her mind still obviously immersed in the shocking news about Josh's Excursion.

"We're ready for the check," Booker replied.

"Oh, yeah." She walked over and slapped their ticket on the table.

Booker tossed a five on top of it before pulling Rebecca from the booth.

"Are you thinking what I'm thinking?" she murmured as they made their way to her car.

"No," Booker said. "I'm not."

But she knew he was. She knew it from the tenseness of his body, the soberness of his eyes.

"What am I going to do?" she asked after he put her in the passenger side of her car and took the driver's seat himself.

"Nothing."

"I have to do *something*."

He started the engine. "No, you don't. Considering the past, there isn't a snowball's chance in hell anyone will believe what happened was an accident. How are you planning to explain what you were doing at his house? And I'm an ex-con. I can't exactly lend you credibility. So we're not going to say anything. Josh's insurance will replace his ride, and that'll be the end of it, okay?"

"But what if it was my fault?"

"If?" he said.

And that was when Rebecca knew for sure: she'd burned Josh's new Excursion to the ground.

REBECCA'S HEART ECHOED the thumping of her hand on Delaney's door.

"Laney, it's me. Open up," she called, shivering. When she and Booker had arrived at Granny Hatfield's, she'd gone inside and tried to sleep. But she'd only tossed restlessly in her bed. When the emotions swirling inside her refused to settle down after an hour, she'd pulled on a pair of jeans and a sweater and headed out, hoping to speak to the one person who'd always been able to make sense of the world. Delaney.

The porch light snapped on and Rebecca stepped back. *Finally. Thank goodness.* But she wasn't very pleased when she saw Conner's sleepy face through the crack in the door, instead of Delaney's.

"Rebecca?" he asked. "Are you okay?"

Rebecca rubbed her palms on her jeans, suddenly resenting Conner as much as she resented all the other changes life had brought over the past year. Now that Delaney was married, she was mostly unavailable. Buddy had postponed their wedding—indefinitely, this time. Her next closest friend was an ex-con. And she was living with Hatty, for God's sake. Could things *get* any worse?

"Um…yeah," she said. "Sorry to wake you, but…I really need to talk to Delaney."

"Rebecca?" Delaney gently pushed Conner out of the way and opened the door wider. "What's going on?"

Rebecca glanced uncomfortably at Conner. She shouldn't have come. Conner was obviously disgruntled at the disturbance and, being so close to the end of her pregnancy, Delaney needed her sleep. "Never mind. I shouldn't have bothered you. I'll call you in the morning."

She turned to go, but Delaney grabbed her arm. "No, come in. I'm worried about you."

Rebecca let herself be dragged inside and breathed a little easier when Delaney insisted Conner go back to bed. "I can take care of this," she said. "You get some sleep."

He shoved a hand through his rumpled hair, gazed with bleary eyes at his wife, then shuffled down the hall.

"Sorry," Rebecca said when he was gone.

"Don't worry about it," Delaney replied. "Come on into the kitchen. I'll make us a cup of herbal tea."

Rebecca followed her and slumped into a chair while Delaney put some water on to boil.

"So what's wrong?" she asked, sitting across from her.

Rebecca poured salt on the kitchen table and began moving it around with one fingertip. When that didn't ease the tension humming through her body, she sighed and said, "I'm in trouble, Laney."

Her best friend stiffened, as though bracing for the worst. "This doesn't have anything to do with Booker, does it?"

"Actually it does. But not in the way you think."

"Then what?" she said, her voice tentative.

Meeting her gaze, Rebecca said, "I burned down Josh's truck tonight."

Delaney stood, as quickly as she could in her condition, and pressed a hand to her chest. "You *what?*"

"It was an accident. He called Buddy today and told him every terrible thing I've ever done. And Buddy said he wasn't sure whether he even wanted to set a date for the wedding anymore. And…and I just felt so helpless and frustrated and angry. I shouldn't have gone out to Josh's place. I know that. But I really didn't mean to burn his Excursion."

"You want to explain how it happened?"

Rebecca told her about how she'd dashed off to Josh's, planning to confront him—and how pointless that had seemed by the time she'd reached his house. When she finished by describing the careless toss of her cigarette butt, Delaney didn't respond. "Say something," she finally prodded.

"I'm trying to think," Delaney replied. "I mean, Josh had no right to do what he did. I can't believe he'd involve himself in your personal life. But I doubt the police will give you much sympathy."

"Josh might not have done anything illegal, but when he called Buddy, I'm sure he left out all the stuff he did to provoke *me* while we were growing up."

Delaney dropped her head in one palm. "You mean like breathing?" she muttered.

Rebecca stared down at the salt granules on the table, feeling almost as minuscule. "Like…like…I don't know," she said. "Why did he have to call Buddy, anyway?"

Delaney wiped the salt Rebecca had poured onto the table into her hand and went to toss it down the sink. "That's what has me stumped," she said, turning on the water. "You guys rarely see each other anymore. You were letting the past go. You were calling a truce. So why the sudden involvement?"

Rebecca got up and began to pace. "I don't know. I haven't done anything *bad* to him for years."

"The last time was when we stole his truck and stranded him and Cindy at the old skinny-dipping spot, remember?" Delaney said.

Rebecca easily recalled the warm, dark night they'd seen Josh at the movies with Cindy Westover. They'd chanced upon his pickup a few hours later, parked not far from Culver Creek with the keys dangling inside, and knew he and Cindy were probably taking a swim—or doing more than swimming. Either way, it had been too good an opportunity to pass up. "That was nine years ago."

"Maybe he's still holding a grudge."

"He was the one who left his keys inside."

"Hormone-induced frenzies don't lend themselves to cautious thinking," Delaney pointed out.

"Then it would've been a bigger mistake if they'd left their clothes in the truck, too." Rebecca folded her arms as she paced; she felt so fidgety, she didn't know what to do with her hands. "In any case, he and Cindy had to walk a few miles in the dark. So what? It wasn't even cold out."

"They had to walk ten miles, at least," Delaney corrected. "But forget I brought it up. This is different. You could be in big trouble here. You didn't just borrow his truck this time—you destroyed it."

"Ten miles is no big deal," Rebecca insisted, because she didn't want to think about the repercussions of the here and now. "Josh and Cindy walked home and found Josh's truck parked in his driveway, keys inside. No harm done. Surely he didn't call Buddy to get me back for *that*."

"Who knows? He has a long list of grievances to choose from," Delaney said.

Most of which he'd enumerated quite nicely for Buddy, Rebecca thought, pivoting at the end of the kitchen and coming back.

"That wasn't exactly the last contact you had with him," Delaney went on.

Rebecca gave up crossing her arms, because she was too nervous to hold her arms so still, and began fiddling with the bottom of her sweater. "But I didn't do anything unkind last summer. I was out of my mind for a little while and nearly tore off his clothes and begged him to take me. What would make a man angry about that?"

"I can't say," Delaney said, leaning against the counter. "I only know you've been different since that night."

"How?"

"Less volatile. More reflective. Certainly far less vocal about your dislike for Josh Hill. Why'd you ever leave the Honky Tonk with him?"

"You already know. I was drunk."

"You seem to remember a lot about that night for being drunk."

Rebecca would've had to be deaf to miss the skepticism in Delaney's voice. "Last summer has nothing to do with now," she said, changing the subject as quickly as possible.

"Who knows," Delaney said.

"*I* know."

"So?"

"So what?"

"What are you going to do now?"

"I don't have a clue."

Delaney pulled her chair away from the table to make

more room for her belly and sank down again. "You couldn't simply have *asked* him why he called Buddy," she said, tucking her long hair behind her ears. "You couldn't have gone to the door and said, 'Keep your nose out of my business.' Instead, you had to toss a cigarette butt inside his SUV."

"Thanks for trying to cheer me up," Rebecca said.

"Sorry."

Rebecca gave up pacing to stand and stare out the kitchen window at the black night beyond. "I need another cigarette."

"Hang on. The desire will pass."

Maybe her craving for a cigarette would pass, but what she'd done to Josh's truck had to be reckoned with. "It's just a vehicle, right?" she said suddenly. "I'll pay for it."

"You'll *what?*" Delaney responded.

"I'll pay for it."

"Uh-huh. You'll write him a check on your big, fat bank account. Or do you think Buddy should help pay for it once you two finally get married?"

If they *ever* married, Rebecca thought Buddy probably *should* help pay for it. "Buddy has some responsibility in all this," she said.

Delaney turned to gape at her. "Why's that?"

"He believed what Josh told him."

"It was the truth!"

"So what if it was? He could've defended me. He could've had a little faith. Instead, he's seriously doubting I'll make him a good wife." Rebecca hated the way her voice cracked on that last statement, especially when Delaney's sudden softening told her she'd heard it.

"Oh, Beck," she said. "Buddy will come around."

"Why'd Josh have to do it?" Despite herself, Rebecca couldn't mask the pain behind her words. "Why shouldn't

I burn his Excursion, Laney? What difference does it make? I can't have a fresh start. I'm damaged goods, even with Buddy. I've always been damaged goods.''

''Don't say that! You have too much to offer the world to let anyone's opinion hem you in, even Buddy's. I can't imagine why Josh did what he did. But you can be anything you want to be, regardless of the past.''

Rebecca curled her fingers into her palms as the reality of what she'd done sank even deeper. ''No, I can't. Because I just proved everybody right, didn't I? These kinds of things don't happen to good people. Only to bad seeds. I'm not marriage material. I'm not even 'friend' material. I dragged Booker over there with me, which means I could've gotten him in trouble, too. I deserve to do hair in Nowhere, Idaho, until I die of old age,'' she said. And then, because she resented Delaney's sympathy as much as she craved it, she left.

THE SMELL OF SMOKE HUNG thick in the air as Rebecca stood facing Josh's house. The lights were out, and the place looked peaceful and sleepy. The fire was out, too, leaving the Ford Excursion looking like a soulless heap.

She'd done that. She'd killed it in her anger, and now she had to pay the price.

Resolute, Rebecca threw back her shoulders and made her feet carry her to the front door. She hated knowing she'd wake Josh at three o'clock in the morning, hated standing out in the cold, humiliated and alone. But she was afraid that if she waited, she'd lose her nerve and never say what had to be said.

Swallowing hard, she fought a sudden mutinous on-slaught of tears and raised her hand to knock.

The light came on. Rebecca quickly stepped into the shadows as the door swung open.

"Back to torch the house?" Josh asked, wearing nothing but a pair of jeans.

Rebecca hunched into her wool coat, wishing she were small enough to disappear. But she refused to let herself move any farther back. She had to own up to her mistakes, accept responsibility, *apologize*. And she had to say those things to Josh. There were insurance issues, which could easily become criminal issues. And there were moral issues, too. She knew no one would ever believe her, but it was the moral issues that had brought her traipsing across town in the middle of the night.

"So—" She cleared her throat because it felt like someone was squeezing it and she wanted to ensure that her voice remained steady and true. If she was going to do this, she was going to do it with dignity. "So I guess you already know it was me."

He crossed his arms and leaned against the doorjamb. Rebecca knew he had to be freezing, standing there barefoot and without a shirt. But he didn't invite her in or ask her to wait while he grabbed a jacket. "I know it was you. And it doesn't surprise me a bit."

Of course it wouldn't surprise him. She was the only one who'd ever done anything bad to him. All the other residents of Dundee turned themselves inside out to give Josh Hill whatever he wanted.

"Right," she said. "Well, I came to—" Suddenly it felt as though she couldn't catch her breath. "To tell you I'll pay for the damage."

"You will?" he said, not hiding his astonishment. Sticking his head out the door, he looked around as though expecting to be ambushed at any moment. "Are you trying to throw me off here? Are you setting me up for something else?"

She shook her head. "I don't have the money to pay the

whole amount right now, which might put you in a bind as far as replacing it. But I can pay as much as—'' She hesitated, knowing that what she could afford would sound paltry to him, then forced the words out of her mouth anyway, because it was the best she could do. ''Three hundred dollars a month.'' *At least I won't be smoking again. I won't have the money for chewing gum, let alone cigarettes.*

He seemed unsure how to respond. ''Let me get this straight,'' he said. ''You're taking responsibility for destroying my SUV, and you're going to pay me three hundred dollars a month to make up for it?''

She jammed her hands in her pockets and nodded.

''It could've gone down as an accident.''

''It was an accident,'' she said.

He cocked an eyebrow at her.

''I know you don't believe me, and I don't want to explain. I'm taking responsibility. That's all you need to know.''

''The insurance would've replaced it.''

''They might have investigated.''

''There were no witnesses. Anything with any fingerprints has been burned to cinders.''

''What are you saying?'' she asked.

''That you had a good chance of getting away with it.''

''I know.''

He scratched his head. ''Then what are you doing here?''

Proving to herself that she wasn't what he thought she was, that she wasn't what *anyone* thought she was. But this was the hard part, the part she'd rehearsed so many times on the way over. ''I came to apologize. I don't appreciate what you said to Buddy, but I should never have come out here and...''

God, did she have to say it? He deserved to lose his

Excursion. He'd always had everything, everyone's admiration and affection. He was sexy and gorgeous and could kiss like the devil himself. And now he was rich while she scraped by doing hair. She'd always lived in his shadow. Even her own father preferred him to the gangly girl with the skinned knee who could never do anything right....

He waited, obviously taken aback but curious enough to give her the time she needed, even though the cold was turning his normally smooth skin to gooseflesh.

Lifting her chin, Rebecca looked him in the eye. "I'm sorry," she said.

She dashed a hand across her face because her vision was blurring so badly she couldn't make out the muddy flowerbeds from the still-steaming Excursion. Then she hurried back to her car.

CHAPTER FIFTEEN

JOSH COULDN'T BELIEVE IT. Somehow he'd pierced the thick hide that had always kept Rebecca Wells so aloof and unreachable and tough—tougher than any boy he'd ever known—and found something soft and sweet and very...vulnerable.

Damn. He shoved a hand through his hair, then tried to straighten the covers he'd twisted into a mess and told himself to go to sleep. Dawn was only an hour or so away, and he'd been up all night.

But he couldn't close his eyes without seeing the tears rolling down Rebecca's cheeks. It was the first time he'd ever seen her cry. Those tears grabbed hold of his insides and squeezed until he could hardly breathe.

Think about what she did to your truck. He stared at the ceiling, preferring the simplicity of the outrage he'd felt before her visit to the confusion he'd experienced since she'd left. She was in the wrong. She'd burned down his brand-new Ford Excursion, for crying out loud. Which meant she *deserved* to pay for it.

He'd provoked her, though. What he'd done seemed pretty innocuous compared to her reaction, but considering the size of the backlash, he'd apparently created some serious waves for her and Buddy. Maybe Buddy had even broken up with her. *Something* must have happened to set her off like that.

He glanced at the clock by his bed and wondered why

he'd never lost any sleep over Mary. Because she was nice and uncomplicated, he decided. Those were good things. He'd heard all about the differences in the male vs. female psyches, the jokes about guys never knowing a woman's mind, the talk about how hard it was to please a woman. But in his experience, keeping a woman happy wasn't so difficult. Give her plenty of attention, a few compliments, some gifts and laughs and candlelight dinners, and everything went smoothly enough.

Except when it came to Rebecca. With her, there were no hard and fast rules. She played in a whole different ballpark.

Punching his pillow, he rolled onto his side and gazed at the phone. He felt terrible to think he might have cost her the man of her dreams—if a milk-toast man like Buddy *could* be the man of her dreams. And he felt even worse that his interference had made her do something as stupid as torching his truck, landing her with three-hundred-dollar-a-month payments she probably couldn't afford. But he didn't really know what to do about the situation at this point, and he wanted to release himself from whatever kept twisting his gut every time he remembered the pain in Rebecca's eyes.

I'll call Mary. She never makes me feel like this, never makes me want to rant and rave or slug inanimate objects.

Of course, if he was being honest, she didn't make him feel much of anything. Certainly she inspired no passion. Nothing like what he'd felt when he held Rebecca in his arms, their bare skin pressed together, their mouths hungry for each other. The primitive drive to possess her had been startling in its ferocity, thrilling, exulting, the absolute pinnacle of sexual experience.

Only he hadn't wanted to tear off her clothes tonight. Tonight he'd wanted to pull her into his arms and beg her to forgive him—and he was the one who'd lost a thirty-thousand-dollar vehicle!

"I'm screwed up," he said aloud. Then he grabbed the phone, determined to put Rebecca and this restless night behind him.

"Hello?" Mary's voice was barely audible.

"It's me."

"Josh?"

"Yeah. Sorry to wake you."

"That's okay," she said. "I like hearing from you anytime. Lets me know you're thinking of me."

Josh winced at the guilt he couldn't fathom, any more than he could've explained anything else about this crazy night.

"Is something wrong?" she asked.

"No, nothing." *Other than the charred hunk of junk that used to be my truck.* "I just want you to come over." *And help me get my head on straight.*

"But it's five o'clock in the morning."

"Your mom's there with Ricky. You can go back before it's time to get him off to school."

"That's true...."

"And it's not like we're on some kind of schedule where we can only make love on Friday nights," he said, even though their relationship had actually settled into something almost that predictable.

"Of course not. I just...I don't want you to see me this way," she said. "I don't have any makeup on."

So? What did makeup have to do with anything? Rebecca hadn't been wearing a stitch of makeup when she'd appeared at his door. She'd stood tall and proud and looked up at him with those clear green eyes filling with tears and—

No more Rebecca! "I don't care about makeup," he insisted. "Just come over. Please."

She giggled. "Boy, are you eager. Did you have a naughty dream? Or have you just been thinking about me?"

I've been thinking about Rebecca, and I can't stop, and it's scaring the hell out of me. I need you to remind me why I'm with you. Help me out here. "It…it just hasn't been a very pleasant night."

"But I look *terrible.*"

Josh rubbed one temple and gave in. He didn't really want to see her anyway, he realized. With or without makeup. And that was when he knew he was even more screwed up than he'd thought.

"Forget it," he said. "I'll talk to you tomorrow."

JOSH LEANED his elbows on his desk on Monday, and stared blankly at the stack of papers and checks awaiting his attention. After the terrible weekend he'd spent, he hadn't been able to concentrate on a damn thing all morning, hadn't been able to muddle through half of what he needed to get done. The memory of Rebecca at his door kept intruding, along with other memories that stirred him just as much, only in a far different way. She'd been so responsive, so aroused by him a year ago last summer—that meant she couldn't hate him too badly, right?

Or maybe she could. He certainly had more proof of her dislike than he did of any softer emotion.

Shaking his head to clear his thoughts, he picked up a stack of payroll checks and started to sign them. The woman had just burned up his Excursion, and he was sitting here doing "she loves me, she loves me not." Of course Rebecca Wells hated him. Torching someone's vehicle wasn't generally a sign of affection. And it wasn't as though he cared for *her,* anyway.

Sure, there were times late at night when images of her haunted him. In his dreams, she always clung to him as he made her cry out in ecstasy, over and over again. Though last night that dream had changed a little. First he'd kissed away her tears, *then* he'd made her cry out in ecstasy. But every man had his fantasies. Some liked cheerleaders, others movie stars. He happened to have a thing for the girl who'd grown up across the street and put honey in his sleeping bag when he and his friends tried to camp out in the front yard.

Frowning, he wondered if that made him a masochist.

"There you are." Janie, the freckled nineteen-year-old who exercised the studs and cleaned the paddocks and stalls, poked her head inside the room. "Mary's downstairs," she said, wearing her tan cowboy hat and widemouthed smile. "Want me to send her up?"

Mary. Josh took a deep breath and rubbed a palm against the stubble on his chin. "Does she have makeup on?" he muttered.

Janie blinked in surprise. "What's that got to do with anything?"

"Nothing," he said. "Tell her to come up."

Janie's steps receded, and Josh leaned back, waiting. He knew Mary expected a marriage proposal soon, knew she was growing almost as impatient as her parents and his. But how did a man marry one woman when way down deep, so deep he'd never admit it to anyone, he secretly desired another? Josh had tried to put Rebecca behind him, knew he'd be a damn fool not to, but this whole Buddy business, and his SUV, and last night…

"There you are, working hard, I see." The petite Mary waltzed into the room in full regalia—dark hair curled to perfection, glossy pink lipstick, a thick coating of mascara on her lashes and a tailored, form-fitting suit. A belt at the waist highlighted her trim figure, but somehow even the thought of what lay beneath did nothing to stir Josh. For the first time, he noticed that her legs were too short.

"What brings you out here?" he said, trying to redirect his mind before he did something really stupid and broke up with her on account of a woman who hated him.

She gave him a promising smile and closed the door. When the lock clicked into place, he knew she'd come for more than talk.

"Don't you have to be at work?" he asked curiously. Mary ran the office of the only attorney in town—the one who'd handled her divorce and everyone else's for the past thirty years—and was usually quite busy.

"Lunchtime," she said. Then she unbuttoned her jacket and let it gape open to reveal a sheer lace bra that left nothing to the imagination.

Josh felt his pulse kick up a few notches and welcomed the sudden infusion of testosterone as she climbed onto his lap. He didn't need Rebecca to make his blood race. He was fine the way he'd always been.

Maybe he *would* propose to Mary. Maybe he'd marry her and come home to her every night and make *her* scream in ecstasy. Only something told him that if she screamed, it would be a calculated response. She'd be offering him what she knew he wanted to hear, not the wild abandon of Rebecca Wells—

Rebecca again. He jerked his hand from Mary's breast and managed to stifle a curse.

"What's wrong?" she asked. Suddenly Josh realized he hadn't even kissed her. Maybe if he kissed her...

"Nothing," he said and bent his head to press his lips to hers, trying to back up and approach their lovemaking from a whole new angle. But she tilted her face away before their lips could meet.

"You'll get lipstick all over both of us, silly," she laughed. "This has to be a quickie. I've got to get back."

"Oh, right," he mumbled, but when he hesitated, she lifted his hand to her breast again. As her nipple responded to the attention he gave it, he felt his desire build—but then she started telling him about some pointless incident that had happened at work, and he almost snapped that he needed to concentrate if she wanted this to happen.

To prevent himself from snapping at her, he started thinking about Rebecca again, and suddenly he didn't need to concentrate at all. He had Mary on his desk and was just about to make her scream in ecstasy—at least that was the next step in his fantasy—when she chose that moment to mention seeing a wedding dress she really liked.

"After we're married, you won't have to wait until lunch to get what you want," she added with a little laugh.

He pictured them making love in twenty years with her chatting about something inconsequential and wearing lipstick she wouldn't let him kiss away, and somehow his desire—and everything else—withered on the spot.

Suppressing a groan of frustration, he withdrew and fastened his pants.

"What's wrong?" she asked again.

"It's not you. It's…it's just not going to happen this time. This hasn't been a very good day."

He saw the same pouty expression she gave her son when he scraped his knee. For a moment Josh was afraid she'd say something like, "Joshy got a boo boo?" Much to her credit, she didn't. "You want to talk about it?" she asked.

Suddenly she looked so undignified on top of his desk, her skirt around her waist, her jacket open, that he helped her off and felt relieved when she started righting her clothes.

"Someone set fire to my Excursion last night."

"You're kidding! Who would do such a thing?"

"I don't know," he lied.

"That's terrible."

He nodded but began to feel a little uncomfortable again when her eyes fastened intently on his face. She had something to say, but he wasn't sure he wanted to hear it. "What?" he asked.

She straightened the lapels of her jacket. "I just don't want you to feel I'll think any less of you after this."

"After—"

"You know…" She nodded toward the desk and all the papers they'd wrinkled before aborting his fantasy. "An upsetting event would impair any man's ability to…*perform*. So don't give it another thought. I certainly won't."

She already had. Josh winced at the insult to his masculinity and nearly told her that he would've been able to perform just fine had her mind been anywhere in the room. If she hadn't given the impression that she looked at sex as *servicing* her man, as relationship maintenance that seemed no more meaningful to her than having the oil changed in her car. Who would find that arousing? He didn't want her to look at lovemaking as some kind of favor. He wanted the absolute honesty he'd experienced with Rebecca. In the few minutes they'd been together, they hadn't been able to remove their clothes fast enough, touch enough, kiss enough…

He shoved his hands in his pockets because he didn't know where else to put them. "Thanks for your understanding," he said so she'd leave. No need to debate the issue. In the first place, he wasn't convinced his lukewarm response was really her fault. She'd come over to give him what she thought he wanted. She deserved some credit for that. In the second place, Mary wasn't used to criticism. She probably wouldn't understand his complaints even if he tried to explain them.

Regardless, the past ten minutes had taught him one thing, and he definitely wasn't happy about it. Mary wasn't his problem; Rebecca was. And he wasn't going to be right in the head until he found some way to get her out of his system.

BOOKER LEANED BACK to accept the beer he'd ordered as Rebecca cast a wary glance around the Honky Tonk. Not much excitement tonight—only two couples swaying on the dance floor to a rather tired Luther Van Dross ballad and maybe half a dozen men at the bar. But it was Friday and early yet. The tempo would pick up as the evening progressed. At a minimum, Billy Joe and Bobby would come for their usual game of darts. They visited the bar as regularly as the hired help.

She shouldn't have come.

"Why'd I let you drag me here?" she demanded, wearing sunglasses despite the dim lighting.

"It's been almost two weeks, Rebecca. You can't hide forever."

Rebecca would've argued that she wasn't hiding from anything. Except she knew she'd never convince Booker. Buddy had broken off their engagement for good just two days after Josh had called him, nearly two weeks ago. On impulse, she'd taken some time off work and scarcely gotten out of bed since then—except to go outside and smoke. Her attempt to quit had failed at precisely the moment her hope of marriage to Buddy disappeared.

"I'm fine," she insisted, reaching for the pack of cigarettes she'd dropped onto the table when they first arrived.

She knew Booker thought she should quit, because she really *wanted* to quit. But he made no attempt to stop her.

"So how's this gonna be good for me?" she asked as she lit up. "Are you going to psychoanalyze me or something?"

He lit his own cigarette. "I thought it couldn't hurt to listen to a little music, play some pool."

She took a sip of the margarita the waitress had delivered with Booker's beer. "I don't feel like playing pool."

"What do you feel like doing?"

"Nothing."

"That would explain why you haven't been working."

Rebecca looked around the bar, hoping for a distraction. She didn't really want to talk about the past two weeks. The argument she'd had with Buddy was still too fresh in her mind. He'd said his mother was coming to visit him. She'd said she wanted to meet her. He'd told her now wasn't the time. She'd felt hurt and rejected and accused him of stalling. He'd said there wasn't any point in "rocking the boat" since they weren't even getting married anytime soon. And things had escalated from there.

"I'm going back to work on Tuesday, if it makes you feel any better," she said.

"That's good." He rested his elbows on the table. "Katie's been worried about you."

Although Rebecca doubted he'd ever admit it, Booker was probably more worried than anyone, except perhaps Delaney, who'd called incessantly. "If you say so."

"When did you tell everyone at the salon about Buddy?" he asked.

"I dropped by the day after it happened. I had to. I needed Katie and Erma to cover my appointments. And someone had to train Ashleigh, the new girl," she said, making circles in the condensation from her glass. "Besides, I figured the sooner I let the truth out, the better. Everyone will have their laugh, then I'll face them all on Tuesday."

Someone started the jukebox and an old rock song by AC/DC vibrated through the room. "No one's laughing," Booker said.

Rebecca didn't answer.

"Have you told your father?"

Giving up on drawing circles, she scowled at her wet finger, wiped it on her jeans and nodded.

"And?"

"He was too upset about Josh's truck to give the lack of a wedding a second thought." She assumed a deep, booming voice. "'For hell's sake, I'm the mayor around here, Becky. What did you think you were doing? You could've gone to jail, dammit. When are you gonna grow up and realize you can't get away with making an ass of yourself at every opportunity?'" She shrugged as carelessly as she could manage. "You know the litany."

"Litany?"

She laughed. "Never mind."

"Doyle lives in a world of absolutes," Booker said, surprising her by commenting further on the subject. "He doesn't understand you."

"He doesn't *want* to understand me," she replied. "In any case, he's right, I guess. What I did to Josh's truck was pretty bad."

"It was an accident."

"We shouldn't have gone out there in the first place."

Booker squinted at her through the smoke of his cigarette. "If Buddy means so much to you, why don't you call him back? You could ask him for a second chance."

Rebecca shook her head adamantly. "No."

"Why not?"

"He doesn't want to talk to me."

"How do you know?"

She stubbed out her cigarette. "Because of what I did to Josh's truck."

Booker had been about to take another drink of beer, but now he set his mug on the table. "How does he know about Josh's truck?"

Rebecca sipped her own drink. "Word spreads fast in this town."

"Buddy doesn't live in this town."

She discovered a sudden interest in those dancing.

"Who told him, Beck?"

She ignored him.

He nudged her. "Beck? Who told him?"

"I did," she admitted at last.

"And why did you do that?"

She slung one arm over the back of her chair, feeling belligerent. "I just don't see any point in pretending to be something I'm not. Buddy's mother said he could never be too cautious, and I told him she was right to be worried about me, that I'll be making three-hundred-dollar-a-month payments to Josh Hill for quite some time."

"And that's why he broke it off?"

"Maybe."

"So what Josh did wasn't enough. You had to finish the job?"

"Quit harassing me," she said. "If Buddy and his precious mother don't want a woman like me to wear his ring, I'd rather find out now than when I'm living in the middle of Nebraska."

"You *wanted* him to break it off."

Rebecca scowled at the accusation. "Of course I didn't."

"Then why didn't you wait to tell him about the fire until everything calmed down?"

"One call from Josh, and Buddy would've found out. He's afraid of marriage, so I thought he should see the real me. I needed to know if he could take it." Rebecca heard her voice wobble and used the excuse of pushing her sunglasses up on her nose to give herself a moment. "Obviously, he couldn't."

"Right."

"What? I didn't end it on purpose," Rebecca said at his knowing expression.

Booker sipped at his beer, then licked the foam off his top lip. "We both know better than that."

"I can't believe you think I purposely blew up my engagement!"

He winked at her, gave a little salute and took another drink of beer.

"I did no such thing!" She drew some more circles in the moisture on the table, then added, "Buddy wouldn't have been happy with me, anyway."

The door opened and a brisk wind whipped into the room. Rebecca looked up to see Mary Thornton, accompanied by her usual entourage. She knew Booker had seen her, too, when he muttered one of his favorite expletives.

"Let's go," he said.

Rebecca took another drink of her margarita and made a dismissive motion with her hand. "I'm not going to leave just because Mary's here. I have no problem with Mary. I have no problem with Josh, either."

Booker cocked a doubtful eyebrow at her as Mary made a beeline for their table, her clique trooping after her.

"I ran into Dilma Greene at the gas station a couple of days ago," she said as soon as she was close enough to speak. "She said it was you who set fire to Josh's truck. Is that true?"

Those at nearby tables turned to gawk, probably shocked to witness the perfect Mary Thornton exhibiting such negative emotion in public.

Rebecca clamped her jaw shut so she wouldn't vent the frustration that had been boiling just beneath the surface since Buddy first mentioned his great-aunt and her father set up that silly truce between her and Josh. Her knuckles went white, but she made sure the words that came out of her mouth were admirably civil. "I've apologized about the truck, and I'm going to pay for it."

"*Why* would you set fire to anyone's truck, let alone Josh's?" Mary demanded.

Rebecca shrugged. "Ask Josh."

"I have. He says he doesn't know."

"Then neither do I."

Mary's eyes narrowed. "You think you can get away with anything," she said, her voice dripping with disgust. "When the rest of us were in school, you'd go joyriding in your father's Lincoln. When the rest of us were learning survival skills on the eighth-grade camp-out, you were tossing Josh's wallet down the toilet of the outhouse to see if he'd go after it. When we were decorating the floats for Homecoming, you were—"

"It wasn't your truck," Booker cut in. "So why don't you let Josh and Rebecca deal with the problem?"

"Josh's stuff is as good as hers," someone behind Mary piped up.

Mary's expression faltered for a moment when she glanced at Booker. But then she folded her arms and drew herself up to her fullest height. "You stay out of this," she said primly.

"Or what?" He chuckled.

Mary didn't seem to have an answer, so she turned back to Rebecca. "What you did really upset Josh. He called me in the middle of the night, acting strange. I couldn't figure out what was going on. Then the next day, he couldn't even—" another of her friends snickered from behind, which seemed to make Mary rethink what she was about to say "—well, he wasn't himself. He hasn't been himself ever since."

"If it makes you feel any better, he's already gotten his revenge," Rebecca said.

"I heard Buddy broke up with you," Mary replied. "And I can understand why he would. Lord knows we were all surprised he wanted to marry you in the first place. But what happened between you and Buddy doesn't have anything to do with Josh."

"Doesn't it?" Rebecca said. Then she got up and shoved past Mary and her friends, suddenly eager for the open space and cool air of the outdoors.

CHAPTER SIXTEEN

JOSH WAS JUST GETTING OUT of the old Suburban he was driving now, which was normally one of the ranch vehicles, when he spotted Mary's brown Camry across the Honky Tonk's parking lot. He hadn't planned on seeing her this weekend. After the incident in his office two weeks ago, he'd told her he wanted to take some time off, maybe go skiing with his brother for a few days. But his brother hadn't been interested in leaving town—at least not with him. Mike was seeing a woman from McCall he'd met at a horse show. He'd probably spend the night with her, if not the entire weekend, just like he had last week. Which left Josh pretty much on his own. He'd considered calling his old buddies Randy and Dexter. But they were both married now, and he wasn't sure he could take any more talk about kids and wives and positive discipline and whether or not perpetuating the myth of Santa Claus damaged a six-year-old's psyche. Lately, when he was with them, he felt like an apple that had been left on the tree through the winter.

He could change that, he thought, eyeing Mary's car again. Mary was a nice person. She claimed to love him, and she had a great son. If he became Ricky's stepdad, he could go right into coaching Little league and soccer with Randy and Dexter, instead of starting at the very beginning, with a squalling bundle that did little more than eat and sleep.

Raising Ricky appealed to him more than anything else about living with Mary. He certainly didn't care for her parents. They still doted on their only daughter, treated her as though she was barely sixteen. But hey, lots of people didn't like their in-laws. He could tolerate having Gene and Barb over for various holidays. If only he could see himself feeling anxious to tell Mary about his day. If only he could see himself wanting to make love to her over and over again, the way he wanted to make love to Rebecca....

Besides, if he didn't want to hold Mary now, didn't even really want to see her, how was marriage going to change that?

It's just too soon. I'm trying to force it when I need to give myself time. We'll fall in love eventually, and then we'll marry and everyone will be happy.

They were perfect for each other. Everyone said so, even his own parents.

Golden Boy marries Golden Girl... Rebecca's words niggled at the back of his mind, but he pushed them away. Now that he'd talked himself into proposing to Mary—eventually—he couldn't see any reason to avoid her tonight. He might as well go in, he decided. He had nothing better to do.

The snap of a twig drew his attention to the back of the building. Someone stood in the shadows beyond the Honky Tonk's floodlights, at the edge of the dirt and gravel that comprised the bar's overflow lot. Someone who seemed sort of familiar...

He closed the Suburban's door and sauntered closer, but by the time he reached the walkway, whoever was lurking behind the bar had disappeared into the darkness. He wondered where he or she had gone but didn't think much about it until he rounded the corner of the building and nearly ran into Booker Robinson coming out the front entrance.

They both stepped back and regarded each other warily. "Where did she go?" Booker asked, his voice clipped.

"Who?" Josh asked.

"Rebecca."

Immediately Josh thought of the person behind the building, remembered the flicker of recognition he'd experienced and knew it had to be her. But he didn't want to give her location away before finding out what had driven her into the cold. "I don't know. Why? What's wrong?"

Booker slanted him a withering glare. "Why don't you ask your girlfriend?"

"Did Mary say something to her?" he asked, alarmed to think that she might have involved herself. He and Rebecca had enough difficulty keeping peace between them without the interference of others.

Booker didn't answer. He was too busy scanning the area. Then he brushed past, straddled his bike and roared out of the lot.

Josh let him go. He needed to talk to Rebecca, had wrestled with himself over calling her ever since she'd set fire to his truck, and figured now was as good a time as any. At least he knew they'd be alone. For a while, at least.

Shoving his hands in the pockets of his coat, he walked to the back edge of the building. There he leaned against the corner and searched the darkness until he made out the shape of someone sitting on a fallen log in the frosty grass.

"Booker's looking for you," he said. He knew his voice had carried across the distance, but he received no answer.

"Come on, Rebecca. I know you're there."

"Maybe I want to be alone," she said.

If she didn't want to be with Booker, she sure as hell wouldn't want to be with him, especially after everything that had happened. But Josh couldn't bring himself to leave. He had something he wanted to say, something he hoped would finally erase the image of tears streaming down her face.

"I want to talk," he said.

"We don't have anything to say to each other. I'll make my first payment at the end of the month."

"This isn't about the money."

"Then what?"

He crossed the gravel lot and lowered himself onto the log, careful not to sit too close for fear he'd chase her off. "Bit dark for those, don't you think?" he said when he saw she was wearing sunglasses.

She shrugged.

"Mary told me about Buddy," he said. "I hope you know I never planned for that to happen."

"That's exactly what you wanted," she said. "Why else would you have called him?"

That was a good question. One Josh couldn't answer simply. He *hadn't* wanted to hurt her. He knew that much. He'd just wanted to...what? What could he possibly have hoped to achieve?

"I didn't think it would go that far," he said, resting his elbows on his knees.

"Well, it did. And now you can gloat."

"I'm not gloating." Truth be told, he felt lousy, deluged by a jumble of emotions he was half-afraid to name. Guilt played a part, of course, for causing Rebecca so much pain. But he envied Buddy, too. After only a few short months, Buddy had been able to capture Rebecca's heart—all of it, judging by how upset she seemed over the breakup. He, on the other hand, hadn't been able to garner anything more than her dislike, and that was after twenty-some years. Even when they weren't fighting, even when he tried the charm that generally worked on other women, she wanted nothing to do with him.

The only exception was that night almost fifteen months ago. If not for those few minutes in her arms, he probably wouldn't care so much. He wouldn't know what he was missing, would never have dared hope he could breach her defenses. But now Rebecca was all he thought about, and it angered him that he cared, that he had to talk himself into seeing Mary, that he had to rely on the expectation of coaching Ricky to make marrying her palatable.

Picking up a smooth, round rock, he tossed it into the trees. "I want to call another truce," he said.

"There's no need. I'm not going to do anything to you. You can go ahead and move on with your life and never think of me again."

How he wished it could be that easy. He'd tried putting her out of his mind, but no amount of effort seemed to make that possible. Thoughts of her came to him at the damnedest moments—like when he was trying to make love to Mary.

"Then what about being friends?"

"That didn't work out so well the last time."

He tossed another rock and listened to it bounce along the ground until it came to a skittering halt. "Well, whether you agree to be friends or not, I don't want any money for the truck. I started the fight, I'll accept the loss."

Rebecca remained still and silent for so long, Josh turned to see if she'd somehow slipped away into the trees. The rustling of his coat as he moved was the only noise, besides the music drifting toward them from the Honky Tonk. But she was still there, hugging herself for warmth and staring out across the parking lot.

"Are you sure?" she finally said without turning to look at him.

"I'm sure."

"That should make my father happy," she said, but the sarcasm in her voice told Josh the statement wasn't as straightforward as it sounded.

"We wouldn't want to disappoint Doyle."

"You couldn't disappoint Doyle. He's always thought you walked on water."

Josh considered this, weighed it against other comments Rebecca and her father had made in the past and had to ask, "Is that what you hold against me, Beck?"

She stiffened. "Of course not. My father likes a lot of people I don't. And he doesn't like a lot of people I do. Take me, for instance," she said with an unconvincing laugh. "Anyway, you can't help how others feel about you any more than I can."

"You don't really believe that, do you?"

"That you can't help how others feel about you?"

"That your father doesn't like you."

"I can't throw a football," she said with a shrug, as though that should explain everything.

"What's football got to do with anything?"

"You'd be surprised."

Josh found another rock and threw it after the first two. Rebecca had never been easy to figure out, and she wasn't proving any easier now. "Are you going to explain it to me?"

"No."

"Then tell me why you hate me so much. How am I any worse than Booker?"

"You're not any—" she started, then stopped. "What does it matter?" she said, instead. "Everyone else has always adored you. You've never needed me."

What if he needed her now? Would that make any difference?

Josh closed his eyes and thought of the night he'd held her in his arms, tried to recapture her subtle scent. But she was too far away and too bundled up. He could only smell the cold air and damp earth.

"What about last summer when I took you home from here?" he asked, despite the warnings in his head telling him not to bring up that subject again. He knew Rebecca would rather not acknowledge the fact that they'd almost made love. He knew it would be smarter for him to pretend the incident had never occurred. But...he had so many questions. Why had their lovemaking felt so right, even though they'd always been enemies? Why had she responded to him as greedily as if she'd lost her heart to him years ago? Why had the feel of her soft, bare skin, the feel of her arching into him, turned him on like nothing he'd ever experienced? And why had she eventually shut him out? Sure, his brother had come home, but Mike wouldn't have bothered them. "Beck?"

"What about it?" she responded, sounding leery.

"You didn't seem to mind me so much then."

Her shrug looked a little forced, but Josh couldn't be sure. "We didn't know what we were doing, remember?" she said. "We were both drunk."

He picked a blade of grass and stuck it between his teeth. "I wasn't," he admitted. Then he got up and strode away so he wouldn't have to stare into her dark lenses and see only himself staring back.

REBECCA PROBABLY WOULD HAVE sat outside the Honky Tonk for hours, if Booker hadn't returned to search for her. The coldness numbed her hands and her feet, but it also seemed to numb her senses, diminishing her desire for a cigarette and slowing the process of her mind to a crawl so she could carefully examine each thought. Only a month ago, she'd been poring through bridal magazines and planning her new life in Nebraska.

Now she'd be picking up her old life just where she'd left it, knowing she might never escape Dundee or her past mistakes. She would watch Josh, her father's standard of the perfect son, continue to be successful. He'd probably marry and have children while she remained single and cut hair until her back ached each day just to bring home enough to cover her living expenses.

But life didn't always go as planned. She, of all people, understood that. She wasn't going to grovel, wouldn't even try to convince Buddy she was worthy of his love. She hadn't done anything to *him*. And she'd already made her peace with Josh.

So why did peace between them still feel like war? She couldn't figure it out.

The loud rumble of a motorcycle drowned out the strains of a Travis Tritt song coming from the Honky Tonk, announcing Booker's return long before his headlight arced into the lot.

There were a few good things about staying in Dundee. One, she knew the others at the salon well enough to ensure that Mary Thornton never received a decent haircut in the future. And two, she still had her friends, Booker and Delaney. Booker would need some help taking care of Hatty. She was too high-maintenance for one person. And Delaney would need some help taking care of the baby, due in only a couple of weeks.

Standing, she dusted off her pants and started for the motorcycle before Booker could park and head back into the Honky Tonk. "You looking for me?"

He cut the engine. "What do you think?"

"Sorry. I've been having a little heart-to-heart with Josh Hill."

"I don't see any blood," he said, removing his helmet long enough to study her. "That's a good sign."

"We called another truce."

"You're smiling," he pointed out. "Must've been some truce."

"I'm smiling because he forgave my thirty-thousand-dollar debt."

His eyebrows shot up. "What does that tell you?"

"That I don't have to pay for the Excursion."

This statement met with a few seconds of silence before Booker went on. "Actually, it says a lot more than that." He zipped his leather coat. "But it doesn't matter, right? You don't like him. He's still the bad guy."

"Right."

Booker smiled and handed her a helmet. "Feels good to let someone else be the bad guy for a change. But I've never seen two people fight something as hard as you're both fighting this."

"I don't know what you're talking about."

"Sure you do."

"No, I don't," she said, hoping he'd let the subject drop.

He didn't. "Then why don't you do yourself a favor and prove me wrong?"

Warning bells went off in Rebecca's head, but she was curious enough to press the issue. "How?"

"Treat Josh as if you like him for a change and see what happens."

"Nothing would happen. Except he'd think I'm certifiable."

"Chicken," he said.

Rebecca felt a scowl coming on. "I'm not chicken."

He started the engine. "In that case you don't have anything to lose, right?"

"Right," she said slowly, because there wasn't a better answer. But she wasn't so sure.

JOSH LOOKED AT Mary as she sat across from him at the diner. They'd never made any promises to each other, yet it felt as though they'd been married for years. Not the steady, abiding, mutual respect kind of married. The "where did love go?" kind of married. The kind where a husband and wife wake up one morning, take a hard look at each other and realize they no longer have any reason to continue sharing the rent, never mind the rest of their lives.

He let his gaze fall to Ricky, who was sitting in the booth beside his mother. Ricky was a great kid. Josh hated to ruin Mary's very obvious plan to give him a father for Christmas. But he wasn't completely convinced that a permanent connection to Mary was the best way to participate in Ricky's future. He could be a friend, a mentor, maybe an uncle...

Why he'd had such a sudden change of heart, he couldn't say. It wasn't five nights ago he'd decided, at the Honky Tonk, that he would marry her. Eventually. Then she'd entered the restaurant and approached his booth this morning and he'd suddenly known: he didn't love her the way a husband should love a wife and time wasn't going to change that.

On the one hand, it was a relief to finally achieve some clarity. On the other, he knew he was going to disappoint a lot of people—Mary more than anyone. A part of him still wondered if he wouldn't be better off settling for less love and more peace—because the only woman who remotely tempted him was Rebecca—but he now knew that was a risk he'd have to take.

Maybe nothing had changed, after all. Maybe he just didn't like what his heart had been telling him....

"Can I go horseback riding today?" Ricky asked, his mouth jammed full of pancake, interrupting Josh's thoughts.

"Swallow before you talk, baby," Mary said.

Josh considered all the things he had to accomplish over the course of his day. The breeding season was nearly upon them; the mares they were trying to breed would be kept under lights beginning in early December, to create a false spring and thereby bring them into heat early, and he had a lot of preparation to do before that. A client from Nevada was supposed to arrive around noon with ten mares. Josh wanted to be there to greet him and introduce him to his stud manager. After that, Conner Armstrong had scheduled a meeting to discuss the progress of the Running Y Resort, in which Josh and Mike were large investors. Paperwork was piling up at the office—the registration papers for various foals from last season, a limited partnership he was trying to put together to buy yet another stallion. And Mike was out of town attending a horse show, drumming up more business. Josh didn't really have time to take Ricky riding, but his determination to maintain some type of relationship with the boy, and guilt for what he was about to tell his mother, made him say yes.

"Yippee!" Ricky cried the moment he heard his response. Wriggling out of the booth by slipping beneath the table, he turned and held out his palm. "Can I have a quarter for the vending machine?"

The vending machine by the exit sported cheap rings, chains, gum and candy, and Ricky insisted on getting a plastic prize-filled bubble every time they came to the diner. But a few quarters was a small price to pay for a little privacy. Now that Josh knew there was no hope for him and Mary, it was unkind and useless to string her along.

"Here you go," he said, handing Ricky every quarter in his pocket and several dollars he could change at the register. "Have fun."

Mary smiled as her son ran off, obviously pleased with his generosity. "You spoil him," she said.

He didn't spoil Ricky the way Mary did. At least he didn't coddle him. But what she did with her son suddenly seemed like none of his business, so he didn't comment. "We need to talk, Mary," he said.

She brightened, and Josh feared his serious tone had misled her into believing he was finally going to propose.

"About what?" she asked, folding her hands neatly on the table.

"About us."

She sat up taller, her smile widening. "I think it's about time we did."

Josh winced as her blue eyes met his and he read the hope and excitement there. "This is going to be difficult," he admitted.

She glanced over at Ricky, who was kneeling in front of the vending machine, pumping one quarter into it after another and eagerly opening each prize as soon as it dropped into the bin. "Why will it be difficult?" she asked. "You can say anything to me. I probably know you better than anyone."

She gave him an intimate smile, and Josh had the impression she was referring to the day in his office when she'd offered him a quickie, and he hadn't followed through. They hadn't had sex since then. She must be wondering what was going on with him. He'd been wondering himself.

"I think we should stop seeing each other," he said, hoping the more quickly he dispensed the bad news, the less it would hurt her.

She blinked at him and made a valiant effort to keep smiling. "You're joking, aren't you? Everyone knows we're perfect for each other. We should've married years ago, right out of high school. But then I got involved with that lousy Glen, and—"

He reached for her hand. "We're not going to get married," he said. "It's taken me too long to figure it out, I know. And for that, I apologize."

"But things have been going so well between us," she said, her voice bordering on shrill. "I mean, if this is about that little incident in your office a couple weeks ago…well, you can't blame me. I mean—"

"That has nothing to do with it, Mary. I just realized that…that we're better off as friends."

Her fingers curled until he could feel her nails digging into his hand. "You can't mean that. You've been under a lot of stress lately, that's all. You're making a rash decision."

Josh knew his decision was anything but rash. But Ricky was back already, his mouth jammed with gumballs, his pockets filled with toys and candy. He was watching his mother curiously. Josh thought maybe he should let it go for now. "We can talk about it later," he said.

Her fingers didn't relax their death-grip. "We've invested more than seven months in each other, Josh. That doesn't disappear in a two-minute conversation."

He looked uncomfortably at Ricky, who'd turned soulful eyes in his direction. "I realize that."

"So you'll think about it? You'll think about it long and hard before you destroy something that was meant to be?"

"Mary, I've—" he started, but Ricky was beginning to frown and ask what they were talking about, and the waitress was hovering at the table next to them, removing dirty dishes, so Josh simply shrugged and said, "Sure."

Mary smiled in relief. "I can make you change your mind," she said. "Do you want me to come over tonight?"

More party favors. "No. I'll call you though, okay?"

"Okay." She glanced around and lowered her voice. "I know I can make you happy."

Gathering her purse, she grabbed Ricky's hand and dragged him out the door just as Judy brought the check.

"Would you like anything else?" she asked Josh, holding a coffee pot in one hand.

An escape from Mary without hurting her, Josh thought. But there wasn't a thing anyone could do to arrange that, so he slid his cup toward her and doubled up on caffeine.

CHAPTER SEVENTEEN

JOSH DIDN'T KNOW what to do with himself. He'd tried to call Mary every evening since Wednesday, but her mother always said she wasn't home. He suspected there'd been several times when she really *was* there, and refused to come to the phone for fear of what he might say. But he couldn't exactly accuse her mother of lying....

Oh well, he wasn't keen on speaking to Mary tonight, anyway. There was no reason to break things off in a hurry. If Mary needed a few more days to accept his decision, he could wait.

That didn't solve the problem of what he should do with his night, however. He'd been busy the past couple of days catching up on paperwork in his office. His eyes were tired and his shoulders ached, but he wasn't quite ready for bed. Not yet. It was only ten o'clock on Friday night, for crying out loud. He was freshly single—not that he'd ever really been attached—and felt like going out. But there weren't a lot of places to go in Dundee. And he didn't have a lot of single friends to hang out with anymore.

He considered his short list of possibilities before picking up the phone. Who said a man had to be single to go out for a drink?

"YOU'RE SMILING at Josh Hill again," Delaney complained.

Rebecca shifted her attention to the couples moving on

the dance floor. Delaney had called a few hours earlier and insisted, since Conner was visiting his grandfather in California for the weekend, that the two of them have a ladies' night out. Rebecca highly doubted her friend had had the Honky Tonk in mind when she'd suggested getting together, but Rebecca had been thinking about Booker and his challenge to treat Josh nicely for a change. Part of her believed that Booker was wrong—Josh hated her as much as he ever had. The other part kept acting like a tape recorder, playing, rewinding and replaying her last conversation with Josh. Especially the bit where he admitted he hadn't been drunk that night at his house.

They certainly had some unresolved issues. She felt it was time to give Josh a wink and a smile—to act as if they actually were friends. And maybe find out what that summer night was all about...

Fate seemed to second her opinion. He'd appeared tonight.

Of course, Delaney didn't know she'd changed tactics where Josh was concerned. In case things worked out badly, Rebecca didn't plan on telling her.

"I'm not smiling at Josh," she said.

"You were. I saw you," Delaney argued. "You've been glancing his way ever since he came in. And he keeps looking over here, too."

"So? We're just being friendly. We've called another truce."

"This is more than friendly. This is flirting."

Rebecca turned and dropped another quarter in the jukebox. "Will you stop? We're not flirting."

Delaney propped a hand on what was left of her hip, and motioned with her head toward the far wall, where Josh stood next to a couple of married friends and their wives.

"He's staring at you right now. See? Wait…he saw me watching and looked the other way."

"He's probably just wondering where Conner is," Rebecca said.

"He's probably wondering how you could set fire to his truck three weeks ago and be smiling so coyly at him now," Delaney replied.

Rebecca adjusted the black leather miniskirt she'd worn for maximum impact. "I don't think he's holding a grudge," she said and chose a song by Tammy Wynette.

"Am I missing something here?" Delaney asked. "What's happened between the two of you since you killed his truck?"

"Nothing." Rebecca widened her eyes and spread her hands palms up so she'd appear innocent. "Really. I apologized for…the accident, and he forgave me. That's it."

"So where's Mary? She's usually here when Josh is, but I haven't seen her tonight."

"How should I know?" Rebecca said. "Mary and I aren't exactly friends."

Delaney opened her mouth to say something else, but just then Billy Joe and Bobby squeezed through the crowd. "Hey, Laney," Bobby said. "How's that bun in the oven?"

"Doctor says the baby's doing great," Delaney said.

"Glad to hear it. How much longer?"

"Just another week or so."

Bobby shook his head. "Jeez, that went quick."

Billy Joe didn't even acknowledge Delaney. He was too busy whistling at Rebecca's outfit to pay any attention to a woman nearly nine months pregnant. "That's some skirt, honey," he said, his ruddy face creasing in an appreciative grin. "What do you say we give it a whirl?"

"Fine by me," Rebecca said, and let him lead her onto

the dance floor. Soon Bobby and Delaney were dancing next to them and, for a moment, it felt like old times. Good times.

Rebecca started to relax. Buddy might have dumped her, but she wasn't without options. And right now, her options weren't looking bad. Booker had driven Granny Hatfield to Boise for the day and probably hadn't returned yet, so he wouldn't even have to know she'd taken him up on his little challenge. Apparently, Mary had other plans for the evening, as well. And here was Josh, all by his lonesome....

She smiled at him yet again. She knew he had to be surprised that she'd suddenly turned on the charm. He'd been watching her with a mixture of distrust and curiosity all evening. But if she kept this up, his curiosity would soon overtake his distrust, and that might be enough to get her what she wanted. One night. Just enough time to satisfy the craving he'd created more than a year ago.

THE MYSTERIOUS SMILE Rebecca gave him whenever their eyes met proved too much for Josh. He broke down and asked her to dance, despite all his resolutions. But he was trying to hold her at a respectable distance. She was the one who kept moving closer, all soft and cuddly, her hair smelling like rain and her skin glowing in the dim light. She felt so damn good that before long his hands slid down to curl over her behind and keep her right where she was. Somehow it seemed as though she *belonged* this close.

"Now this is the kind of truce I like," he murmured, feeling desire lick through his veins. He automatically recalled the taste of Rebecca's kiss, and became obsessed with her mouth. His gaze lingered on her lips, then took in the green eyes that slanted up at him so mischievously— and all the blood in his head began to head south at a record rate. Maybe it was this phenomenon that was costing him the ability to reason, but he couldn't figure out what, exactly, had changed between them. Why were they in each other's arms? Alcohol certainly had nothing to do with it this time. They hadn't been at the Honky Tonk long enough to get drunk.

Yet, here they were, clinging to each other as if they couldn't get close enough. It took all of Josh's self-restraint not to bend Rebecca over his arm and kiss her as if there was no one else in the world, regardless of the fact that they were in a public place.

"I never thought we could stick to a truce," she said, pressing her cheek to his shoulder. "But I think this is going to work out just fine."

"Beats the hell out of finding pincher bugs in my locker," he responded. Then, just because she was molded so perfectly to his body and he couldn't resist, he traced the curve of her ear with the tip of his tongue very subtly, so no one could see.

She shivered and melted into him and he began to think about how badly he wanted another chance to have Rebecca in his bed....

He slipped his thumb under her blouse to lightly graze the soft skin at her waist. "You feel good, Beck."

"I could feel better," she said, her fingers playing with the hair at the nape of his neck.

"Is that an invitation?" he asked.

"What do you think?"

"It sounded like an invitation to me."

She nearly leveled him with a temptress's smile. "Didn't we start something a year ago that we never finished?"

Josh blinked at her. "You didn't want to finish."

"Can't a girl change her mind?"

His first impulse was to take Rebecca by the arm and steer her out of the Honky Tonk and straight to the old

Suburban he was driving until the insurance check arrived and his new Escalade SUV was ready. She might have torched his Excursion, but now she was setting other things on fire—things he liked hot. Only he hadn't decided whether it was wise to take whatever was going on between them to the next level. He was supposed to be getting her out of his system, not allowing her to inflame his deepest desires. And there was Mary. He might have tried to break off their relationship, but she hadn't really accepted it.

"I don't know. The night's young," he said, stalling. *If I have half a brain, I'll run out of here as fast as my legs can carry me.*

She tilted her head back to look up at him and he caught a faint whiff of spearmint and alcohol on her breath. Liking the scent, he bent closer, giving her a brief kiss. The tavern was dark and smoky, the music loud, creating the illusion of privacy. Still, nothing in Dundee went unnoticed. He just couldn't make himself pull away. Every dream, every fantasy he'd ever had centered on Rebecca.

"That's no answer," she said.

He tightened his embrace. "What exactly do you have in mind? Your sudden departure last time wasn't particularly enjoyable. I'd like to know a little earlier if you're going to bail out on me."

"That depends," she said.

"On what?"

"On how things go."

Nothing about Rebecca was ever easy. Even when *she* propositioned *him,* he couldn't tie her down. But he had to admit that her unpredictable nature was part of her allure.

Of course, that same trait could bring even a strong man to his knees....

"What about Delaney?" he asked, although his conscience was screaming, "What about *Mary?*"

Rebecca arched her brows, her expression world-wise and slightly cynical, yet feminine in the extreme. God, there was something about this woman he craved.

"She can't come with us," she said.

"You're going to leave her here?"

"She's nine months pregnant, due in a week. She'll be more than happy to go home early."

"Are you going to tell her you're leaving with me?" he asked, nuzzling her neck.

Another sexy smile. "No. That'll be our little secret."

Her voice had turned husky. Josh felt his groin tighten as he tried to read what was going on behind her eyes. Was she setting him up? It wasn't like Rebecca to be this nice, this…open. At least to him. If he took her home, would she make love with him tonight, then spit in his face tomorrow?

Chances were she would. But tomorrow suddenly seemed very far away.

"So?" she asked. "What do you say?"

What *did* he say? Getting together with Rebecca after someone as steady as Mary would be like trading the safety of the bunny hill for the steep depths of the hardest ski run on the mountain. With Rebecca, he'd go careening down the slopes, gathering speed until he was flying through uncharted territory with only a vague idea of the obstacles and pitfalls he might encounter. Life would be anything but safe or secure. But it would be exciting. And somehow he knew, for better or for worse, that this was the woman he could love for the rest of his life.

He'd never been a big fan of the bunny hill, anyway.

Taking a deep, decisive breath, he brushed a quick kiss across her forehead. "I have to do something," he said. "Send Delaney home, and meet me outside in fifteen minutes."

Then he called Mary, insisted her mother let him talk to her when she tried to say Mary wasn't home, and broke the news as gently as he could. On his way out, he told his brother to get a hotel. After what happened a year ago, he wasn't about to risk another interruption. Not tonight. Tonight Rebecca was his.

REBECCA ANGLED HER HEAD to better receive Josh's kiss and buried her hands in his hair, which was thick and had just enough curl to give it body. He smelled of the leather coat he'd been wearing, and some sort of aftershave. Taken together with the feel of his bare chest against her naked breasts, the sensation was overwhelming. She could scarcely breathe for the desire that threatened to consume her.

This was nothing like it had been with Buddy. Nothing at all, she thought dimly. Thank God she hadn't settled.... She wouldn't have wanted to miss something like this.

It occurred to her that Josh was the reason she hadn't settled, but she didn't want to give him too much credit, not when he'd interfered in her life just to hurt her.

He rolled her beneath him on the bed, covering her with his big body even though he still had on his pants and she her skirt, and angled his hips so that she could feel the delicious pressure of him. She wrapped her legs around him to draw him closer, feminine satisfaction heightening her pleasure when he groaned and deepened his kiss.

"You kiss so well," he said, running his tongue lightly over her bottom lip and tugging it gently into his mouth.

She could've said the same to him, but she was too busy reveling in his solid weight anchoring her to the mattress. If he did other things half as well as he kissed, she had a lot to look forward to. The next few minutes would finally put an end to the curiosity and yearning she'd experienced for so long.

"Do you like this?" he asked, gently suckling one breast, then holding it so he could witness her nipple's response in the light from the hall. She watched him, strangely captivated by the eroticism of what he was doing.

"Do you?" he prompted.

She let her lips curve into a smile and nodded.

"Then say it. I want to hear you say it," he said, gazing at her with half-lidded eyes that made him look lazy and relaxed even though she could feel the tautness of his body.

"I like it," she muttered, her breath ragged.

"You want more?"

"Um-hum."

"Tell me what else you'd like."

"You want to hear me talk dirty?"

"No, I want to hear you say you want *me*," he said. "That it wouldn't be the same with anyone else. That no one else will do."

Rebecca felt far more comfortable with the purely physical. The physical she could close off when she needed to; it didn't threaten her. But he was asking her to combine the sharing of pleasure with something far more personal, and she couldn't do that. She wouldn't bare her soul for Josh Hill. She had certain defenses against him she refused to tear down, even now, and precisely because she *did* want him, and only him, inside her, meant she could never say what he insisted on hearing.

"I wouldn't have let you bring me home if I didn't want to be here," she said, skirting the issue.

He leaned up on his elbows, a frown on his face. "That's the best you can do?" he asked, sliding one hand beneath her skirt. "Come on, Becky. I want to hear you say my name. I want to be sure you know it's *me* who's making you writhe and cry out.''

When she said nothing, his hand stopped its gradual ascent on her thigh. ''Beck?''

''Josh, let's...let's not play games,'' she said hoarsely. ''It's not as though we have any illusions about each other, right?''

He pulled his hand away. ''What illusions are you talking about?''

''That anything will ever come of this. I mean, we've been enemies too long for that.''

His eyes grew watchful in a different way. ''So what are we now?''

Rebecca paused. She could tell this was suddenly veering off-course, but she couldn't figure out how to steer it back without giving too much of herself away. Was he hoping for some type of confession that would finally cede him the victory of the battle that had waged between them since they were kids? Because she could never give him that. She'd held a grudge against Josh Hill for twenty-four years, and she wasn't going to let it slip away now. It was her talisman, her protection from the devastating charm he used to conquer everyone else, her only insurance that he would never find her wanting as her father always had. ''For the moment we're lovers, I guess,'' she said.

''For the moment.''

A foreboding note had entered his voice. It made Rebecca a little uncomfortable. ''Yeah.''

''And in the morning?''

''Look, let's not talk, okay? That'll ruin everything. Tonight is tonight, and tomorrow is tomorrow.'' She reached for the zipper of his jeans, eager to get back to what she'd been enjoying so much, but he pushed her hand away.

"What's wrong?" she asked. "Why'd you bring me here if this isn't want you want?"

"It is what I want."

"Then what's wrong? What are you waiting for? I want the same thing."

He shook his head. "You're not ready," he said, rolling off the bed.

Rebecca couldn't believe what she'd just heard. What the heck did he mean, *not ready?* She'd never been more ready in her life!

"What are you talking about?" she cried, sitting up and pulling the sheet over her breasts to cover herself. In the face of his sudden rejection, she felt newly vulnerable. "Is this some sort of revenge for the Excursion?"

"No."

"Are you getting back at me for walking out on you a year ago?"

"No."

"Then what? You want me as badly as I want you. You can't hide it, you know."

"I'm not trying to hide it," he said. "I've already admitted as much."

"Then why aren't you making love to me?"

"Because I want it to mean something, okay? I can sleep with anyone, but it's just another screw unless…unless you care."

"You're joking."

"I'm not. I won't touch you again until you can look me in the eye and tell me I'm the only man you want. And that you'd trade anything to have me."

Rebecca clenched the sheet with both hands. "Are you *crazy?*"

Cupping her chin, he angled her face up until they were nearly nose to nose. Rebecca thought he might kiss her again—hoped he would. Everything he'd said had to be an unkind joke. How like Josh to do this, to taunt her this way....

"Maybe I am crazy," he said, "but nothing's going to happen between us until you find the guts to take the same risk I'm willing to take. I go, you go. We jump together."

"I don't understand this," she protested.

He bent and picked up her bra and blouse from where he'd tossed them on the floor and handed them back to her. "Then I'll make it easy. If you can't care about me, I don't want anything to do with you. Now get dressed, and I'll drive you home."

OF ALL THE dirty rotten things Josh had done, Rebecca thought this one was the worst. *If you can't care about me...* As if he cared about her! As if he wasn't practically engaged to Mary Thornton! As if he'd ever want more from her than a quick tumble!

Except that he could've had his tumble, and he hadn't taken it.

Not that she cared. She didn't really want him anyway.

A pang in her chest told her she'd like nothing more, but she ignored it and continued to stare out the car window as he drove her home, wondering where she'd gone wrong. At the Honky Tonk, she'd had him eating out of her hand. She'd known he'd ask her to dance, and he did. She'd known he'd take her home, and he did. When they'd reached his place, events had taken an even better turn. So how had *he* ended up in charge?

She couldn't say exactly. It was somewhere between the time he removed her blouse and the time he started asking her to tell him things she couldn't say. Which meant she'd denied him first, right? But somehow that didn't matter.

Any way she looked at it, he'd won this little skirmish. No doubt about it.

Damn him! She'd never been able to best him. Not really.

He pulled to the side of the road in front of Granny Hatfield's and let her out without saying a word. After she slammed his door, he drove off, and a minute later she was watching his taillights disappear around the corner.

"Jerk!" she muttered, cutting across the wide front lawn to let herself in.

Booker was sleeping under a quilt on the couch, the television on, as she tried to slip through the living room. Before she could escape to her room, however, he stirred and called her name.

"Beck? That you?"

She hesitated at the foot of the stairs, afraid he might guess where she'd been. He seemed to have a sixth sense where she and Josh were concerned.

"Beck?"

"Yeah, it's me."

"Where've you been?"

"The Honky Tonk," she said, having to invest some real effort in making her voice sound happy enough.

"After I brought Granny home, I went by the Honky Tonk."

Rebecca's heart dropped to her knees. "Oh. Was Delaney still there?"

"No, but Bobby was. He said you went home with Josh."

"Josh left a few minutes before I did."

"Yeah, well, nice try. But it didn't fool anybody." He flipped off the television and rose up on one elbow. "So was it everything you thought it'd be?"

"No."

"That's too bad."

"Why?"

"Because everyone's blaming you for why he broke up with Mary. I was hoping you'd at least get something out of it."

Chills suddenly cascaded through Rebecca's entire body. "Josh broke up with Mary?"

"That's what I heard."

"When did he do that?"

"Tonight, I guess. Just before closing she came to the Honky Tonk looking for him. And she was mad as hell." Yawning, he rolled over. "I guess he didn't mention it."

"No," she said. "He didn't."

CHAPTER EIGHTEEN

"HOW'D IT GO last night?"

Rebecca blinked and sat up, wondering how she'd managed to answer the telephone in her sleep. "Delaney?"

"Your powers of perception are improving."

"What time is it?"

"Eight."

"*Eight?*" Rebecca shoved a hand through her hair and grimaced at her bleary-eyed reflection in the mirror above her dresser. "You woke me up at eight on a Saturday morning?"

"You have to work today."

"Not until eleven."

"Okay, I couldn't wait any longer to hear how things went with you and Josh last night."

Rebecca could have waited until *much* later to fill Delaney in. "I don't want to talk about it."

"That bad, huh?"

That good. Almost. "He's not...realistic," she said, knowing her complaint sounded weak. But it was difficult to come up with anything worse. Josh had been loving and attentive and sexy as hell. Everything had been perfect until he'd suddenly changed direction.

"Really?" Delaney was obviously not convinced. "I've gotten to know him a little bit through Conner and this whole resort business, and he seems pretty realistic to me.

He seems nice, too. I was actually hoping you two could find some common ground for once.''

"He's not what he seems. It's an act," Rebecca said, even though she knew it wasn't true.

"Right." Delaney chuckled. "So, did you two—"

Rebecca cut her off before she could get any more specific. "No."

"Sure seemed like things were drifting that direction when you were plastered to him on the dance floor last night."

Plastered to him on the dance floor? Rebecca rolled her eyes toward the ceiling. How many other people saw it that way? "I wasn't exactly *plastered* to him," she said.

"Any closer and you would've been inside his clothes."

Cursing her own stupidity, Rebecca flopped back onto her pillows. "That's probably what Mary heard when she arrived, then."

"How do you know Mary arrived?"

"Booker told me she came to the Honky Tonk around midnight, looking for Josh."

"Uh-oh. Did she ever find him?"

"Not while I was with him."

"Thank God for small favors. I don't know exactly what their situation is, but I know she feels pretty possessive. How long were you at his place?"

Not long enough. Rebecca pulled her covers over her head to shut out the light, wishing she could close off the memory of Josh and what had happened just as easily. "About half an hour."

"That's it? What went wrong? You're really making me curious, you know that?"

Letting her breath go in a long sigh, Rebecca turned onto her side. "We realized we're not compatible."

"After what you two have been through, that came as a surprise?"

"There is one interesting thing," she said, ignoring the sarcasm.

"What's that?"

"Apparently he broke up with Mary last night."

"He did? When?"

"According to a very reliable source, he must've done it before we went to his place."

"Oh." Delaney seemed to think this over. "Good. That was decent of him."

"I don't think Mary would agree with you."

"I don't care about Mary. I care about you."

"Well, don't get too excited. It doesn't mean anything."

"How do you know?"

"I was there," she said, even though the way Josh had behaved seemed to signify that it *might* mean something. *If you can't care about me, I don't want anything to do with you...*

"Whatever you say, Beck. I just want you to be happy."

"I am happy," she said, but it was a lie. She'd never felt more unsettled and...*slighted* in her life.

"So it's already over between you and Josh?"

"It was over before it ever started," she said, but despite everything, she couldn't help crossing her fingers that maybe, just maybe, the future would prove her wrong.

"You'll find the right man someday."

"I hope so. How's the baby?"

"Good. I'm getting close. Maybe I'll go into labor on your birthday."

"Since I'm not going to be in Cancun, I hope *something* good happens that day. A party at the Honky Tonk doesn't sound as exciting as it used to."

"Don't tell me you're getting tired of playing darts with Billy Joe and Bobby."

"I'm just ready for there to be more to life," she said.

WHEN REBECCA ANSWERED the phone several days later, she expected to hear Katie on the other end of the line. She'd overslept after a restless night, couldn't find her keys and was already fifteen minutes late for her first appointment. "I'm coming," she said without waiting for a hello. "I'll be there in five."

But it wasn't Katie's voice that came back to her. It was her father's. "Where?"

Rebecca stopped dashing through the house and set the shoes, lipstick and gum she'd gathered for her departure on the kitchen counter. "Oh, it's you."

"Is that any way to greet your father?"

"Sorry. I just wasn't expecting to hear from you." Turning toward the small bulletin board that hung on the fridge, she stared at a photograph of her entire family from last Christmas. She'd set it aside when she was cleaning out her purse, and Hatty had tacked it onto the fridge.

"Where've you been?" he asked. "Your mother wants to know why you haven't been by."

She hadn't visited since the anniversary party because she hadn't wanted to face their disappointment. Neither did she want to deal with any more criticism because of what she'd done to Josh's truck. Even if her father was finished with the subject, her sisters and brothers-in-law would want to hear all about it. They'd laugh and send knowing glances at each other and shake their heads.

"I've been busy," she said.

He grunted. "The least you could do is call once in a while."

"You could call me once in a while, too, you know. The

only time you stop by the salon is when you want me to cut your hair.''

"Yeah, well, we're both busy. So what's going on? Are you in some sort of trouble?''

"What makes you think that?''

"We haven't had any crises in the last few weeks. We're about due, aren't we?''

Rebecca decided to hang up before the conversation deteriorated further. "I'm late for work. I'd better go.''

"Josh Hill called here yesterday,'' he said.

Rebecca paused, feeling an odd sensation in her stomach. Word had spread all over town that Josh had broken up with Mary, but she hadn't heard from him since last weekend. She knew she wouldn't, either. He'd told her that certain conditions had to be met if she wanted to be with him again, and the desire to capitulate on every count—the whole, "I want you, I need you, I can't live without you,'' routine—was sometimes so strong she craved it more than she'd ever craved a cigarette. But she wouldn't let herself need Josh Hill. She'd given up nicotine *again*. She'd beat her addiction to Josh, too, even if it took the rest of her life.

"What did he want?'' she asked.

"When I heard who it was, I thought he was calling to ask me for the money to replace that Excursion you burned, but he said the insurance covered it. After that, his call was a bit strange.''

"Why?''

"He wanted to know how long it had been since we talked.''

"You and I?''

"Yeah.''

"What would make him ask that?''

"I don't know. I told him it'd been a few weeks, that I

couldn't remember exactly, and he said he'd teach you to throw a football if that would help.'' Her father cleared his throat. ''You have any idea what he meant?''

''No,'' Rebecca lied, gripping the phone more tightly as she realized Josh was on to her. He was starting to see through her, to see everything, and it wasn't fair. This wasn't a frontal attack. He was breaching her defenses where they were the weakest. She'd offered him her body, but that hadn't been enough. He had to mess with her mind, instead. Or was it her heart?

Somehow it would've been far less frightening if he'd given her a quick tumble and moved on.

IT WAS DARN LONELY on the nights Booker went out with Katie. The following Friday, Hatty went to bed early, as usual, and Rebecca sat in the living room by herself, watching television. After an hour or so, she read a few chapters of a book and tried to sleep even though it was only eight o'clock. Then she gave up on sleeping, watched some more TV and considered calling Buddy simply for something interesting to do. She hadn't talked to him since their big breakup three weeks ago and was curious to know if his dog had recovered from hip surgery. His sister had been studying for the bar. Rebecca wondered if she'd passed, and whether Buddy had ever finished the new hardwood floor he was putting in the small house he'd inherited from his grandfather.

Not too long ago, they'd intended to make that *their* house, *their* hardwood floor, *their* dog.... But somehow, losing the house and dog and Buddy's romantic interest didn't hurt anymore. Once her pride had recovered, everything else bounced back as though she hadn't just lost the man she'd been planning to spend the rest of her life with. From there, it hadn't taken long to realize that she missed

Buddy's friendship more than anything else. Especially on nights like this, when she wanted to see Josh Hill but wouldn't let herself.

She longed to talk to Buddy the way she talked to Delaney, tell him what Josh had said, explain how badly she'd wanted him to make love to her last weekend. She even wanted to analyze possible motivations for his refusal and have Buddy help her try to figure out what it all meant.

But it probably wasn't smart to talk about Josh. It wasn't smart to think about him. Every time she did, she became angry over what he'd done to her—or what he hadn't done, to be more specific—and swore up and down that she'd never let him break her.

Then she imagined how he'd react if she ever capitulated, and wondered if it would really be so bad to give him what he asked.

Drive by his place. See if he's home.

The temptation seemed innocuous enough. Except that the voice in her head sounded suspiciously similar to the one that constantly whispered, "One cigarette won't hurt. What's one cigarette?"

"I'm not going anywhere near Josh Hill. I won't let him win," she said aloud. Then she called Buddy, because calling Buddy was a lesser evil than going out to Josh's place. But even after she'd talked to Buddy for almost thirty minutes, during which they fell into a quick and ready friendship, she still couldn't stop thinking of Josh.

Just drive by. Once. What's it gonna hurt? You know you want to see him.

Rebecca glanced at the clock. It was nearly eleven. Finally. Though she hadn't mentioned Josh to Buddy—considering their background, it was a bit early in their friendship to include love-interest discussions—she knew he'd think she was crazy to pursue him. She could hear him saying, "That's the guy who called me." She could also hear Mary Thornton saying, "You think you can get away with anything."

But she wanted to go out to Josh's ranch, anyway.

Good thing she never listened to anybody, she thought, and grabbed her keys.

REBECCA SAT in her Firebird, engine running, and stared longingly at Josh's house. At first, she'd pulled to the side of the road a quarter mile short of his place, just to be cautious in case he was up and about or had company. But no extra cars cluttered the drive, and the lights were all out. She felt fairly safe creeping closer.

She parked right in front and shifted to rest one arm on the seat, the other over the steering wheel. What would happen if she actually went to the door? Would Josh invite her in? Would he forget all that crazy talk about risk and "I go, you go" and the meaning of sex? What was the point? They were doomed before they began. He had to know that as well as she did.

But she couldn't put what she felt for him to rest. Thoughts of Josh swirled around and around in her head, wearing her down, wearing her out.....

She tried to remember the last good night's sleep she'd had and couldn't. She'd been worried about Delaney, of course. Delaney had started having a few isolated contractions several days ago, which meant the baby could come anytime. Then there was Booker, who refused to give up on Katie, even though she had an undying crush on Mike Hill. For all his bravado, she knew he could get hurt and didn't want to see that happen.

But underlying everything else was the constant magnetic pull of Josh Hill, which responded to no reason.

For the tiniest moment, Rebecca imagined telling him

what was banging around in her heart. Maybe if she set the truth free, she wouldn't feel as if she was about to explode.

But she couldn't tell Josh she loved him. She could never really hope he might love her back. And what about how foolish she'd feel when things fell apart and the entire town had a good laugh because she'd thought herself capable of winning Josh's heart? Even if he started seeing her, her family's smug patronizing would veil a calm assurance that he'd wise up at some point. And what about Mary? Josh had always seemed so lukewarm about her. Was that the best he could offer a woman?

Rebecca knew she could hate a man and fight with him constantly. She could also love a man and fight with him constantly. But she couldn't live with an impassive partner. It would completely strangle her passion for life.

Finished. Done. Decided. There'd be no strangling for her, she decided.

On that note, she put the transmission in drive and checked her rearview mirror. A pair of headlights stabbed the black night behind her. She felt a moment's panic as the two beams reflected in her mirror, momentarily blinding her before she could shove the car's gearshift into park and cut the engine to douse her own lights. With luck, whoever it was wouldn't notice her. With luck, they'd drive right by. But the next house was five miles away, which didn't make for a very steady stream of traffic, at least this late, and she had a sick feeling that the person coming down the road was Josh.

Curling her nails into her palms, she kept her head down and waited. The engine hummed closer. The truck—she could definitely tell it was a truck now, as she could see the top of it despite her position—slowed, seemed to hesitate in the middle of the road, then turned into the drive.

"Damn," she muttered. Had he seen her? Would he surprise her by coming to the window? Realize she'd been spying on his house like a lovesick fool?

Her face burning hot with embarrassment, she raised her head to peer over the door panel. Then she breathed a giant sigh of relief when Mike got out, slammed the door of his truck and headed to the house.

Ahh…a reprieve. Rebecca knew when she'd tempted fate far enough. As soon as Mike disappeared inside, she started her car again and drove off as fast as she could without squealing tires and spewing gravel.

MARY CAME IN to get her nails done the next day. Rebecca tried to focus on little Jessica Ball, whose bangs she was trying to trim, but it was pretty difficult to ignore the fact that Mary was staring daggers at her from across the room.

"Sit still," she muttered, shoving a toy in the child's lap.

When Rebecca had Jessica's bangs straight, her mommy paid for the haircut and the two of them walked happily down the street. Rebecca thought it a perfect time to escape—er, to grab some lunch. But she'd barely reached the door when Mary said, "Rebecca, can I talk to you for a minute?"

Rebecca hesitated, tempted to give Mary a firm no. Then she reminded herself that she wasn't moving to Nebraska, that she wasn't moving *anywhere,* at least in the near future, and decided it was probably best not to let the hostility between them linger. Josh hadn't broken up with Mary because of her. Rebecca hadn't even heard from him since the night he'd said all those crazy things, things she was sure he didn't mean in the first place. That he'd happened to break up with Mary the same night was just a coincidence. Maybe if Mary understood that, they could return to being more discreet enemies.

"Sure," she said. "Do you want to go in the back?"

Mary glanced at Mona, who was watching them both curiously, and shook her head. "No. You'll probably tell everyone here what I said the moment I leave, anyway, right?"

Rebecca didn't bother denying it. She knew she'd cave in to the pressure of having Katie, Mona and Ashleigh, the new girl, nag her for details of their conversation before Mary could so much as pass through Dundee's main intersection in her Camry. "Probably," she admitted.

"Well, I just wanted to say that I wish you'd told me you and Josh had something going, instead of sneaking around behind my back."

"Josh and I didn't have anything going, and we weren't sneaking around behind your back."

"Don't lie to me," she said.

"I'm *not* lying."

"My next-door neighbor told me Josh spent the night with you a couple of weeks before he broke up with me."

"And how would your next-door neighbor know that?"

"Randy told your sister, who told her best friend, who told her mother, who is my next-door neighbor," Mary recited smugly.

"It's not true," Rebecca said, and felt okay with the lie since Josh *hadn't* spent the night in the way Mary meant it.

"So you two aren't having a little...fling?"

"No."

"Then I guess you won't mind me telling you that he's going to come back to me eventually," she said.

Rebecca hated the sinking sensation that came over her and struggled to keep her face blank. "He is?"

"Of course. He still loves me. He's just suffering from

a bad case of the jitters. It happens all the time. A guy gets too close to marriage and starts to buck.''

Horse talk again. Maybe Mary *was* perfect for Josh. "Seems to me he bucked you right out of the saddle," she said.

"Not for long. That's the point I'm trying to make," Mary said. "I just wanted to let you know—so you won't get hurt." With that she studied her newly manicured nails and blew on the wet polish. "Have a nice day."

THAT NIGHT after Granny Hatfield went to bed, Rebecca tried to entertain herself by playing twenty-one with Booker. But her heart wasn't in the game. She kept thinking about Josh getting back together with Mary and how much she'd hate running into them. And she kept wondering why Josh getting back with Mary would somehow be more difficult for her to get over than her own breakup with Buddy.

"Quit thinking about him," Booker said.

Rebecca glanced at the cigarettes in his pocket but refused to ask for one. She hadn't smoked in weeks. For the most part, she'd managed to get over her cravings. But there were still times....

"Who?" she said, as though she could fool him.

"You know who," he said simply. "You want another hit?"

Rebecca looked at her two cards as though she didn't already know what they were—a king and a deuce. "What the hell," she said, "give me one." She'd probably take his bust card, but standing on a twelve was far too conservative for her.

He slid her another card. When she saw it was an eight, she smiled broadly. Sometimes it paid to be aggressive. "I'll stand," she said.

He turned over his cards, and Rebecca felt her momentary joy evaporate. He'd been holding a queen and a jack. So much for the success of her big risk.

"How are things between you and Katie?" she asked as he dealt her another hand.

"About the same as they are between you and Josh," he said, his focus on his cards.

Rebecca studied what he'd dealt her. "You've been calling her. You've been seeing her occasionally. That's a lot better than what's happening with me and Josh."

"If you're not seeing Josh, where do you go when you leave here late at night?" he asked.

He'd noticed? She should've known he would. "You don't want to know," she said. "It's too pathetic."

He cracked a rare smile. "Yeah, well, I'm beginning to feel pretty pathetic myself. Katie told me she's in love with Josh's brother last night."

"I told you that before you ever got to know her," Rebecca pointed out.

"It was a little different coming from her. Your timing was certainly better."

"How's that?"

"She waited until *after* we wound up in her bed."

"Ouch." Rebecca considered her cards again. A queen and a three. Not a big improvement.

"It's a good thing we're not in Vegas," she grumbled.

"You going to take my bust card?"

She answered his challenge by motioning for another card. "Probably."

Sure enough, he gave her a jack. Then he turned over a ten and a two and promptly garnered all the change in the center of the table.

"You beat me on a twelve?"

He stacked the money in front of him like chips. "When I'm playing with you, I always stand on a twelve."

"Why?"

"Why do you think?"

"Because I always bust?"

He grinned.

"I don't always bust!"

"You take a hit on anything less than eighteen, which means your busting average is a lot higher than most."

"I'm just not myself tonight," Rebecca said. "My birthday's coming up and, instead of spending it in Cancun with Buddy on a warm beach, enjoying our honeymoon, I'm going to be here."

"Buddy wasn't right for you."

Rebecca didn't want to admit that she'd finally reconciled herself to that fact, so she said nothing.

"Besides, Delaney's due to have her baby any day," he added.

"True. I would've hated missing the birth."

He dealt them each another two cards, and she felt vindicated when she won three bucks. "Take that," she said, tossing her cards on the table.

"You were holding a nineteen," he said.

"So? I still won."

"I was holding a fourteen. Short of receiving a six or a seven, there wasn't any way I could beat you."

"A minor detail," she said, motioning for more cards. "You going to forget about Katie?"

He cocked an eyebrow at her. "Sure. At about the same time you forget about Josh."

"I'm not holding out any hope where he's concerned."

He grinned. "Is that lie meant for me? Or just for you?"

"You think you know everything," she accused.

"I know Josh could do a lot worse."

She caught his eye and smiled. "So could Katie."

"REBECCA'S OUT THERE again," Mike said, peering through the blinds of the front window.

Josh glanced up from the kitchen table where he'd been busy devouring an entire cookie sheet of nachos and resisted the urge to get up and see for himself. He knew he couldn't appear too eager or he'd scare her off. He also knew if he wanted a relationship with Rebecca Wells, he had to make her meet his terms.

But he could offer her a small concession. "Turn on the porch light."

His brother sent him a quizzical look. "Why? You want her to come in?"

Josh felt excitement stir low in his belly and knew there could be no doubt about how badly he wanted just that. Sending her away the night he'd brought her home was the hardest thing he'd ever done. But if he'd given in to his baser yearnings, they'd be enemies again by now. He had to make her open her heart before anything else could happen. "I do."

Mike scratched his head. "You didn't get enough of her that night you made me pay for a hotel?"

"Not by a long shot." Josh was beginning to wonder if he'd ever get enough of Rebecca. Regardless of everything she'd done to him in the past, somehow she belonged to him. He couldn't understand why or how, exactly, but the fiercely proud girl he'd hated most his life had worked her way so deeply into his heart, he doubted he'd ever get her out.

Still, she had to come to him, had to admit she felt something, too, or there was no hope for a future. "I didn't sleep with Rebecca that night," he added. "I've never slept with her."

"In my mind, that's a good thing," Mike said. "Why ruin a perfect record?"

Josh considered his brother's words as he ate another cheese and sour-cream-topped chip, but Mike continued before he could formulate a response.

"You're not going to listen to me, are you? You want her to come in."

"Yep."

"And you want to sleep with her tonight. Is that where you're going with this?"

Josh washed down his food with the last of the soda he'd bought at the Quick Mart on his way home from his folks' house, sat back and folded his arms. Right again. But would tonight be his night? Rebecca had been driving out to his place about every other night for the past ten days, which meant she was tempted. *Something* had to be bringing her here.

But, Lord knew, she was a stubborn woman. Getting her to open herself to him emotionally was proving even more difficult than he'd anticipated. If not for her midnight appearances, he might have believed he'd never reach her. But she wanted to give in, or she wouldn't keep coming out here.

He smiled at her stubbornness. If she ever gave in, he was going to have his hands full. But he didn't care, as long as she came to the door with the understanding that she'd belong to him in the morning as much as she belonged to him in the night.

"Josh? Are you even listening to me?" Mike asked.

Josh blinked and realized his brother had been waiting for an answer. "What did you say?"

"I asked if you wanted to sleep with her tonight."

"I want to sleep with her every night," he admitted, and grinned as he watched his brother's jaw hit the floor.

CHAPTER NINETEEN

REBECCA SAT UP STRAIGHT when she saw the porch light come on. It pierced the dark, misty night like the beacon of a lighthouse, beckoning her closer. But she wasn't sure she could trust it to lead her to a safe harbor. Josh was inside. She'd followed him home when she'd spotted him in town just half an hour ago, being careful to stay at a distance. She'd told herself she just wanted to catch a glimpse of him. But even after he'd gone inside, she'd sat across the street on the shoulder of the road, wanting to go to the door yet refusing to let herself do it. After thirty minutes, she'd been about to head home when that blasted porch light had come on, making her hesitate.

Safe harbor... There were things about Josh that seemed safe. The way she felt when she remembered him saying, "If you can't care about me, I don't want anything to do with you," was one of them. The fact that he expected her to care about him indicated he was willing to care about her, right? He'd talked about risk, said, "I go, you go." That meant *something*.

But...she bit her lip. There were definitely things about Josh that were not safe. He was her childhood nemesis, the one who'd stolen her father's love and attention. She'd have to let go of the grudge she'd held against him all these years, forgive him at last, if they were ever to have a chance. But if she did, the softer feelings she had for him would completely consume her. She already knew that.

And then what? There were no guarantees. In a few weeks, she'd probably be nothing more to him than another soul falling to worship at his feet.

She recalled the conversation she'd had with Mary last week in the salon and wondered if Mary could be right. Was Josh simply running from commitment? Would he wise up and go back to her? Mary's confidence had to come from somewhere. And she had everyone's support. All of Dundee thought she and Josh went together like apple pie and ice cream. On the other hand, the entire town would shake their heads in stunned disbelief to hear that she and Josh were seeing each other.

She rubbed her nose with her hand for warmth. Now that her birthday had almost arrived, the nights were cold and often wet. She should have brought a heavier jacket.

She should go home....

Turning the key in the ignition, Rebecca started her car, but before she could pull onto the highway, one final glance at Josh's house told her something had changed. The blinds in the kitchen window had been raised, and Josh was standing there, hands on his hips, watching her. Challenging her.

As she suspected, he'd turned the light on for a reason. He knew she was there.

Any embarrassment she might have felt at being caught hovering near the object of her fascination was lost as she gazed at him. Regardless of how hard she'd tried to hang on to it, her grudge over the past was gone, she realized. And all those softer emotions? It was too late to do anything about them. She wanted Josh Hill about as badly as any woman could want a man.

And not just for the night.

Taking a deep breath, she turned off the engine, got out and walked to the house. *I'm a glutton for punishment,* she told herself. She and Josh had too much history. If her father found her lacking, so would he....

But she and Josh had a hell of a lot of chemistry, too. Was that enough?

Josh saved her the trouble of knocking. He swung the door open as soon as her foot hit the step. Then he stared out at her, waiting. "Well?"

He wasn't planning to make this easy. She looked back at her car and considered beating a quick retreat, but rejected that idea when he stepped outside to bar her escape. "Oh no, you don't, you little coward."

"I'm not a coward!" she protested.

He reached out to catch her by the shoulders. "If you're not a coward, then say what you came to say and forget about running."

She wasn't going anywhere. Suddenly she knew that like she knew the sun would come up in the morning. Letting her arms wrap themselves around him, she wished he'd just kiss her and stop with all the demands. But when she tried to distract him by pressing her lips to his, he fended her off. "First you have to *tell* me."

She stared up at him, amazed that she could be so in love without having known it.

He seemed to soften a little. He dropped several brief kisses on her forehead, her temple and each cheek, but he paused just short of her mouth. "I don't hear anything, Rebecca."

"I...I'm willing to risk it," she murmured.

"Risk what?" he countered, his mouth still hovering temptingly close to her own. As he rubbed his nose against hers, she caught her breath in anticipation and felt the last of her pride, her fear and her denial give way.

"Risk everything," she admitted. "It's hopeless to fight it. I want you too badly."

He grinned and hugged her. "That's my girl. That wasn't so bad, was it? And it'll get easier as time goes by."

"You expect me to say things like that a lot?" she asked doubtfully, slipping a hand inside his shirt to feel the ridges and contours of his muscles.

He finally kissed her, hard and hungry and demanding. "I do. I predict you'll tell me you love me someday," he whispered, his hands now buried in her hair, his lips next to her ear. "I'll hear it over and over again when I make love to you, right before I make you cry out in ecstasy." He grinned. "But knowing you, that'll take a while."

"I hope you're not talking about the ecstasy part."

"I'm talking about the 'I love you' part."

"Oh, good. That can wait until you say it first," she said, finding his lips for another breathtaking kiss.

Finally, he pulled back to look down at her and chuckled as he ran his thumb over the curve of her jaw in a touch that was so possessive, so tender, Rebecca thought she must be dreaming. This was *Josh* touching her. The man she'd been absolutely certain she hated...

Suddenly she couldn't blame her father for admiring him. How could she, when she saw everything her father saw and more?

"That day might come sooner than you think. I'm halfway in love with you already," he said. "Maybe I always have been."

Rebecca blinked up at him, wanting to capture those words and let them burn inside her like a candle in the window of her heart. "Could you say that again?"

He laughed and gave her a meaningful pat on the behind. "You heard me. Now go to my room and take off your clothes. I want to see that tattoo."

REBECCA STARED at Josh while he slept. God, he was handsome. She loved him so much it hurt. So much it terrified her. What if he woke in the morning and realized he'd made some sort of mistake? That she was nothing special, after all, just the girl from across the street who'd poured bleach on his lawn when they were in junior high?

He'd certainly known who she was when he made love to her, though. He'd made that abundantly clear. He'd kissed her neck and nibbled on her earlobe and murmured that he'd never wanted a woman more than he wanted her. And right before he'd brought her to a shuddering climax, he'd slowed his thrusts to the point of driving her crazy with frustration.

"Look at me," he'd commanded. When she'd opened her eyes, he told her he was punishing her for all the rotten things she'd done to him over the years. He'd proceeded to build the tension in her body ever so slowly, until she was nearly begging for release. And then the exquisite wave of pleasure finally broke over her, and it was far too powerful to hold anything against him.

Still, she'd insisted on reciprocating.

She smiled in satisfaction as she remembered him trembling on the brink of his own climax. His gaze had locked with hers in that final instant and his eyes had filled with some unspoken emotion that made her feel both feminine and powerful. Josh wanted her. He *really* wanted her. Not only that, he knew every skeleton in her closet *by name*— and it didn't seem to change anything.

She shifted so she could better see his face in the dark, too afraid to sleep for fear she'd wake up and everything they'd felt and experienced would be different. Come morning, Josh would have to confront his brother, and his family, and everyone else in town who could never imagine the two of them together. Come morning, they'd have to make some sort of decision as to whether there'd be another night like this.

Suddenly her father's voice closed in on her, sounding loud and unmerciful in her ear, making her doubt. *We haven't had any crises for the past few weeks...we're about due, aren't we?... You're not invited to the anniversary celebration unless you can behave yourself...*

And then there was Mary: *I heard Buddy broke up with you... I can certainly understand why... He's coming back to me, you know. It's just a matter of time—*

"What are you thinking about?" Josh murmured.

"Nothing," she lied.

He reached out and ran his thumb down the side of her face. "What I'm thinking is that you're beautiful," he said.

She tried not to smile, not to relinquish any more of her heart, but it was too late. She had no defenses left. She was hopelessly and irrevocably in love, and she had no idea whether it would turn out to be a good thing. She was gambling on the one man who had no reason to even like her....

"Don't you think this is kind of funny?" she asked.

"What?"

"The fact that we're lying here naked together after all we've been through. I'm the one who told everyone in school that your penis was three inches long, remember?"

He grinned. "Yeah, but that was just foreplay."

"What about tomorrow?" she asked.

"What about it?"

"What happens then?"

"Tomorrow I'm going to figure out a way to convince you to make me breakfast—naked," he said. "But we've got a few hours to work up an appetite, and I plan to make the most of every minute." Scooping her closer, he rolled on top of her, then kissed her gently. "You ready to tell me you love me yet?'' he whispered, pressing his forehead to hers.

''Hell, no,'' she said, even though her heart and her mind were screaming just the opposite.

He chuckled. ''That's too bad. I guess it's going to take a little more convincing.''

''I won't crack,'' she insisted.

He licked one taut nipple. ''We'll see what you have to say in five minutes.''

REBECCA SAT at his kitchen table, wearing nothing but one of his T-shirts, her hair an unruly mess, her lips still swollen from his kisses, and Josh thought, ''That's the way I like her best.'' Any makeup she'd had on last night was long gone, but Josh didn't think she needed makeup—not with the natural beauty of her clear green eyes. Or maybe it was the quick-changing expressions on her face that appealed to him and not any particular feature. She could say more with one glance than most women could say in a fifteen-minute monologue.

He tried to keep his gaze from straying to her long, slender legs, propped up on the chair next to her, so he wouldn't burn himself at the stove, but it wasn't easy. He'd made love to her several times during the night—and still felt like he wanted to drag her back to his bedroom. He smiled as he remembered thinking he could get her out of his system. Now he knew what twisted logic that really was.

''What's so funny?'' she asked.

''Nothing.'' The bacon he was cooking popped. He jerked his hand away to avoid being spattered by the grease. ''Breakfast is almost ready. Want some more orange juice?''

She shook her head.

He flipped the pancakes on the griddle. "I hope you're hungry. I've got enough food here for ten people."

She didn't answer.

Wondering why she'd suddenly grown so quiet, he glanced over to see her staring out the window, a brooding expression clouding her face. "What's wrong?" he asked.

"Nothing."

"Come on, Beck. You can't lie to me. What's going on?"

She folded her arms and scowled at him. "You always took Mary *out* for breakfast."

He raised his brows. "So?"

"We're eating in."

He leaned one hip against the counter, still holding the fork he was using to turn the bacon. "And…"

Her eyes lowered to her empty plate, and she began toying with her napkin. "You obviously didn't mind being seen with Mary."

"I don't mind being seen with you, either."

"Then why did you want to have breakfast here, instead of going to the diner?"

He took the bacon off the stove so it wouldn't burn. "First of all, you're drawing some pretty major conclusions from one day. That's hardly a fair sample. Second, I thought it'd be more fun to make you breakfast. Granted, I'm not a very good cook, but breakfast is one meal I can manage. Then you wouldn't have to get dressed," he added, hoping to tease her out of her sullen mood.

It didn't work. "You didn't mind it when Mary got dressed?"

"No."

"Because you wanted to take her *out* to the diner, where there'd be other people."

"No."

"Then why?"

He sighed, not particularly anxious to analyze his actions. Taking Mary out to breakfast put a decisive end to their time together and allowed him to get to work. "Because I couldn't see her lounging around my kitchen," he admitted.

"Why couldn't you?"

He forked the bacon onto a paper towel-covered plate and poured most of the grease into a jar. Then he broke a couple of eggs into the pan, which he put back on the burner. "I don't know. I think I was afraid she'd get too comfortable."

Rebecca studied him. "*I'm* lounging around your kitchen," she pointed out. "I'm even wearing your clothes."

"I know," he said. "And the crazy thing is, I like it."

WHEN REBECCA RETURNED home shortly after ten o'clock, she found Hatty's old Buick gone and the house empty. Which was a relief. Now she didn't have to answer any awkward questions about staying out all night. And without anyone to waylay her, she was able to shower, change and dash to the salon in time for her eleven o'clock perm with Mrs. Londonberry.

"You're sure quiet today," Mrs. Londonberry said as Rebecca put the rods in her hair. "You feeling okay, dear?"

"Fine," Rebecca said. In fact, she'd never been better, or had more pleasant memories to mull over. But she was afraid that stating her feelings too emphatically would draw unwanted attention. This relationship between her and Josh was still new enough that she wasn't really sure whether or not she could trust it.

"You look really happy," Ashleigh said, kneeling in

front of the shelves while restocking the hair care products. With Rebecca still working at the salon, it was taking Ashleigh longer to establish a clientele than it would have otherwise. But she seemed content to clean, organize and answer the phone. And Erma had come to depend on the extra help.

Mona paused while sterilizing her nail instruments at the utility sink. "Come to think of it, I haven't seen you smile this much since— Hey, don't tell me you and Buddy are back together!"

"No," Rebecca said quickly, keeping her attention on Mrs. Londonberry's iron-gray hair.

"Then what's going on?" Katie asked. She was sitting in her own seat, flipping through a magazine while awaiting her next client. "You seem different today."

"I'm not different," Rebecca said, wondering how everyone could tell that the world she was living in today wasn't the one she'd been living in yesterday.

The buzzer squawked over the door, and Booker and his grandmother entered the salon.

"I'm here for my appointment," Hatty announced as though she expected Rebecca to boot Mrs. Londonberry out of her seat.

Booker shot a not-so-covert glance at Katie, who whirled her chair around and immediately began rummaging through drawers.

Rebecca could feel the tension between them, but she was too preoccupied to focus on it. She'd forgotten that she was supposed to cut and perm Hatty's hair today. Hatty normally had Erma do it, but Erma had been taking more and more time off. "I'll be with you in a minute," she said. "Go ahead and have a seat."

As Hatty settled herself, Booker unzipped his jacket and

sauntered over to Rebecca's station. "How'd it go last night?"

Rebecca cleared her throat, looking around to see who might be listening. "Fine," she muttered.

"That's it?" he asked, grinning wickedly.

Mrs. Londonberry put down the magazine she'd been perusing and stared up at them. "What happened last night? Did I miss something?"

"Nothing happened," Rebecca said, but Hatty must have had her hearing aid turned all the way up because she didn't miss a beat when she shouted across the room. "Something must've happened. You never came home."

Ashleigh rocked back on her knees. "Aha! Is Rebecca seeing someone new? Already?"

Rebecca didn't want to admit to anything. She wanted to wait and see what happened with Josh before everyone starting talking about them. She could only imagine what her father and sisters...and *Randy* would have to say.

"Sure she's seeing someone," Granny belted out. "It's that cute boy, Josh Hill. Booker told me he has a thing for her. He wants her bad—isn't that what you said, Booker?"

Silence engulfed the salon.

"Thanks a lot," Rebecca muttered to Booker.

"Josh Hill?" Mona repeated, sounding as surprised as though Granny had just said she was seeing Brad Pitt.

Booker shrugged, obviously trying to play off Granny's blunder. "Sure, why not?"

"Why *not?*" Mrs. Londonberry cried. "Because he's supposed to marry Barb and Gene's daughter, Mary."

"Didn't you hear?" Ashleigh stood and began to gather up her boxes. "They broke up."

"They broke up on account of Josh having a thing for Rebecca," Granny said.

"But you and Josh have never gotten along," Katie said, her eyes sliding toward Booker.

"Is it true, Rebecca?" Mona asked.

Rebecca shrugged. "Not really, no. I mean...Josh and I are...friends."

"I don't spend the night with *my* male friends," Ashleigh said.

Closing her eyes, Rebecca felt a doomed sensation come over her. She'd never be able to stop the rumors that were going to fly all over town, never be able to reel in what had just gotten out. No one would believe Josh could want her. They'd laugh, and she'd look like a fool. Especially since she was no longer sure that what had happened last night had the meaning she'd thought it did. Her time with Josh seemed almost too perfect. "No one said I spent the night with him."

"Then where were you last night?" Mona arched her brows at Rebecca while carrying her instruments to her station.

"She certainly wasn't at my place," Granny said with a cackle. "But that's okay. If I were her, I would've stayed with Josh, too. He's a looker!"

"I'll admit he's cute," Ashleigh said. "But is he everything he's cracked up to be?"

"He told me Buddy was in the market to breed a horse," Katie said, seemingly to herself.

"I don't think Barb's going to be very happy about this," Mrs. Londonberry chipped in. "She just told me yesterday that she expects Mary and Josh to get married this Christmas."

Rebecca dropped her scissors on her rolling tray and sighed. She supposed there was little point in asking everyone to keep this quiet. Insisting on secrecy would only ensure that the news traveled faster.

"Is that why Josh came in here to get his hair cut?" Katie wanted to know.

"No," Rebecca said. "You guys are making a big deal out of nothing. Mary told me he's going back to her. So it's not what you think."

"Then what is it?" Mona asked.

Rebecca wished she had a good answer to that question. Josh had said he wanted their lovemaking to mean something. He'd treated her as though he cared about her and said some very flattering things. She just didn't know how serious he was when he said them. And putting the whole town in an uproar couldn't possibly help.

"We're—" She grappled for some statement that might calm everyone down. But then the phone rang and she hurried across the salon to answer it, grateful for the unexpected reprieve.

"Hair And Now," she said.

"Rebecca?"

"Hi, Laney."

"It's time."

"For what?" she said, still preoccupied with the catastrophe at hand.

"For the baby."

"Oh!" She stood straighter. "Right now?"

"Right now. Are you going to join us at the hospital?"

Rebecca glanced over at Mrs. Londonberry and Granny Hatfield, and considered the long list of appointments she had on the books. "Of course I'm coming," she said. "Are you sure you'll be able to make it all the way to Boise?"

"The contractions are still mild. I don't think we'll have any trouble."

"Great. I'll see you there." Rebecca hung up. Then she begged Ashleigh to take whatever appointments she could and cancel any she couldn't, told Booker she'd probably be home late, and escaped the salon.

But she knew her leaving wouldn't stop the others from talking. And she hated the thought of what they might stir up in her absence.

CHAPTER TWENTY

THE HOSPITAL ROOM WAS DARK and mostly quiet. There were the usual sounds of footsteps, hushed voices and equipment rolling down the hall, but they didn't disturb a peace that, in the tired aftermath of such intense excitement, felt almost profound.

Delaney lay sleeping beneath a light blanket, her face serene. Conner, the concerned and doting father, had finally dozed off in the chair next to her bed. Rebecca held Delaney's new baby girl. She'd considered leaving many times. The baby had been born nearly eight hours earlier and it was getting late. But Rebecca was still too emotionally charged and enamored with little Emily to go anywhere, despite the exhaustion that edged closer as the clock ticked toward midnight.

In the light spilling through the partially open doorway, she studied the miracle in her arms. Emily was wrapped tightly in receiving blankets and wearing a knit cap to keep her body temperature stable; only her tiny red face and long perfect fingers showed. But she had that sweet smell so peculiar to newborns, and the slight weight of her felt satisfying in Rebecca's arms.

Toying with Emily's hands, Rebecca admired them with the same reverence she'd experienced during the birth. "You're incredible," she murmured, brushing a kiss across her satiny cheek. "Seeing you come into the world makes me believe in all things that are good, little Em."

"Sounds like you're ready for a baby of your own," Delaney said.

Embarrassed to realize she'd been overheard, Rebecca glanced up to find Delaney watching her, a gentle smile curving her lips. "I should find a husband first, don't you think?" she replied, trying to steer the conversation away from the emotional.

Delaney arched her brows. "They may not be absolutely necessary, but I think it's definitely the better way to go." She leaned up on one elbow to see Conner, still slouched on the chair and dead to the world. "He made a pretty good coach today, don't you think?"

"Oh, he got in my way a few times, but I forgive him," Rebecca said. She'd actually told Delaney, repeatedly, that she'd wait in the lobby with Aunt Millie and Uncle Ralph, Delaney's adoptive parents. She hadn't wanted to intrude— and she hadn't particularly wanted anyone to see the tears streaming down her face as she watched Delaney's baby take her first breath. But Conner's mother hadn't arrived from California yet, and the doctor allowed two visitors in the room. Delaney and Conner had both insisted she share the experience with them.

"He gets in my way sometimes, too," Delaney said. But the tone of her voice suggested she liked having Conner in the way.

"I'm glad you two are happy," Rebecca said.

Delaney smiled proudly at her sleeping husband before turning back to face Rebecca and her baby. "I know you are. I just wish things had worked out for you and Buddy. Were you thinking about him a few moments ago?"

"No, why?"

"When I first woke up, you seemed to be in your own little world."

Rebecca *had* been in her own little world, but she'd been

thinking of Josh, not Buddy. But for some reason, it was difficult to talk about Josh, even to Delaney. Ever since their phone conversation, in which Rebecca had claimed she felt nothing for Josh, she'd purposely not mentioned him to Delaney again. It'd been easier to let her best friend—and everyone else—believe she was pining for Buddy. Pining for Josh felt too much like crying for the moon. But the added closeness inspired by having so recently shared Emily's birth seemed to demand less caution and more honesty. "I'm over Buddy," she said.

Delaney blinked in surprise. "That was quick."

Little Emily began to squirm, rooting for her mother's breast, and Rebecca reluctantly passed her to Delaney. "I don't think we were right for each other to begin with," she said. "And..." Making the admission that was on the tip of her tongue was still difficult. Fear threatened to choke her. But, considering Hatty's announcement at the salon today, Rebecca knew there was little point in withholding the truth. "...And I think there might be something between me and Josh, after all."

Delaney had been looking down, trying to settle her baby to nurse, but now her head snapped up. "Seriously? You're finally admitting it?"

Rebecca nodded.

"To him? Or just to me?"

"Last night he made me admit that I wanted to be with him."

"And what did he say when you did?"

"That I'd tell him I love him someday."

Delaney's eyes rounded. "What do *you* think?"

Suddenly Rebecca felt fidgety and thought of having a cigarette for the first time in well over a week. Resolutely shoving the temptation away, she clenched her fists. She'd come too far to slip up now. "I think I could tell him I love him *today* and it would be a terrible understatement."

Worry instantly shrouded Delaney's face. "Oh, no..."

"That's all you've got to say?" Rebecca asked.

"What else is there? You and Josh don't have a very good track record. I'm almost afraid to guess what you might do to each other."

"We've never tried going in this direction before," Rebecca said.

"That's true, but—" Delaney tucked her hair behind her ears and nibbled her bottom lip "—can you see yourself *marrying* Josh someday? Having his children, Beck?"

Letting her gaze fall to Delaney's newborn, Rebecca nodded. "At this point," she said softly. "I can't imagine having anyone else's."

JOSH SNATCHED UP the phone on the first ring. He hadn't heard from Rebecca since she'd left his house nearly fifteen hours earlier and, as midnight turned to one o'clock, he was beginning to worry that making love to her had been a one-shot deal. Considering Rebecca's unpredictable nature, it was entirely possible she'd done an about-face and would never want to see him again. Maybe he hadn't made it clear enough that what had happened this morning was actually positive. For the first time in his life, he hadn't felt compelled to take the woman he'd spent the night with somewhere impersonal, like the diner, for breakfast.

When he'd stopped by the salon earlier, he'd learned that Delaney was in Boise having her baby and Rebecca was involved in the big event. But he'd expected her to call him at *some* point. He'd certainly left enough messages at Granny Hatfield's.

"Hello?" he said. It was Rebecca's birthday today—

now that it was past midnight—and he wanted to be the first to acknowledge that. But it wasn't Rebecca.

"Josh?"

"Mary?" he said. He hadn't heard from her since he'd broken things off, but he'd suspected at the time that she thought he'd change his mind and come back to her. In their last conversation, she'd said as much. "You'll never find anyone like me, Josh. You'll wake up someday and figure that out," she'd said. But she'd also rejected his offer of friendship, so he hadn't expected her to contact him.

"Who else did you think it would be, calling this late?" she asked. Her words were slightly slurred and could barely compete with the music blaring in the background.

"Where are you calling me from? The Honky Tonk?"

"Yeah."

He stopped the playback of the football game he'd been watching so he could hear her better. "Sounds like you're having a good time."

"No. No, I want to go home."

"Is there any reason you can't?" he asked, not quite sure why she'd called or where she was leading him.

"I-I need…"

She finished her sentence, but she was mumbling worse than before and Josh couldn't hear her for the noise. "What?" he said.

"I need…ride home."

Obviously, she'd had too much to drink. But Mary never went anywhere alone. "Where are your friends?"

"I don't know. I think Candace…"

Again, what she said was lost. "Can you repeat that?" he asked, plugging his other ear in an effort to concentrate on her voice.

"…left with Leonard. And Wendy…don't know." He

thought he heard her sniffle at the end of these sentence fragments and wondered if she was crying.

"Is something wrong?" he asked. But he couldn't get a coherent answer out of her and he didn't think she could hear him any more clearly than he could hear her.

He sighed. He really didn't want to leave the house. He was still hoping to hear from Rebecca, and he wasn't sure she had his cell number. Most people didn't use cell phones in Dundee; the coverage was too spotty in the mountains. But he couldn't leave Mary stranded at the Honky Tonk. "I'm coming," he said. "I'll be right there."

When he finally got an okay out of her, he hung up and grabbed his coat before dashing outside. Grimacing at the rusty, dented Suburban that had become his usual mode of transportation since Rebecca burned up his Excursion, he shook his head.

"And *she's* the woman I want in my kitchen," he muttered. Then he climbed into the Suburban, started the engine and backed out of the drive.

JOSH FOUND MARY at a table near the jukebox, nursing another drink. As far as he could tell, she was alone. But her mascara was smeared and her clothes looked disheveled. When she saw him, the corners of her mouth turned down in a pouty, sullen expression.

"What are *you* doing here?" she said.

"You called me, remember? You ready to go home?"

"No."

He glanced around the smoky tavern to see Billy and Bobby Jo and a couple of other guys playing darts. A few pool players huddled over the tables in the back, and a handful of couples were dancing. But the place wasn't nearly as busy as it would've been a couple of hours earlier. Probably because it was almost two in the morning—closing time.

"It's late," he said.

She stared at her drink without answering.

"Mary? Do you want me to take you home or not?"

"How could you?" she suddenly demanded. "Do you know what you've done to me? Everyone expected us to get married. Everyone! And then you dump me for that…that tramp Rebecca." She shook her head wildly as though words alone couldn't describe her humiliation.

"I'm sorry," he said. "We've already been through that. I hope you find someone a lot better than me who—"

She held up a hand. "Stop. I don't want to hear it. There *isn't* anyone better than you."

Josh would have been flattered had he thought she meant that the way most folks would've taken it. But he knew she saw him more as a status symbol than anything else. "You're a bright, attractive woman, Mary," he said. "You don't need me to prove that."

"Oh, yeah?" She grimaced. "If I'm so bright and attractive, why am I divorced? Why—" Her voice cracked but she sniffled and continued. "Why wasn't I enough for Glen? Or for you?"

Josh reached out to cover her hand with his. "It wasn't that you weren't enough for me, Mary. I think I just had my eye on someone else, someone who's been part of me for a long time."

"Rebecca?"

He nodded.

"But everyone's always thought you didn't like her!"

"For most my life, I thought so, too."

"What changed your mind?"

He smiled, remembering all the years he'd known Rebecca growing up. He could still recall the time she'd lost a baby tooth in third grade and had to go see the nurse. And the time she'd found a worm in the schoolyard and chased Monti Blevons the entire recess for grinding it to dust. Then there were the later years, when she slowly shed her tomboy dress for girl stuff. Seeing her in her first formal at Homecoming had taken his breath away. Of course, she was someone else's date. They'd scowled at each other and brushed past without speaking. But he'd *wanted* to dance with her. "Truthfully?" he asked.

"Truthfully."

"I think it was that fight with Buck Miller."

"In the seventh grade?" Mary said.

Josh nodded, even though he suspected he'd loved Rebecca before that—since the day he'd first seen her and she'd tilted up her sharp little chin and glared down her nose at him.

"It's pretty hard to compete with giving Buck a bloody nose," Mary admitted. "I'm not the rough-and-tumble type."

"Rebecca is a hard act to follow," Josh agreed. "But don't get me wrong. There are those who are grateful for that." He chuckled. "Sometimes I'm one of them."

"You think you two can make it work?"

"I have no clue," he said. "Rebecca always seems to make things more difficult than they have to be. But if I have my say, we're going to try."

"Well…" She dried her eyes and glanced at the dance floor. "Can I have a last dance?"

DUNDEE AT LAST. Thank God. Rebecca was so tired she could hardly keep her car on the road. She knew she should probably have gotten a hotel in Boise. But she hadn't wanted to stay. It was her birthday. She'd arranged to have the day off work—and not so she could sleep in some hotel room by herself. She was hoping Booker might take her out for a late breakfast. And when she'd called to tell her mother about Delaney's baby, Fiona had insisted she come for the traditional family dinner party, to take place in the late afternoon.

But Josh was the real draw. After everything that had happened, she was anxious to see him again. Being tortured by him, using the same techniques as last night, sounded like a pretty good birthday activity. Receiving some sort of birthday gift from him wouldn't be bad, either.

Should she call him as soon as she got home? Or, better yet, simply go over and crawl into bed with him? Besides the—

The sight of Josh's Suburban sitting in the parking lot of the Honky Tonk jerked Rebecca out of her daydreams and sent prickles down her spine. What was Josh doing at the Honky Tonk at two o'clock in the morning? she wondered, throwing on her brakes. It was closing time. He'd been up late last night. And from the looks of the parking lot, he was nearly alone.

Nearly alone? Nearly alone took on a whole new meaning when Rebecca spotted Mary Thornton's car parked only a stone's throw away.

Wheeling around, she gave her Firebird more than enough gas and pulled into the lot, spewing gravel as she slid to a sudden stop next to the Suburban. It was Josh's vehicle, all right. She'd spent too many years being hyper-aware of anything to do with him to mistake the distinctive dents and dings.

She got out, tossing a baleful glance at Mary's brown Camry, and marched into the Honky Tonk. She could scarcely breathe for the fear squeezing her chest, but anger pulsed through her like a tidal wave, overcoming everything else. She wasn't about to walk away and pretend she hadn't seen what she'd seen. Only a coward would refuse to face the truth. And she would never be that kind of coward.

"I go, you go, huh?" she muttered as her blood pressure soared.

The inside of the Honky Tonk looked almost like a different place without all the familiar faces crowding the bar. Bear, the weekend bartender, was busy drying glasses. He jerked his head up when she came in because she'd flung the door so hard it banged against the outside wall, drawing everyone's attention.

Josh and Mary were on the dance floor, moving slowly to Faith Hill's "There I'll Be." Judging from their delayed response, her presence took a moment to register. When it did, Josh released Mary. "There you are," he said with a smile as he moved toward her.

"Don't come near me," she said, putting out both hands to ward him off. Her voice was higher and louder than she would have liked. If there'd been any chance that their audience might have gone back to whatever they were doing, that was no longer the case. But it was difficult to think about being discreet when she was so furious. "I believed you! I trusted you! I...I almost told you I love you!" she shouted.

Over in the dart area, Billy Joe and Bobby whooped, "Watch out, Josh. She's not happy, and she's going to make sure you know it."

"She'll be fine once I get her home," he said calmly, then gave her that cocky grin of his. "You almost told me you love me?"

"No. And I won't, either. I'm not going home with you. I'm never going home with you again," she shot back. "I don't even want you to forgive my debt. I'll pay you for the stupid Excursion, every cent. Because I don't want to owe you anything. I don't even want—" *Oof!*

The sudden jolt of being tossed over Josh's shoulder rendered Rebecca incapable of speech, effectively cutting off her recital of what she didn't want. She'd expected him to argue with her—or apologize and offer some flimsy excuse. He did neither. He simply carried her toward the exit as though this sort of thing happened every day. "Careful, Beck. Don't cut off your nose to spite your face," he said.

"I don't know what you're talking about," she cried. "Put me down!" She started banging on his back and kicking so he'd have to let her go, but he merely secured her feet so she couldn't hit anything he cared about. Rebecca knew she wasn't putting much effort into the fight, anyway. She *wanted* to be in Josh's arms. She *wanted* him to convince her that what she'd seen wasn't what she'd thought.

"Would you look at that," Billy Joe said in obvious amazement. "I've never seen anyone get away with *anything* with Rebecca."

Evidently he hadn't been keeping close track, Rebecca thought. Josh had always gotten the best of her.

"Where are you taking her?" Bobby asked.

"I told you," Josh responded without bothering to glance back. "Home."

"Whose home?" Mary asked.

Rebecca managed to look up in time to see her watching them with her mouth agape, eyes round with disbelief.

"*Our* home," Josh told her as he paused to shove a chair out of their path.

"Put me down," Rebecca said again, but her initial anger was dwindling fast. *Our* home? Our home suggested a lot of earth-shattering possibilities....

"Wow," she heard Mary murmur as Josh shouldered open the door, a note of envy in her voice. "He never treated me like that."

"Like what?" Billy Joe asked.

"Like he loved me," she replied and the door banged shut.

CHAPTER TWENTY-ONE

"YOU HUNGRY?" Josh asked.

Rebecca's automatic response was no, but when she took a moment to consider, she realized she was actually famished. She'd been so caught up in the birth of Delaney's little girl that she'd scarcely eaten all day.

"A little," she admitted.

"What would you like?" Pocketing his keys, he led her through the front door and into his kitchen, where he paused to open the refrigerator.

"Anything."

"An omelet?"

"Sure." She sat at the kitchen table while he pulled out the eggs, cheese, onions and mushrooms and carried them to the counter.

"Are we going to talk about what happened tonight?" she asked. After depositing her in the passenger seat of his Suburban, he'd gone around and climbed into the driver's side, started the engine and headed out of the lot. As an afterthought, she'd asked him to stop and let her out so she could get her car. She didn't exactly want the entire town to see it sitting at the Honky Tonk in the morning. Past experience had taught her that wasn't such a good thing.

"There's nothing to say," he told her. "You thought something was going on with me and Mary but it wasn't what it looked like. That's all."

"That's not all."

"There's more?"

Rebecca considered all the questions she'd like to ask. There was that little "our home" comment he'd made, and the way he'd carried her out as though he had a right to do so. But probing for his reasons could possibly lead to a very serious discussion that might not end the way she wanted it to. And it was her birthday. Better to save the serious stuff for another time. "I guess not," she said.

He grinned and started chopping onions.

"You look smug," she said.

"I'm just thinking."

"About what?"

"You."

"Could you elaborate on that?"

"Everyone's so afraid of setting you off. They don't know the real you."

"But you do."

"I'm beginning to understand a few things."

"Like…"

"That spiny front you present to the world protects a very soft heart."

Rebecca wasn't pleased that his comment made her feel so vulnerable. "And this assumption is based on the fact that I let you get away with what you did tonight?" she asked, folding her arms and leaning away from the table. "I was just too tired to fight. I could've made you let me go if I'd really wanted to."

He chuckled as he cracked the eggs into a bowl, his fork making scraping sounds as he added some salt and started whisking everything together. "More bluster," he muttered, shaking his head.

"What?"

He threw her a swift glance. "Nothing."

"Don't bait me right now," she said with a scowl. "I just want to relax."

"Okay, so tell me about Delaney and Conner's baby."

The sizzle of the eggs in the pan, along with the smell of the food, was comforting. It felt good to be sitting in Josh's kitchen, letting him take care of her.

Rebecca covered a yawn, thought about snuggling up with him and drifting into a contented sleep, and some of the tension in her body eased. "It was wonderful. I've never seen anything like it, Josh. At times I laughed, and I cried, and then there were moments when I was so worried about Delaney I thought I'd die. For the first time in weeks I wanted a cigarette. But I stuck it out. And then, after the baby was born and I held her in my arms, so much longing swept through me I could hardly—"

At the stunned look on Josh's face, Rebecca fell silent.

"What?" she said hesitantly.

"You said 'longing.'"

Rebecca's cheeks started to burn. She *had* said longing. In her excitement, she'd forgotten to downplay certain aspects of what she'd experienced.

"You said when you held the baby, so much longing swept through you that…what?" he prodded.

She tried to think of a way to make what she'd said sound plausible in the context of witnessing Conner and Delaney's baby being born. But longing wasn't typically an emotion she'd feel at the birth of someone else's child— unless she wanted a baby of her own.

"That I couldn't breathe," she finished. She'd wanted to take things slow with Josh, learn to trust him before exposing any more of her softer side. But her feelings were too strong and too close to the surface to pretend. And she wasn't good at it, anyway.

He set the pan on the opposite burner, left his spatula on

the counter and came over to squat before her. "So you want a baby, Beck?" he asked, resting his elbows on his knees and looking up into her face.

She nodded. Her heartbeat was thudding through her entire body as she anticipated his response and, for some crazy reason, she felt a rush of tears. Swallowing hard, she blinked them back, but the lump in her throat threatened to choke her. She wanted a baby, all right. She wanted Josh's baby. Somehow it seemed as though a family with Josh Hill was all she'd *ever* wanted—even when she'd been pouring bleach on his lawn.

"Can you wait till we get married?" he asked, taking both her hands.

"Married?" she echoed in surprise. "We've only been together one day."

"We've known each other practically our whole lives. I don't need any more time than that. Do you?"

"No." She definitely needed no more time than it would take to say "I do."

He pulled her slightly forward and kissed the end of her nose. "So you'll be my wife?"

Because she didn't trust her voice, Rebecca nodded, wondering if she was going to wake up in the morning and realize this whole conversation had been a dream. But it felt very real when Josh reached up to wipe away a tear that had gotten stuck in her eyelashes, blurring her vision.

"When do you want to have the wedding?" he asked.

She sniffed. What was wrong with her? She cried probably one-tenth as often as most women. She was Rebecca Wells—proud and tough, with a bad-ass reputation. Granted, her reputation protected her on some occasions and plagued her at others. But with Josh her reputation no longer mattered. He didn't see her the way other people did. Not anymore.

Maybe that was the reason she was crying. She knew he was looking at the real her—and that he actually liked what he saw.

"I guess there isn't any reason to let all those cookies go to waste," she said.

"Cookies?"

Too busy figuring out a date, she didn't explain. "Is three weeks too soon?"

"Not for me. If you want, we can elope tonight."

"No way," she said. "My father's got to see this."

WHEN THE TELEPHONE RANG, Rebecca thought it was the buzzer on Hatty's oven. In her dreams, she kept trying to turn it off, but no matter how many times she twisted the knob, the noise wouldn't stop. Then, suddenly, silence was restored. She settled herself more comfortably on Josh's shoulder and was about to sink back into oblivion when a solid knock sounded on the door.

"Josh? Is Rebecca with you?"

It was Mike. Rebecca sat up and shoved a hand through her disheveled hair, then remembered to pull the blankets up to cover herself, in case he decided to enter.

"Yeah, I'm here," she said.

Their voices finally roused Josh. He stretched and rose to his elbows to squint at Rebecca before scooping her toward him and burying his face in her neck. "What is it?" he mumbled against her skin.

"It's your brother."

"Do I have a brother?"

"He doesn't belong to me," she said.

"Oh, yeah." Rolling away, he scrubbed his face with one hand. "What is it?" he called.

"Booker's on the phone," Mike said.

Reaching over to the nightstand, Josh grabbed the receiver and handed it to her. "It's your roommate," he grumbled.

"Do I detect a little jealousy?" she asked.

"Damn right."

There wasn't anything to argue about if he was going to agree with her, so she pulled him down next to her and contented herself with threading her fingers through his hair. It was such a possessive thing to do and so utterly fulfilling....

"Late night, huh, babe?" Booker said as soon as Rebecca answered.

"Yeah. Delaney had her baby."

"I heard. A little girl. It's all over town."

"Already?"

"That surprises you?"

"Not really."

"What's up?" she asked.

"Thought I'd better warn you that your family's looking for you. They're about to call the highway patrol and they'll probably follow with the morgues in Boise. They've talked to Delaney and know you left the hospital last night. They're afraid you might've ended up in a ditch. And I wasn't gonna be the one to tell 'em you're sleeping with Josh."

"Gotcha." She let the silky strands of Josh's hair slip through her fingers again. "The morgues, huh? That's not good."

"What's not good?" Josh murmured.

"My parents think I've gone missing."

"So what are you doing for your birthday?" Booker asked.

Josh kissed her temple and placed a possessive hand on her breast, obviously trying to distract her. "I think we're going shopping."

"'We?'"

"Josh and me."

"For a birthday present?"

"For a wedding ring."

"No shit?"

Rebecca smiled, remembering how Josh had called her Mrs. Joshua Hill while he was placing little kisses along her collarbone—and then considerably lower—last night. "No shit. How are things with Katie?"

"Not anywhere as good as they are with you and Josh."

"You really like her, don't you?"

"Hell, no. I don't like anybody," he said, but Rebecca could tell he was lying.

"If she's as smart as I think she is, she'll wise up someday."

"It's pretty tough for a lowly mechanic to compete with a big-ass horse breeder."

Rebecca playfully batted Josh's hands away. "Yeah, well, they're not all they're cracked up to be."

"Next time try saying that like you mean it," he said.

"That might be the best I'll ever do," she admitted. Then she told him he owed her a birthday present, hung up and called her mother.

"There you are," Fiona said, obviously in the middle of what her father called a dither. "Where have you *been?* Are you all right?"

Rebecca skipped the first question to focus on the second. "I'm fine."

"Your father's definitely *not* happy with you, Rebecca Paige Wells. You made him miss an important meeting this morning."

"I did?"

"Yes! When you didn't come home last night, he was sure that hunk of junk you call a car had finally given out on you and you were stranded on the side of the road somewhere. Or worse. He's driven all the way to Boise looking for you."

"And now he's going to be upset that I'm okay?" she teased.

"You know what I mean."

Rebecca smiled to herself. "Yeah, I do. But there's nothing to worry about. And you can tell him..." When she hesitated, Josh lifted his head and looked up at her expectantly, and the magnitude of what she was about to do suddenly hit her. She was going to marry her childhood nemesis. She was going to bear his children. Her mother-in-law would probably hate her forever, but Rebecca had never been happier in her life. "...Tell him I'm getting married, after all. That should make everything better."

"You're *what?*"

"I'm getting married. And Greta can do the wedding in ivory and green, if she wants. It doesn't matter to me."

"Are you drunk?" her mother demanded.

"No!"

"You don't sound right. And I don't know if marriage is such a good idea, after all. Your father and I have talked about it, and we really don't think Buddy will make you a good husband. I mean, maybe if he'd agree to move *here*.... We don't think you should leave your friends and family. We'd never get to see our grandkids and—"

"Don't worry, Mom," she interrupted. "I'm not moving to Nebraska."

A moment of silence met this statement. "Well...that's a relief, at least."

"And you *did* make all those little poem scrolls. We should probably use them, don't you think?"

"They were an awful lot of work...."

"Exactly. What time is dinner?"

"Five. We're having your favorite—homemade pot pie and German chocolate cake."

"Can I bring a guest?"

"Booker?" she asked, obviously not pleased.

"No, my fiancé."

"Oh!" The tone of her mother's voice instantly changed. "Of course. It'll be good to see Buddy again. Doyle has a few things he wants to say to him."

"Uh…we'll see about that," she said and hung up.

"We're making the big announcement today?" Josh asked, putting the phone back in its cradle.

"I thought it might be a good time. The whole family's gathering for my birthday."

"Then we'd better get going. I want to have your ring."

"It's Thursday. Don't you have to work?" Rebecca asked.

"That's the beauty of being in business with your big brother," he said. "Mike will cover for me. He owes me for all the time he's spent in McCall."

"Hey, you two interested in breakfast?" Mike called from the kitchen.

"Boy, you do have it good," Rebecca said.

"Not half as good as I'm going to have it," he told her and drew her into his arms. A few minutes later he yelled for Mike to eat without them.

JOSH TOOK A DEEP BREATH as they pulled up in front of the Wells family home. He knew relations between Rebecca and her father were strained. They had been for years. And he had no idea how this latest development might change things. He hoped he wouldn't have to tell Doyle Wells exactly what he thought of the way he talked to and about his daughter. But Josh knew he didn't have the forbearance to put up with more of what he'd seen in the past. Rebecca was going to be his wife now. That gave him the right to protect her, even from her father.

"Are you okay?" he asked as she eyed the cars around them. Randy and Greta's blue minivan was parked behind Doyle and Fiona's Lincoln Towncar in the drive. Delia and Brad's red minivan was parked at a sloppy angle right at the curb, along with Carey and Hillary's truck.

"The whole gang's here," Rebecca said, giving him a smile that didn't look nearly as self-assured as she probably thought it did.

"They're just your family," he told her. "No big deal, right?"

"Of course."

"You ready?"

"Sure." She scrambled out of the Suburban and marched decisively toward the house.

"Whoa, what's the hurry?" Josh asked, breaking into a jog to catch up with her.

"I want to get this over with, that's all."

"Not a real positive slant, Becky. What's going on?" he asked.

"They're not going to believe it, you know. Especially my father."

"We've got proof." He held up her hand, on which sparkled a much bigger diamond than any she'd initially picked out. She'd lived on a shoestring for so long, she didn't seem to understand that ten thousand dollars to him wasn't the same as it was to her. During their shopping, she'd told him several times that she felt too guilty about his Excursion to let him buy her anything very expensive, that a simple gold band would do. Which made it all the more fun for him to insist she have a full carat marquis with the best clarity they could find. He'd never forget the look on her face when the salesperson slid the ring he wanted her to have on her finger. Her eyes went wide. She stared at it. Then she turned to him. ''This is obscene,'' she whispered, but she laughed as though obscene wasn't a bad thing at all, and he'd known then that it was perfect—just as flamboyant and beautiful as she was. Any woman who occasionally dyed her hair some wild color, sported a butterfly tattoo on her belly, and mentioned having his name tattooed on her hip (okay, maybe he'd suggested that in the throes of passion last night, but she hadn't disagreed), had to have something flashier than a simple band.

''They might try to talk us out of it,'' she said. ''They're not going to think we have a chance in hell of staying together.''

''Fortunately, they're not the ones who get to decide.''

She bit her bottom lip. Josh bent and kissed her, his movements quick because he could hear the front door opening and knew they wouldn't be alone much longer.

''I love you,'' he whispered, because it was true. For the first time in his life he felt he could offer his whole heart. Rebecca wouldn't be the easiest woman in the world to live with. He already knew that. But he knew something else— he couldn't live without her.

A tentative smile crossed Rebecca's face as she looked from her ring to him. ''I love you, too.''

Josh could tell by the stilted way she said it that she wasn't comfortable expressing her feelings so openly—at least to him. She preferred to avoid that kind of self-exposure. But he knew she meant what she said and that eventually she'd learn to trust him. After twenty-four years, he'd finally won the girl who'd always thumbed her nose at him. And his obsession with her wasn't about challenge or conquest, as he'd once believed. It was about something far simpler—it was about falling in love.

"I thought you said you'd never tell me that," he taunted.

Her smile turned into a devilish grin. "It's okay. You said it first."

"Rebecca?" her father called, stepping out onto the front stoop. "Is that Josh Hill you've got with you?"

"Unless Buddy's grown a foot since we've seen him last, that's not the guy from Nebraska," Randy said as he and the rest of the family gathered behind Doyle.

"It *is* Josh," someone else marveled.

"God, now I've seen everything!" Randy said.

Rebecca slipped her hand inside Josh's and pulled him forward. He could tell she was much more settled than she'd been just a moment before. It made him proud to think he had such a bolstering effect on her. He'd be good for her. He'd love her and take care of her his whole life. And she'd be good—er…keep things exciting for him.

"I want to introduce you to my fiancé," she said to her family. Then she flashed her ring and let her sisters and mother "Ooh" and "ahh."

"What happened to Buddy?" Doyle asked above the melee of voices.

Josh shrugged. "You were right. He wasn't the man for her."

Doyle chewed on a toothpick while he considered them for a few seconds. Then he moved the toothpick back to the corner of his mouth so he could speak. "You think you can handle her?"

"Do you know of anyone who'd have a better chance?"

Doyle scratched his head. "Now that you mention it, I guess I don't." He chewed on his toothpick some more. "What're your parents going to say?"

"It doesn't matter."

He accepted this without comment, but Josh got the impression his answer had somehow been the right one. "It'll take a strong hand."

"I know."

Doyle's eyes lighted on Rebecca and seemed to soften. "But I'll admit one thing."

"What's that?" Josh asked.

"She's worth the trouble."

Rebecca must have been listening because she looked up at her father and something passed between them, the depth of which Josh could only guess at. Stepping through the cluster of women surrounding her, Doyle embraced his youngest daughter. It was about the roughest hug Josh had ever witnessed, but it was a start. And it made Rebecca smile.

Fortunately, she didn't hear what Doyle muttered next. "But one's enough. Pray you don't have a daughter just like her."

* * * * *

Visit Dundee, Idaho, again next spring.
Will Rebecca's friend, Katie Rogers,
end up with Booker Robinson,
Mike Hill—or someone else?
Watch for Brenda Novak's

A FAMILY OF HER OWN.